Freaks' Amour

Freaks' Amour

by

Tom De Haven

William Morrow and Company, Inc.
New York   1979

Library of Congress Cataloging in Publication Data

De Haven, Tom.
    Freaks' amour.

      I. Title.
PZ4.D3225Fr   [PS3554.E423]   813′.5′4   78-10277
ISBN 0-688-03408-X
ISBN 0-688-08408-7 pbk.

BOOK DESIGN   LESLIE ACHITOFF

Printed in the United States of America.

First Edition

1   2   3   4   5   6   7   8   9   10

For Santa, who said: "Goldfish! Make them goldfish.
Next question. Ask me anything."

Thanks to James Landis, Maria Guarnaschelli and Francis Greenburger for their help, encouragement and patience.

Very special thanks to Craig Nova, without whom . . .

Contents

Prologue: Bedtime Story

(1988-2001-2-3 . . .)

When we were twelve, thirteen, fourteen, our father often came lumbering into our bedroom late at night after he'd boxed and shelved all of his slides and cassette tapes, after he'd finished a bottle of wine or a liter of beer. He'd switch on a light, then shake my brother and me by the shoulders until we sat up and knuckled our eyes. "Don't try and fool your da, you guys weren't sleeping," and he'd shuffle away across the floor with his long and atrophied right arm bumping alongside him. Its bloated wrist and kielbasy-fingered hand fishtailed and swished on the linoleum as he walked. He'd grab a desk chair and carry it back, set it down in the alley between our twin beds and straddle it. He'd stare at the wall for a moment, pondering. He'd smile next and I'd know what he was going to say. So would Flour. It was always the same thing.

He'd remind us that we'd been conceived (pretty amazing odds: two sperms colliding with two eggs following our parents' inaugural bang) on Caliban's Night—"that was April the 18th, 1988"—just an hour before number 221 Blofeld Street, Jersey City, New Jersey, burst into smithereens.

Da would scratch his throat, or suck at his grayed front teeth, and then he'd whisper like carbonation:

"You shoulda seen your mother that day, that night. I'm telling you, kids, pretty."

No doubt. We'd seen pictures of what she looked like as a young woman. There were plenty hidden around the house. Pretty she'd been, all right. Once. An oval face, a complexion as perfect as a bar of cold-cream soap, dark-red hair and deeper red lips, eyes green as mint. But Flour and I never knew that woman. The woman we called mother, her skin was galaxied with small scales like green sequins, her irises had no pigment, she was bald as a muskmelon . . .

They were married, Joe Fistick and Helen Doremus, in a Catholic church. Da was an atheist and would've preferred a chop-chop civil ceremony, but Ma, not so much a good Catholic as a conscientious parishioner, insisted upon a sacramental exchange of vows. They were both twenty-seven.

After the wedding there was a small party back at their new apartment above a pasticceria on Rose Avenue—just cold cuts and seeded rolls and half a keg of dark beer for twenty friends. Neither Ma nor Da had any brothers or sisters, and their parents were dead. Around eleven, the party broke up. Ma went around collecting the paper cups and fluted plates and chucked them all into a trash-can liner, and she wrapped any leftover deli meat. (Da never failed to mention these picayune details, as if they were clues to a personality or a murder.) Then she went into the bathroom, to change, and Da—as I got older, I started to picture him at this stage walking around the apartment with an anticipatory erection already puptenting his trousers—made sure the door was locked and chained. He turned off the lights, threw open the bedroom window. A warm night (he'd say), stars like salt, a scimitar moon. In the breeze, an oily trace scent of burnt pork rinds, a heavy coffee aroma from the Maxwell House plant.

And later (were those four gametes fusing already in our mother's belly?), they lay on the bed, on top of the covers, holding each other, their breaths sieving out slowly through closed teeth. From the street down below: a scraping car muffler, a distant cop siren, then:

"The blast nearly shook us right offa the bed. I wasn't worried, but. I figured it was another one of them oil tanks in Linden, or something "

But it wasn't. It was a house that blew, an ordinary two-story nine-room house with cedar shakes, right there in Jersey City. And the blast which shimmied and painted the night, Caliban's Night (so named by one of the New York newspapers a few days later, as soon as the first mutations began) was nuclear. It granulated more than twenty homes and apartment buildings, leaving a huge bowl in the ground, and it puffed a furious gassy fallout into the air.

Da would wrinkle up his face, that broad doughy face set with huge phlegm-yellow popeyes and polluted with hard white swellings like candied almonds that ran undulant across his brow and clustered at his temples . . .

More than 1200 people died, either in the explosion or, later, from radiation poisoning. And 77,000 others—mostly in Jersey City, in Hoboken, Union City and Bayonne, but there were some cases, too, in other towns in Hudson County, and in Newark and on Staten Island, and across the river in Manhattan, even a few (ask the meteorologists why) as far away as Perth Amboy, New Jersey, and Patchogue, Long Island—they had their chromosomes mugged. They mutated. They turned—gradually or quickly, but with absolutely no homogeneity in their turning—into Freaks (capitalized, by the news media, so there'd be no confusing them with the ordinary variety of bent homo sape).

Human fingers reshaped themselves into rasorial bird claws, skulls ballooned or stretched until they resembled butternut squash. Arms—like Da's right one—grew as long as boa constrictors and then became paralyzed. Flesh thickened into pachydermal hide or cloaked itself with monkey fur. Teeny blind eyes (some human and some not) burst through cheeks and palms and (just like Mary Shelley's nightmare) the nipples of breasts. And, like what happened to Ma, and was passed on to me, pores gave birth to fish scales and gills.

Except for cats (and why those guys were exempt from mutation is anybody's guess), all living things local to the blast site were vulnerable to the fallout. In time, all species had their Freaks. Some dogs developed leathery plates that interlocked on their flanks or long gladiate ears that dragged the ground. There were bees that swelled up to the size of soccer balls (luckily, most of them soon died), and wasps that grew as long as wieners with stingers big as pine needles. Some pigeons sprouted mink-type fur. Some trees began to secrete a smelly brown gelatin. Leaves died and were replaced by foliage that looked like yellow fiber-glass attic insulation.

And on and on, and on, including pet goldfish that quadrupled in length and mass and started to anally extrude tiny, green-dappled hard-shell eggs . . .

Blofeld Street was a two-block inclining dead end in the Heights section of Jersey City. The houses were two-family, mostly, and mostly run-down. Black and Indian families, some Egyptian, Italian, Vietnamese. Number 221 was owned by a carpenter named Perez who'd come up from Uruguay after the food riots there in 1982. He bought the house for a song, renovated it himself, then rented it out. Perez died from radiation poisoning, so when the official investigative commission finally convened in Hackensack in the fall of 1988, his widow was subpoenaed in his place. She arrived at the hearings in a bone-white and cumbersome antiradiation suit. She must've looked like a spacer. She produced a signed lease showing that the last occupant of 221 Blofeld Street had been a man called Thomas nmi Poole.

A white man, she said, in his late thirties.

Medium build, average looks, no missing fingers, no moles, no scars.

No, she didn't know what he did for a living. And, no again, she hadn't been inside the house after Poole rented it. Yes, she thought it was slightly strange that a single man (as he'd declared he was) would want a nine-room house, but that was really none of her business. He paid the rent, always on time, always in cash. That's all that counted.

Had she ever talked to him—about politics, perhaps? Yes, she'd talked to him, but only once. And about whiplash. (Da would vocally italicize that: *whiplash.*)

Why about whiplash, the panel was curious to know. Because, Mrs. Perez answered (her voice, I'd imagine, broadcast through a tiny crosshatched circle in her helmet's double-thick porthole), because the last time she saw Poole he'd been wearing a heavy white plastic neckbrace. A minor car accident, she testified he'd told her.

And that was all she had to tell.

But who was this Thomas Poole? (Da would wag his left pointing finger at me, at Flour, as if he were a public prosecutor.) Had he died in the accident? Had it even *been* an accident? (Da's breath would roar down his nostrils like twin rocket exhaust.) And what exactly had been detonated, what sort of device?

After two months of public hearings, the commission reported: no answers. The Blofeld Hole, where the house had stood, revealed nothing in the way of clues. Still radioactively hot and already teeming with fantastic flora, the ravine contained no bomb or reactor scrap, no bones, no miscellany: all that had been had been pulverized.

Da often paused here, for effect, and slotted his tongue back and forth . . . or crossed one leg over a knee . . . or cut his eyes from his lap to my brother's face or to mine. If he cut them to my face I'd glance away, afraid he'd forget my leer was involuntary, a muscular birth defect, and misconstrue it as an expression of ridicule. Without facts (he'd resume), speculation boiled everywhere, like mosquitoes after a week of crashing summer rains.

The two most popular theories about the explosion ascribed blame either to a blundered military project (like the outbreak of lethal Four-star Flu in eastern Kentucky in the fall of '85) or to yet another whopper terrorist exploit (in the same, but icier, vein as the so-called Plague O' Boils bombs that were detonated in Jerusalem in '81 and Johannesburg in '82). Naturally, the Pentagon denied all "paranoid slanders," and no liberation group, not a single one of any complaint or persuasion, left, right or occult, claimed responsibility for the Blofeld blast.

There were also, of course, the more bizarre hypotheses, full of such cosmic characters and sentiments as God, the Devil and Reckoning Day. Da would smile, then twist his mouth out of shape. "Reckoning Day, shit! Why should we 've been singled out?" Good question. Jersey City was no Gomorrah, just an old arthritic community across the water from New York City, where a couple hundred thousand people went about their daily business inside fatigued buildings or out on treacherously potholed streets, within an envelope of carcinogenic smutch, and then regularly voted for the Democratic ticket.

Sometimes, Da would end his narrative right there, at the baffled commission and the conflicting theories. He'd stand, hawk sputum into a hankie or knead the red-limned black splotches on both his cheeks and toss off several bare specifics:

The county quarantine lasted nearly a year, was lifted eventually on May 24, 1989,

Over 600 blast mutants committed suicide in just the first nine months after Caliban's Night,

The first serious clash between Freaks and the nonaffected occurred after a metamorphosed husband murdered his unaltered wife with a Louisville Slugger because his new looks disgusted her and she planned to divorce him. A small riot erupted outside police headquarters while he was being arraigned—a few broken bones, a slit jugular, somebody's calf was bloodied by a zip gun.

And then Da would tell us good night and shamble from

the room, and Flourface and me would dash to the door, and listen: to our father thump-thumping down the hallway, to the desperately sweet words he'd say to Ma upon reaching their bedroom and finding her awake, and to her clipped and nasal (she suffered year-round from sinus blockage) demands: "Turn out the light before you get undressed. And don't try anything when it's dark, Joe. Let's have no repeat of last night's little episode." They slept in twin beds, like ours, that were separated by a wall of junk-on-chairs, plastic hampers and teeter-tottering stacks of books and magazines, our mother's early-warning system.

But, other times, Da would only peek at his watch and tell us more story.

"You boys . . ."

We boys, my brother and myself, were born, fraternal twins, on January 24, 1989, the same day that a Soviet space station, the *Resolute and Progressive Progeny of Lenin*, lurched from its earth orbit and had to be destroyed by remote control before it could plummet and pancake the city of Amsterdam. We were delivered by cesarean section (since it was impossible to exit through Mother's birth canal, a gauntlet of razor scales) in a special Freaks-only psychiatric ward at Jersey City Medical Center. Our mother had been confined there since late July. She'd tried to kill herself, although she swore (and would still swear today, if you asked her about it) that she'd cut both of her wrists with a paring blade merely to clean them of scales.

I was baptized Charles. Flour was baptized Alan.

Ma had plenty of company there in the psycho ward. Few Freaks accepted their fate with any particular mental grace. Some did, though. Da, for example. What really bothered him were his inability to work (how could he drive a Coca-Cola truck with a stunned arm that stretched now two and a half meters?) and the inconclusive report of the Blast

Commission (the name referred not only to the Blofeld Street explosion itself but also to the commission's chairperson, Dr. Wilma J. Blast, of MIT).

His physical transformation never fundamentally confused or humiliated our father: "And I'll tell you why—this should be valuable to both you boys. I was—and I still am—the same person inside I'd always been. Short-armed or long-armed, it made no real difference. I knew who and what I was. No mystery. I was still Joseph Fistick, a guy with a grade-A brain and a good disposition. See?"

His self-esteem bothered me, even when I was twelve, thirteen, fourteen. It made me feel guilty, since I had none of my own. I had skin like a fish, I grinned like a skull: no self-esteem.

This should be valuable to both you boys.

It was never valuable to me.

It was, I think, to my brother.

Da's self-esteem verged on vanity, but it wasn't quite. He was almost vain, and he was also a stoic—a special kind of stoic. When he was sixteen, he'd been paralyzed for seven months after being inoculated against swine flu. When he was nineteen and his mother died suddenly on the toilet, he'd cleaned her and put her to bed before telling his father. When he was twenty-one, he'd gone down the cellar and discovered his father's still-warm corpse slumped on the dirt floor below the electric and gas meters—skull bulleted, face like a burst pomegranate. Da could accept and live with all those sorts of crises and losses, but only as long as he felt he understood why they'd happened. An allergic reaction to an iffy serum. The seepage from a cerebral artery. Melancholy, alcohol and a revolver handy. "Disruption of your entire life without a good reason, though—well, that could drive anybody crazy." A special kind of stoic.

He became obsessed by the explosion.

"I've showed you guys my scrapbook, haven't I?" he'd ask us, and I'd nod (even though I wished he'd just go away—

go away and let me sleep) and so would Flour. It was spiral
bound and had a pebbled red cover and heavy black pages.
It was taped full of old letters from the Department of
Defense, the FBI, the White House, a couple of dozen con-
gressmen, the Nuclear Regulatory Commission, the Environ-
mental Protection Agency, each one thanking Da for his
telegrams and assuring him the disaster hadn't been forgotten, that several investigations were still quietly continuing.

But all those other investigations ended the same way as
the first one had, with no answers. And so Da commenced
an unofficial, unbudgeted, scattered and gimcrack inquiry of
his own, which lasted over twenty years . . .

Although both the State of New Jersey and the federal
government inaugurated special financial assistance programs
for the victims of Caliban's Night, the combined monthly
checks ("They were green. One was pale green, the other
was dark.") weren't enough to support individuals, much
less entire families, in the blurringly inflationary next-to-last
decade of the twentieth. (Here, Da often recalled out loud
and with a grimace the price of, say, Gerber's mashed
carrots in the winter of '89.) So naturally those Freaks who
weren't totally incapacitated tried to resume their careers
once the initial traumas had passed. Not many had luck.
For one thing, they weren't permitted to leave the county
for almost a year. And once they could leave—after all the
geiger counters stabilized at the noise level of light sleet on
car windshields—they found Normals not so keen on working side by side with somebody whose right ear might resemble a burnt pita loaf, or had a bottom lip in triplicate, a
perfectly formed thumb sticking out of his bald and parti-
colored pate. They found Normals anxious, even at times
hysterical, about "catching" fallout. They found Normals
quite willing to believe all the grisly fabrications about Freaks
which appeared in supermarket tabloids ("BLOOD IS THE
LIFE," CLAIMS FREAK WETNURSE) or sprang from the tongues

of nightclub comics ("These two Freaks are crawling down the street—right?—and the one . . .").

This was 1989 (said Da), the Year of the Earthquakes. There'd been eleven major churnings in Europe, China, Japan and California alone. It was the same year as the first bacteriological conflicts in the Middle East (quadrillions of oil-eating critters turned loose in the hot sands). It was the same year the first cases of Zorba's Plague (from Greece) were verified in Ohio and Texas. It was the same year the United States launched its first orbiting nuclear bomber, the *Pantagruel*.

Da tried to find office work, couldn't. He was forced, finally, to start his own business. What he did, he borrowed cash and bought a good used camera. Then he began prowling the neighborhoods snapping candids of Caliban Freaks. At first, with the quarantine on, he practically had the whole field to himself, and luckily there was enough global interest then in the disaster—especially in Japan and the Netherlands —that he had no problem selling nearly all of the stuff he shot. And his freelancing had a nice fringe benefit, too: he could talk to people on the street and in their homes, talk and ask them questions. The photos not only fed us and paid the rent for a while, they also financed the early stage of Da's solo investigation of the Blofeld Blast. He purchased transcripts of the commission hearings, a tape recorder, cassettes.

Eventually, the market for proletarian Freak portraits withered and Da changed professions again: from photography to larceny, sometimes grand but mostly petty. Dragging that clunky arm of his along from shoplift to hijack, he must've been the most awkward crook in the annals of crime, but he managed. Somehow—he usually worked with several other guys—he managed. After that, he got involved briefly with video-bootleggers. Then, at the age of thirty, he had a heart attack, so he gave up his felonies and settled for welfare, except for an occasional fling too good or easy to pass up.

"I always regretted," he'd say, "that I had to do things like that—steal, I'm talking about. But I did it for a good reason, see that? And youse were the good reason. You guys and naturally your mother . . ."

Our mother was released from the hospital in the summer of '89. She wasn't, however (said Da), any more resigned then to her cosmetic fate than she'd been a year earlier. She was angry. She was depressed. She spent her days locked inside her bedroom. She bought half a dozen wigs and mail-ordered jars and blocks of theatrical makeup. She camouflaged herself, but the best facial disguises were necessarily the thickest and only made her resemble some whore in Imperial Rome. She spurned our father and ignored us. She prayed the rosary and fasted, promised God and certain selected saints total and absolute devotion upon her miraculous corporeal reversal. When nothing happened she abandoned her faith.

She carried tenpenny nails in her pockets, as weapons. Da would break off the narrative here and tap at the fleshy bulb of his nose, where there was a ragged scar. Then he'd stretch his left palm into the light: "All these other scars here I got for trying to touch her, just for trying. She cut my nose the time I criticized her for smearing you guys, youse were still babies, with her liquid makeup."

She frequently called the police and accused Da of beating her.

"Now that," Da would tell us, "was the worst of it. I've never struck her in my life and yet she had these, whatyoucall, delusions I did. The cops would come and she wouldn't have a bruise on her—but they wouldn't care, they'd arrest me anyway. None of them were Freaks—any Freak who'd been one was retired on disability. Shit, boys, cops weren't

different from any other Normals. If we looked twisted outside, imagine what we must look like inside. All told, I spent
thirteen separate nights in jail, on account of her slanders.

"And I'd come home the next morning and she'd say
You got just what you deserved. I'd ask her how come she
was doing this to me"—Da would bulldoze the pad of his
left hand across his face—"and she'd start to yell—crazy,
out of control—that I'd been beating her ever since she got
sick, ever since Caliban's Night. What could I say? She was
afraid of monsters. She'd been a beauty. What could I say?
I said nothing. I knew I wasn't any monster. I left her alone
because *I* knew what Joe Fistick was. I kept waiting for her
to see. I'm still waiting."

After this, silence would fill up the bedroom and crush
my stomach like heavy gravity on some other planet.

Then he'd kiss us both, turn out the light and shamble
off to his own room, to Ma and to her frost and fire.

I didn't believe he'd never beaten her.

I never saw Ma with a bruise, either, but still I didn't
believe he'd *never* beaten her.

His arm went *thoomp, thoomp, thoomp.*

When Da was gone, Flour would snap the lamp back on
and look over at me. His eyes were small and ochery, like
two kernels of Indian corn. His jet lips would break into a
huge smile. He'd wipe his pajama sleeve across his brow in
a showy burlesque of relief, he'd blot it against his cheeks
and chin. His face was as white as milk curd. He'd be wide
awake and want to talk. He always wanted to talk. About
anything, anything at all. About what it must be like living
up in the moon colony—"It must be strange, it must be
great!" About taking a bike trip to the shack we'd built in
the Blofeld Hole—but he never stopped to consider that,
to get there, you had to ride through Normal sections of
the city. Screw doing that! And he'd want to talk about
Reeni Stankunas, the little furred classmate we were both
in love with, and about me: about my scales, my gills, the

way I could breathe underwater for as long as I wanted. He was jealous, a little, wished *he'd* been the fish twin, instead of the motley one. He was all the time urging me to go down to Liberty Park and slip off one of the piers and *stay under* so he could watch bubbles, count minutes. I'd say: "Come on, Alan, cut it out, will ya? I'm not goin' down any freaken park, so just lay off."

"You got the best skin of anybody," he'd say then, "and you don't deserve it."

"You want it? Take it! You want it? Just take it!"

I wished he could've.

He always wanted to talk for a while after one of Da's bedtime stories. I never did.

"What's the matter with you, Grinner?"

"I feel sick."

Laughing, Flour would leap from under the covers, he'd bound across the floor and snatch up a box of fish meal. He'd start tapping flakes into his tabletop aquarium. Fat Freak goldfish snicking toward the saturated food, gobbling it up. Flour, knees bent, would seek his wavering reflection in the glass, he'd smile and wiggle long skinny fingers hello. A ceramic merman and mermaid with tridents (Flour referred to them as "Grinner" and "Ma") stood wedged in the rolling tank bed of colored pebbles intermixed with green-speckled eggs no bigger than pencil erasers.

"I feel gypped," I'd say from my bed. "Why didn't they go on a honeymoon? They coulda been in Canada."

"Who cares? I like my looks fine." He'd peek vainly at his profile and push out his lips.

"I'm scared."

He'd turn then and glare at me. He'd finger one of the nine clumps of pale-red, almost pink, hair that made his scalp seem archipelagic. He'd wag his head. "Bad as her," he'd say. "Friggen mama's boy."

Later, when the lamp was off again and Flour was sleeping, I'd quietly get up and fetch the penlight that I had concealed in a balled pair of athletic socks in my top dresser drawer. I'd bring it back to bed closed in my fist. Burrowing under the blankets, I'd flick its stud. A tiny 3-D image of a nude Normal girl would quiver on my thigh. She'd smile and breathe heavily as I rubbed myself. I'd be thinking of Reeni Stankunas, I'd be staring at the Normal girl. Then, then my brainstem, my spine, the eyes in my head—they'd all explode, just like the Blofeld house, as my semen tore through the hologram and splintered, devoured, all of its light . . .

Part One:
The Grinning Man
(October, 2010)

1
Freaks on the Boards

Coned in glacial-blue spots, we're standing, Reeni and me, in wedding livery and ponderous masks of lacquered papier-mâché, on opposite sides of a broad canopied bed. Her mask is smooth, gleaming, the cheeks are crayoned rosy—a shy maiden's blush. Cerulean eyes carefully painted, as round as wheels. A cascade of artificial red hair. My groomhead looks solemn, is handsome in a stylized mode: enameled dash eyes, a modeled nose, straight and thin-bridged, a short furrowed mouth, a chasmal chin cleft.

We are playing newlyweds on Caliban's Night.

Suddenly: a chaos of fiery lights. We shield our faces with our forearms, we stagger and topple over like a pair of St. Pauls, we effervesce and dissolve.

Gradually, the flame colors cool and soften; they pale and pale and pale . . .

We've assumed our second tableau. Reeni is sprawled across the nuptial bed, her white-gloved fingers scrabbling the bridemask. I stand palsied downstage, sheathed head crooked sideways, like a lynched effigy's, hands fisted and crossed over my glossy tux lapel.

Lemony daylight.

Jerk-jerkily I straighten and slowly lift the mask from my head, stare unmoved at its princely features. I fling it away and leap to the pier glass. A Freak now, my face is scored by scales, gills cantilever on my throat. My eyes bulge as though nine tenths plucked from their sockets, my lips, slender as earthworms, are taut and stretched into rictus.

Grinning, I turn and face the audience. I raise my arms, I clench my fingers, I tear at my clothes, I tear them off. In a gorilla crouch I circle the bed, and my cock, as green and scaly as the rest of me, bobs and swings and flops.

Still in her mask, Reeni cowers, watches, grabs fistfuls of pillow.

I attack, the blades of my hands blurring up and blurring down.

Her mask cracks open, it falls away in two clean halves.

She breaks my grip and we kneel on the bed barely a meter apart, breathing hard, jaws thrust, spines belligerently oblique.

She draws off her prosthetic gloves, touches her face tentatively, curiously. Short, stubby fingers press outthrust skull bones, probe the brow shelf and the flat nose with its pinhead nostrils, the milky moles that bivouac her cheeks, the perimeter of her lipless mouth, the rims of her ears. They comb the bristly dark fur that surrounds her face like a cowl and mantles her neck. Her hands fall now to the frilly gown collar, they drop lower, they gather buttery cloth and pull: pearly buttons fly.

She plunges at me, clawing my shoulders. I push her down, battering her breasts, chopping her throat, and I mount her.

Howls and bloodshed, both simulated and real.

Freaks' Amour . . .

2
Backstage with the Fisticks

Streaming with bloody perspiration, sticky with semen, scratched, chafed and puffy-eyed, we took our bows, we dodged Baggies full of ground glass, a pear core, a bouquet of wizened tea roses bundled in rain-bleached newsprint. The houselights wobbled up, I squinted, Reeni batted away a melt-rubber warted dildo fat as a cuke. The orchestra was half empty—a scattering of torpid zombies in skullcaps and scarves, pea coats and vinyl gloves . . . some arty types, a clump here and there, in scribbly brass wigs and pastel body suits trimmed with flat strips of juicing neon. The loge and balcony were filled, were turbulent bays of fuzzy sweaters and electric-color sport shirts, of raucous laughter, flatulent jeers and curses like crackling bolts of cooking grease. A hacked doll's head missed my shoulder by a fraction.

We took a final bow, I stretched out my arms, opened my hands: on both palms, the red overlapping lozenges of the atom symbol, the ink feathered by sweat.

Nobody applauded, not even the zombies.

Finally, the curtain slammed down, huffing dust, and Reeni and I collected our masks and torn costumes and limped offstage. Going back to the dressing room we passed three strippers waiting in the wings, Normal black girls with cleavage razor-cut to their collar bones, jellied red mouths and long fatty legs in fishnet. Blankly, they watched us squeeze by then closed ranks behind us and mumbled jokes.

One of them I heard call Reeni a troll, and my chest went tight.

I locked the door. Reeni threw herself facedown on the studio couch, her breath coming jerky. Her fur was sticky and peaked in places, there were some cuts on her hands, thumb bruises purpled her wrists. I had a few broken nails, a swelling lip, I stung all over. I took out the first-aid kit. "Take care those cuts for you now?"

"I'll do them myself. Just let me have some peace, Grinner. For coupla minutes."

I pulled up a chair. "Hey. You really hurt or something?"

"I'll be okay." She propped herself on an elbow, she mumped her cheeks and hissed out her breath. "Leave me alone but." And collapsed, rolled over and faced the pasteboard wall junkied with pinholes. I noticed an oozing gash in her leathery heel so I tried to play medic, with Q-tips and Mercurochrome. But she flipped around and punched my hand away. I said: "Relax, just calm down. We'll be home tomorrow. One more show and that's it for a while."

"Grinner . . . ?" She tucked her lips, tiny red strings made fidgeting orbits around her eyeballs, like they always did when she was under stress.

"What?"

"Nothing." Already, a scratch across her nose was crystalizing into a hard-candy scab. "We'll talk later. I'm tired."

I nodded and left her alone, went and scraped crud from the bottom of a coffee mug with a spoon handle and splashed in some brandy. I washed down a few salt tablets. I felt tired myself, and a headache was spreading from the base of my skull. I plopped into a slingback chair.

In just short of five weeks we'd performed *Freaks' Amour* sixty-three times—in Kansas, Missouri, Minnesota, Michigan, Indiana, Kentucky and now, finally, in Ohio. Toledo. We'd drawn good crowds, done good box office everyplace. Lots of times: standing room only, extra shows. And not just in the strip clubs, either. We'd sold out legitimate the-

aters, civic centers, two or three college gyms. We were
making money, squirreling it away. I figured we'd do a
brief East Coast tour in March, a swing through the South
in April and May, the state fair and straw-hat circuits during the summer. After that we'd have enough saved.

I unpacked the mucilage from my shoulder bag and pasted
the bridemask together again. I set it down to dry on top
of the dressing table, gobbled more salt, lit a cigarette. Reeni
shifted over onto her back, gazed blinkingly up at the leprous
ceiling.

"When we get home and have a little time," I told her,
"I'm gonna see if I can't make us some new masks. Out
of rubber. More lifelike, you know? These ones are too much
trouble, always busting. Just 'cause Beef used papier-mâché
doesn't mean we got to. I mentioned the idea to Studebaker,
he thinks it could work. Reen?"

She rolled to her feet. "Christ!" she said, and padded
across the floor, dug through her paraphernalia case. Took
out a squat jar of Vaseline, unscrewed the lid. My stomach
churned as though mice were drowning in there.

"Reeni, hey, we got another show in a coupla hours. You
don't wanna do that."

"What do you know what I don't wanna?" She scooped
out a lump of petroleum jelly with one hand, a cached silver
locket with the other. Inside the locket were three little goldfish eggs, the hard-shell kind, no larger than acne pimples.

I tried again: "Do me a favor, don't."

She turned her head and shot me a squint, grabbed my
bag and fetched out a tube of potato chips.

"What are you," I said, "depressed again? You depressed?"

She laughed between teeth like calcified postage stamps.
She sniffled and poked one of the eggs with the point of a
nail file. She watched oily black yolk dribble on a potato
chip and soak in.

"You better resurrect by eleven."

She didn't reply, just fed herself the chip, and chewed.

"Aw Reen, what're you depressed about?"

She frowned at me, she winced as the cramps started in her belly. She lay down again on the couch. "You wanna cover me?" I obliged her, draping her with the tattered wedding dress and my tuxedo jacket. Her shoulders bucked, her hands spasmed. She pressed her mouth shut and swallowed vomit. She was dead in about a minute. I thumbed down her eyelids. I stood there grinding my teeth as unnatural rigor, speeded as trick photography, seized and contorted her corpse. Then I went and reburied her locket in the Vaseline. I considered flushing the last two death eggs down the toilet, but that only would've caused a blazing argument later, something I wanted to avoid.

Recently, we'd had too many arguments. They mostly ran like this: Reeni would declare she wanted to retire the rape show once our tour ended. I'd respond angrily, calling her a fool, a coward, a zombie. She'd suck at her gums, as if in reaction to a sourball, and turn her back on me, or maybe she'd shuffle a deck of cards for a game of solitaire, or resume mending one of her seven identical bridal gowns. I'd cool, but not much, and try talking reason. I'd ask her if she wanted to stay a Freak for the rest of her life. "Syntha-skin," I'd say. "What do you think, it's cheap? You quit now and how're we gonna afford it?" Mum, she'd start to pace the motel room carpet . . . or rigidly snap down a row of laminated playing cards . . . or shut one rufous eye and aim thread at a sewing needle—miss, miss again, again. Finally she'd look at me: "Well, maybe I don't want it any more." And that's when I'd get really hot, I'd seethe like a furnace, take a punch at a lamp. Doorknobs I'd designate sitting targets for savate. Passion would rip through me like a squad of poltergeists.

Then, in a hoarse shout: "My brother's how come you wanna quit—isn't he?" To punctuate, I'd boot a wastebasket.

"Go to hell," dashing her words into my face as if they were three separate hunks of jagged scrap metal. And then,

usually, she'd go directly there herself, to hell, for a couple
of hours—after ingesting yolk which she'd smeared on a
slice of bread or pooled along a celery stalk.

I soaped my hands at the sink and scrubbed off the atom
symbols. I washed my genitals and salved the raw spots on
the shaft. I gargled with brandy to rinse out the coppery
blood taste—one of Reeni's fingers had rasped my gums.
I put on my robe and belted it. I walked back to her body.
I pulled my jacket off her face. Her jaw hung open. The tip
of her tongue seemed yeasted.

I stood there, staring at her. I wished I had a cup of coffee, I remembered coming into a room and finding my twin
with his arms around Reeni. Her arms encircled his waist,
her face was buried in his chest. . . . *Nothing going on,*
Grinner . . . swear . . . trust me . . . he was only try-
ing to make me feel better . . . And I said: *Can't I do*
that? Isn't that what I'm supposed to do? And Flour just
smiled his black smile and rolled his shoulders, prizefighter
fashion . . .

About forty minutes later I was stippling a chipped eyebrow on the groomhead with black enamel when somebody
tapped on the dressing-room door. My fingers prickled and
so did my arms, my calves, the small of my back. Three
weeks earlier, in Urbana, one of our "fans"—a kid with
tousled greasy madman's hair and wearing a flicka T-shirt
that played crashing Pacific breakers across the chest—had
sneaked backstage, barged into our room and gouged out a
chunk of my neck with a plastering trowel. I'd bled like a
pig as he sprinted away with a tag of my nubby flesh sticking
to his tool.

There were more knocks on the door.

I glanced around, seeking a weapon. I settled for the nail
file. "Who's there?"

"It's Viller, Fishdick—come on!"

I opened up, and Milty Viller, manager of the Spicee

Theater, a thickset guy in his fifties with a stiff gray brush and a porous nose, thrust a parcel into my hands. "It was delivered a few minutes ago. For your wife."

I thanked him and started to close the door, but he straightarmed it. "Got a few minutes?"

"My wife's sleeping."

"Come on down my office then."

"Give me a second," and I shut the door, tossed the package on a chair. Likely, it was another rat's heart swaddled in tissue, or dogshit in candy foil. I just hoped it wasn't another shoe box from home. I whipped off my robe, zipped into a jumper, tugged on a pair of gloves. I wasn't leaving the building so I skipped making up, left off my wig.

Viller's office was cramped and stale-aired. It had a desk, two chairs and a bookcase full of gray looseleaf binders. Everywhere, model space stations and orbiting bombers, meticulously painted and decaled with national flags, rested on plastic bases glued with identifying plaques or hung from the ceiling on picture wire.

He told me to watch my head and dropped into the chair in back of his desk. "Most people who come in here and see my collection," he said, "they always say the same thing. They say, Why you wanna be reminded?" He laughed. "But the ships themselves—they're beautiful. Don't you think?"

I nodded, noticing the *Progeny of Lenin*, all wheels within wheels and red and gilt, turning slowly on its wire. Viller saw me eyeing it. "That was one of the greatest. One of the earliest, but still. Great."

"And from what I heard," I said, "one of the scariest."

He rubbed his chin. "Oh sure. But like, I can separate the design from the function." He grinned slyly. "And nobody's telling me it just *fell* out of its orbit. Bet we had something to do with that. Don't you think so?"

I moved my shoulders.

"Bet we did. Nobody wanted Russian missiles floating like

angels overhead." He pulled a face. "Now everybody's got 'em floating around up there."

He smiled again. The gaps between his teeth looked grouted. A front tooth was chipped on a perfect diagonal— it resembled a toy guillotine blade. "You worry much?" he said.

That took me by surprise. "What about?"

"About what everybody else worries about. Disaster. The end of the world."

"No," I said. "Not about that."

"Me neither. What the hell. Fact, the only thing would bother me is if people *stopped* worrying. The heebie-jeebies are great for business. Least, for our kind of business they are."

I said I guessed so, I pulled at the fingers of my gloves and gazed at the model of a Chinese orbiter—a silver reticulated dragon—that sat on Viller's desk. I supposed the real one was burnt junk, a shrapnel asteroid. China had been taken out in '03—a joint, synchronized Soviet-American attack. Hot China it was still called today, seven, almost eight years later.

I said: "What?" Viller had said something.

"I asked you how come you didn't throw any shit back at the audience." He wasn't smiling any more. "They expect it. They throw at you, you throw at them."

"We got fined for doing that in Columbus, so . . ."

"Just don't worry about fines, okay? At the late show, you throw."

"All right." I started to get up.

"Wait a sec. That's not what I wanted to see you about." He gestured the V-sign. "Two things. First, you're not peddling death eggs, are you? Either here or at your hotel, or wherever?"

"I got nothing to do with that. I don't sell."

"Glad to hear it. Otherwise, I'd have to warn you. We had some visitors before, while you were on stage. Two guys.

The laminated credentials, the little star—know what I'm saying? They asked some of my girls if you or your wife offered anything for sale."

"They still here?" My guts spun like a cyclotron.

"No, they're gone."

"We don't deal, Mr. Viller."

"Personally, Fishy, I wouldn't care if you did. Like space stations and those heebie-jeebies, eggs and zombies are good for business. People are curious, they're angry, they're addicted—they come pay to see a Freak show. But. Just be careful."

"I got nothing to worry about. As far as eggs go."

"Terrific. Now. That second thing we should talk about . . ."

I clenched my hands, jammed them into my armpits. I glanced away, off into a corner of the room, and tried to control my jitters. *Got nothing to worry about*, I'd said. *As far as eggs go*. Wrong! I had Reeni. And Reeni had eggs. I had Flour. And Flour was the eggman. The bollixed nerves in the pit of my stomach broadcast false hunger pangs. I needed to smoke, but I'd left my pack in the dressing room. There were cigarettes on Viller's desk, a few dozen standing up inside a glass bowl shaped like the U.S. orbital station *David Eisenhower*. I considered mooching one, then decided not to. Even the chummiest Normal was still a Normal, and I always tried hard never to set myself up to be stung. I breathed deeply in and out, making believe there was nicotine in the air. I could've used some salt, too. And I wished to Christ I'd flushed away those last two death eggs when I'd had the chance. Two agents. Using a stiff plastic ID to slip the lock on my dressing-room door. Discovering Reeni's impermanent corpse. Unscrewing the lid from the Vaseline jar . . .

"You're sweating," said Viller. "You all right?"

"It's warm in here."

"It's cold in here." When he smiled, his eyes closed.

"Okay," and rubbed his hands together. "What're your plans for after the show? The two of you."

"We're going to bed."

Two agents finding the locket.

"Well, maybe that's not the greatest idea. Listen, there's some people I know who— Well, they asked me if you'd be interested in doing a third show. At a private party. Not scum I'm talking about—these are quality people, I can vouch. They wanna see you but this ain't exactly the sort of place they feel comfortable in."

"How much?"

"Fifty. Apiece."

"No way, Mr. Viller."

"Hundred. Apiece."

"Nuh-uh. For two bills each but, we might."

"For a twenty-minute show?"

"You know how many Rent-a-Freaks never came home after some private party?"

"I already told you: I can vouch!"

"Four hundred, Mr. Viller, that's the rate. I'm really sorry."

"You're out of your mind, Freak!" He came stamping around the desk and threw open the door. I stood up and, "Wait, hold on," he said. He pulled the door closed. Returning to his desk, he barked a cheek on one of the six sharp points of a suspended scale-model Israeli orbiter. He cursed, blotted his scratch with a lilac hankie, dropped into his chair. "All right, forget the party. You interested in doing pictures? I can get a photographer up your hotel room."

"Hard or soft?"

"Shit, I couldn't move soft so easy. They'd have to be hard. An hour it'll take you, a hundred fifty. And we can get one of the strippers here for mixed threesomes. Well?"

"Two hundred apiece. And forget the stripper."

He sighed noisily. "A hundred apiece and I'll be god-damned if I *will* forget the stripper. I'm offering you a nice pink or brown Normal chick with great big tits. What are you, nuts?"

I shook my head. "We'll take the hundred apiece. But it's gotta be just me and Reeni."

He clasped hands below his chin and stared malignant beams.

I got up. "I'll remember," I said, "to throw stuff back at the midnight show."

"But before you do that," he said, and frowned, "whyn't you put a little more passion in your act? The first show was a little too lovey." He looked down at the bloodstains speckling his handkerchief. "Your wife's got a little skin showing on her face. Why not make it purple for the nice people who come to see you?" He raised his eyes.

I nodded and went out. I was glad I hadn't tried to grub one of his cigarettes.

3
Floury Words

Nothing had been disturbed and Reeni was still dead when I got back. Relief, like soda water hectic in my circulatory system. I locked the door behind me and bolted down salt pills galore. I took Reeni's pulse: the faintest perk. She was beginning to resurrect, still had a long way to come. Thirty, forty minutes. I didn't much feel like reading so I unpacked our little video player and the cassette caddy. Reeni had selected most of the cassettes we'd brought along with us: several anthologies of classic movie love scenes, some animal documentaries (anything about eagles, hawks and falcons, or about extinct species, like African elephants, fascinated her; she loved to admire instinct and grace, to weep over irreparable loss), and a smattering of old and not-so-old television comedy shows. I snapped in an *I Love Lucy* I'd started to watch a week and a half ago, back in Ann Arbor. Fred Mertz staggering into the Ricardos' railroad sleeping compartment with toothpaste rippled across his moon face. Then I played part of an episode of *Candy and Cavity*. The program had been my favorite when I was nine. Watching it again now I couldn't really figure out why—unless I'd been in love with the blond girl who played Candy, and played her usually without a blouse on. Candy was a white prostitute and Cavity was her black pimp; his running gags were splitting trouser crotches and a crusading sister who was a cop on the morals squad. The playlets generally revolved around mix-ups and light crises at a hooker hotel called the Royal Shebang.

I touched a button on the top of the video player and froze a frame: a close-up, side view, of a Candy breast, small and plump as a Bosc pear, freckle-dusted and tipped with a waxy red nipple. I gazed and gazed, and only got blue; a twinge of yearning turned sharply into a mock-diarrhetic cramp. Bleakly, I glanced over my shoulder at bundled Reeni, and some mind pocket teemed suddenly with overlapping memories. Automatically, they were distilled to one idealized composite: the two of us naked in bed, watching videotapes with the sound turned off. Feeling wilted and flushed . . .

Before we were married, before we signed up with Ralph Studebaker's Rent-a-Freak Service, before we conceived *Freaks' Amour*, we used to make love so often—the slow, synchronized, tireless kind, our despised bodies vitamined with hope. It was our spirits, I'd always say, that climaxed so powerfully; our spirits, not our queer genitals. We were confident then that soon, very, very soon, we'd both shed our Freak skins, and swap our eccentric eyeballs for new ones from an organ bank, that we'd sleep gassed in a sanitized operating room as our delinquent muscles were surgically corrected, and as the custom-made Syntha-skin was superimposed and melded to our raw forms, and as our new faces were sculpted, sculpted to copy accurately the photographs we'd provided. To be made new and not-different, to become Normals, and anonymous—that's what we'd always talked about and plotted together. Our joint escape into the world. *Safe!*

The two of us naked in bed, watching videotapes . . .

"I'm cold," Reeni whined, postcadaveric, and her teeth chattered. She rubbed her arms, she gulped brandy, choked and spat. I knelt and chafed one of her troglodytic feet between my hands. She tipped up the brandy bottle again, this try she managed to swallow. "What time?" she asked.

"Going on eleven."

"I'm cold."

"So button your coat."

"I'm cold."

"All right, so Christ, you're cold! What do you want me to do about it?" I called her a zombie and some other names. Then I sucked my teeth and apologized.

But she wasn't listening. "I'm cold," and stared vacantly, and quaked.

I helped her stand up and walked her slowly around the room. Then I sat her down at the dressing table and combed tangles from her fur. She exposed her tongue to the mirror and folded it and fluttered it so nimbly it blurred. She caught me frowning. "I'm okay now," she said leadenly. "I'm really okay." And smiled. And lurched sideways and puked an oily black soup full of stringy ham bits, corn niblets, sails of lettuce and lima beans like clods of paste. I cleaned it all up, using one of my frilly stage shirts. Dully, she watched me swab. Then, "I'm cold," she said.

Twenty minutes later, she'd warmed up some, the fogs had thinned in her eyes. I asked her how the death had gone. "How close did you get to the lights?" I was trying to be pleasant. I was still pissed.

"I didn't bother trying to swim or nothing. I was just out there. You know. Passive."

I dropped the subject.

"What's this?" Reeni picked up the package that Milty Viller had brought. She frowned and shook it close to her ear. She tore off the wrapping.

It was a blue Miles shoe box, lashed around and around with electrician's tape. The box corners were crumpled, and the blue looked sun-faded. A box just like the ones she'd been sent in Fort Wayne, St. Cloud and East Lansing.

She unwound the tape clumsily and flipped off the lid.

Three India relish jars, cushioned by cotton batting. Each jar was filled with tens and tens of death eggs that hung suspended in clear gelatin. A little serrated-edged slip of ruled paper was wedged down between two of the jars. Reeni picked it out and glanced at it. From where I stood, rigid as a statue, I recognized Flour's small and crimpy penmanship. I squeezed my cigarette pack and heard filters snap.

"Cut the drama, kindly." She carried the shoe box into the toilet and closed the door. I pounded on it.

"A few for yourself is one thing. Helping him distribute—"

"Will you please let me pee? Such a harp."

I paced. She flushed and came out. I grabbed her elbow, made her look at me. "You wanna get arrested?" And told her about the narcs who'd been around. "Do you?"

"Let go me."

"Reen, you gotta quit helping him, I mean it. You're gonna get in trouble."

"You ever gonna let go, or what?"

I swallowed hard and released her. Crossing the floor, she made a big deal of kneading her elbow. She unzipped one of the four clothes bags that were hooked to a hat rack and tugged on the beaded sleeve of her bridal gown for the late show. The wooden hanger went gyring off, clattered on linoleum. With the gown bunched up and draped over an arm, she said in a small husky voice: "This is the last package I'll be doing for him anyway. No more opportunities."

"Here we go again."

"Yeah, here we go."

"Aw Reeni, why you doing this to me? You *can't* quit the show."

"Grinner, you're turning my stomach."

Irritably, I scratched at the webbing between my fingers.

"I don't feel like playing monster any more," she said. "Isn't that a good enough reason for quitting?"

"No, it's not. Okay? It's not good enough. What's wrong with the show? It makes money, don't it?"

She laughed and spilled her bridal gown on the studio couch. "Come off it, Grinny. What's wrong? We go on stage nine times a week and show any son of a bitch Normal with ten bucks for a seat that all us Freaks are nothing but animals. Like they always figured. That's *what*."

"You're being melodramatic. I don't like to point this out, but—"

"Look, I know it's partly my fault. Maybe it's totally my fault. I was all for doing the show, you never twisted my arm or nothing. But." She shrugged. "Doing the show depresses me. I don't like any of the people we meet. They scare me, they hate me. I don't like any of the places we been. They're like foreign countries. I like it home, Grinny. I wanna go home. I wanna stay home, I think."

"Like got nothing to do with this. It's making us a living. It's supporting you and me *and* my parents *and* your father. Am I making all this up or is this the truth? If we stop now, just say we do, then what? We sell eggs?"

"I'm only doing Flour a *favor*! I told you that ninety-nine times. And I'm not doing it for free. You're the one always talks about making money. So I'm making money."

"I'd rather get hit with a goddamn pear every night than wind up dead. And I mean *really* dead, like with a bullet in my face. Not dead for an hour on some idiot drug."

"Who's being melodramatic now? Nobody's gonna wind up dead with a bullet in his face. Flour's safe, nobody knows where he is—so don't even talk so stupid."

"All right! All right, I won't—if you don't say any more about this quit stuff. Studebaker's booking us another tour and we're gonna do it."

"I can't talk to you any more, Grinner. I don't know why I even bother. This next show is the last one I do."

"You say now. We'll see."

"Fine, Grinner. Good. Let's just see."

* * *

At the midnight performance I made one of her ears bleed.

Afterward, we dressed in heavy silence. I sat at the table and smeared liquid makeup over my face and throat. I blended it and feathered it, very very carefully. I put on a brown shag wig and a corduroy cap, wriggled my fingers into a pair of flesh-colored latex gloves, and screened my eyes with dark glasses.

In the mirror I watched Reeni force her sagging woolly breasts into hollowed-out and pointed prosthetics and then fit the prosthetics into a padded bra. She buttoned on a long-sleeved white blouse. Her front looked pneumatic. The idea was, large breasts drew attention away from her face. She put on black glasses like mine, and a sticky-backed aquiline rubber nose. Gloves and a puffy down parka. The hood concealed most of her cheek and brow fur, but there was nothing she could wear to camouflage her knuckly facial moles—just as there was nothing I could do about my stretched and leering lips.

It was chilly outside. The streets were empty. The moon was in full phase and its pocks were crisp. Once, I thought I glimpsed the ruby lights of a space station. More likely, it was only a high-flying plane.

". . . them . . . telling you." A not-quite whisper from a shadowed tenement stoop.

Automatically, Reeni and I quickened our pace.

"Wait up, you . . ."

My calves tingled, hot currents zagged through my lungs, my heart whammed against my rib cage. Reeni stopped breathing in, just exhaled a steady panicked hiss. (Beef and Pigeon Mary had been jumped one night late last year in New Hampshire, beaten unconscious with softballs and fists and other blunt objects. Some of his teeth were shattered and stolen for souvenirs. Her arm feathers were set ablaze. I wondered if Reeni was remembering, too . . .)

"Eggs? Eggs?"

At that, we both stopped.

Zombies. Only harmless zombies.

There were three of them, Normals, two young guys and a girl whose unwashed dark hair was so gummy it framed her face like a casque. They caught up to us at a streetlamp. All three wore identical long black woolen coats and grimy fur hats. They smelled rank and their eyes looked sugar-glazed.

"We . . . wanna buy . . . some eggs," the girl managed to say. Strung on a sneaker lace that was looped around her neck were a scuffed brown leather ankh, the head lopped from a ceramic Infant of Prague statuette, and a small plastic pig charm.

I said: "Why do you think we'd have any?"

"You, you're F-Freaks . . . aren't y-you?" stammered one of the guys. The corners of his mouth were hived with sticky spittle balls. "Freaks."

So much for our disguises.

The other guy just stood there with his head down. His left glove smoldered and smoked: a cigarette coal was tangled in the wool.

"No eggs," Reeni said. "Go away."

I wondered if, like me, she guessed this might be a set-up charade. Two agents concealed in some doorway nearby . . .

The girl brushed a plastic mitten back and forth below her nose and said: "If . . . you have any . . . we . . . please . . . we can pay. We . . . don't . . . wanna spend . . . the night here."

"Here," I gathered, meant alive, inside their always-cold bodies.

"Let's go, Reen," I said.

We left them and walked on. Suddenly there was a howl behind us.

The quiet zombie's glove had burst into a torch. He was slamming it against the brick side of a building. His companions hugged themselves ineffectually and looked away.

I gritted my teeth, I ground them, and looked away.

Reeni swore and dropped her stuff. She snatched my shoulder bag and ran gawkily down the street. She smothered the flames with a bridal dress, then came back with the girl and sold her three death eggs. One hundred dollars each, which was larceny.

Reeni stopped on the pavement in front of our hotel, a slouching graystone warren called the Seville. "I don't know about you, but I gotta get something to eat. That diner's open." She jerked her head toward a tinny bunker.

"There's some fruit left in the room," I said. "Just have a piece and let's go to sleep."

"You go up, you want. I need some real food." And she went cutting across the street. Reluctantly, I followed her.

We took a rear booth and kept on our hats and coats and gloves. We both ordered hot turkey sandwiches, green salads with oil and vinegar, and almos-coffee.

I ripped fringe around a sugar packet, and "Sorry I got so mad before," I said. "We're tired. It's been a long five weeks, yeah?" I tore too much wrapper and sugar trickled. "Friends?"

"You started it, Grinner."

"I'm not asking you to do the show for the rest of your life. Just through the summer, that's not—"

"This ear better work tomorrow," she said and tugged gently on the right lobe.

"It don't work?"

"No, it don't. Thank you very much."

"It was an accident."

"It was like."

"I'm really sorry. Really."

The waitress returned, bringing us two styrene bowls of soupy stew with grease blebby on the beef cubes and two paper cones half filled with stale gray sickroom water.

"All right," said Reeni, "funny. Now take it back and give us what we ordered."

"That *is* what you ordered. Right there." The waitress was tall and lardy. She had coiled red hair and a long pink face. She glanced back a smile at two cabbies in leather jackets who were staring our way from revolving counter stools.

Reeni said: "This is all very fucking boring, I hope you know."

"You best watch that mouth in this place, you just best," the waitress snapped. Then she looked over and down at me. "Your mouth, too." The cashier who'd been picking his back teeth with the corner of a color photograph broke into wheezing laughter. I tossed aside the napkin I'd begun to shred, folded my hands together in front of my lips. Stared at a gravy stain on the place mat.

"Come on, you gonna take this stuff back or not?" Reeni had her hands braced flat on the tabletop. "Just yes or no?"

"I only wrote down what you told me. And there it is." She was clicking a pen now.

"So you're saying you won't. Give us what we want."

"Look, you can call the manager but I got the evidence all wrote down." She leafed back through her pad, pointed finally to a blue scrawl that resembled a brain wave.

"No, it's not necessary to call any manager," Reeni said, then she broke off her phony nose and flipped it casually, like an oyster cracker, into her bowl of stew.

I bought cupcakes at a machine dispenser and we ate them back in our room; for beverages, tap water. Then we went to bed.

I was still awake but playing possum an hour later when

Reeni crawled from under the covers, unlocked her case and took the relish jars out into the corridor. The elevator clanked up and stopped at our floor.

When she came back, I peeked and watched her bury a brick of currency in her suitcase. She rolled into bed and fell asleep. I thrashed around for another half hour until finally, selfishly, I tried to wake her up for company. As I squeezed her waist she said something in a sticky mutter. I squeezed again, harder. And she said: "Flour, come on, don't ask me to do that!" I pulled my hand away, made a fist and struck myself painfully on the hip. Chills went squirting east and west from my spinal column. I plumped up two pillows and smoked, I continued shivering. I reached down into the wastebasket and snagged the cupcake cellophane and licked it for its last few crumbs of devil's food and bits of icing. Then I balled it up and pitched it angrily— at my brother, sitting hunched over his worktable.

He batted it aside, looked up and measured me coolly with his tiny red-brown eyes. He scratched a kalsomine cheek, pursed his black lips. *Oh quit it, Grinny! What're you so afraid of?*

You stay away from her! And keep your fucken opinions to yourself. My cat, Baudelaire, rubbed himself against my calf, wandered away, went into convulsions, shook them, jumped onto a chair and cozied down.

What, I can't talk to her? Flour said. *She's gonna marry you so I can't talk to her no more?*

She's not gonna change her mind, Flour. Just 'cause you tell her to. She's gonna have the op. She wants to. You're just confusing things.

If she's gonna, then she's gonna. What're you so afraid of me for? With an eyebrow tweezer, he resumed his careful transfer of midget green-mottled eggs from a sheet of waxed paper into a series of emptied rouge compacts. Behind him, more than a dozen goldfish, their flanks bulging, swam frenziedly back and forth inside their forty-gallon aquarium . . .

4
"We're Entertainers!"

Next morning, we rose early and ordered breakfast—corn toaster muffins and synthetic cocoa—from room service. We ate hungrily in bed. After we finished, Reeni hopped up, snapped open her luggage and whipped out a pair of cranberry harem slacks and a striped polo shirt to wear on the flight home.

"That's short-sleeved," I said. "You can't wear that." I'd woken up cranky, probably because I'd slept so piss-poorly, plagued with feverlike dreams: Flour and me burying my cat, Baudelaire. Burying him over and over again, and being startled silly every time that he leaped, alive again, from his shallow back-yard grave, clay gobbing his calico fur . . .

With a robotic arm, Reeni flung her shirt over a shoulder. She gave a steamy sigh like a dry cleaner's press, gummed her mouth, flashed the vealy gray tip of her tongue. And glared. Blood jots, as motile as sperms, rioted through her eyes. She planted a fist on a brindled hip and called me chickenshit. I told her to think reasonably—did she want to be stared at during the flight?—and she took a shower.

The tint was wretched on the television, there were green convulsions on most channels. I'd get a picture and lose sound. I'd bang the top and the damn set would switch off. Eventually, hunkered down in front of the screen and finagling with a few side knobs, I got a wavy picture and brittle sound to synchronize on a local station. I watched Japanese blood cartoons until the news came on. The French orbiter,

Three Parts Gaul, One Part Divine, was still threatening to nuke the city of Toronto; the Canadian government, nevertheless, was still refusing to recognize rebel Quebec as an autonomous state. Food riots in Bolivia, in Cuba, in Spain, in Southern Ireland. Yet another tinhorn emperor's coronation in some bubonic African country. And in the States: more sunbelt factory failures . . . thousands of lethally carcinogenic Cornish Game Hens mistakenly sold in Delaware and Pennsylvania market chains . . . the Agriculture Department's investigation of last summer's supercorn crop fiasco was continuing . . . the President yesterday canceled talks with the new fascist Prime Minister of Iron England (and the rumor was: the Prez has breast cancer and is scheduled to undergo radical mastectomy) . . . a new wave of scattershot bombings in New York City were being blamed on several apolitical nihilist gangs, particularly the Antichrist Newsboys . . .

Toledo Weatherwatch: Rain, with a chance of Saskatoon neutron fallout.

Then there was a local story about a family named Gruskin. Pictures of the parents, both about fifty, and of their two grown sons. They'd all committed suicide in a garaged car with the motor idling. Footage of the coppery coffins being loaded into hearses, the slow cortege, the grave site clumped with mourners.

I went and grabbed a smoke, and when I looked again a short reporter with a little brown mustache like two sardines butting heads was standing in front of a marble cenotaph: "Those weird and grim rumors have now been confirmed by this sad and tragic funeral today. Death-addicting eggs *are* being sold and used here in Lucas County . . ." Blah-blah-blah. They'd found eggshells littering the car footwells, they'd found death eggs in the family refrigerator. ". . . Al Beimdeck, Toledo-11 News . . ."

I wondered if the four Gruskins had reached the godlights and liked what they'd seen before poisoning themselves. I doubted it: I'd never heard of anybody reaching them yet on an egg down. I'd never reached them. You just swam and swam, your soul tired and straining, aimed at the six blue twinklings in the far, far black distance . . .

I reached out to whack the set off, but stopped when a feature came on about the murder of a local inventor named Sam LaPilusa. His body had been discovered minus its head and left hand. And in the victim's home the police had found: a miniature reactor and electronic paraphernalia galore, a liquor case filled with shards of milky crystal like nougat breakage, and three dozen commercial microwave ovens jam-packed with dinnerware and wooden toys—all badly burnt or scorched.

A snapshot of LaPilusa taken just three weeks ago appeared on the screen. He was a long-faced, sandy-haired sober-looking guy with an aristocratic nose. His left hand was thickly bandaged. He was wearing a heavy neck brace.

I killed the set and went and stood at the open window, popping salt pills. To the west, the sky was a herd of ponderous gray clouds, their underbellies sutured black. Most of the tenement buildings in this part of the city were boarded up with sheets of tin. There were taverns and junk shops, laundromats and gypsy parlors, some movie theaters. We'd passed one revival house yesterday that was showing *Freaks Amok*, the uncut version. I'd thought that film had been vaulted after the trouble it caused in '05. (I remembered all the Normals the film had brought to Jersey City, motoring through the streets with their white, brown and black faces pressed against car windows, pointing . . . remembered Ma keeping Flour and me indoors for weeks on end . . . remembered watching arson fires from our bedroom window . . . remembered Da coming home one night with his right arm hacked and soaked with blood . . .) There'd been a long line of children queued at the ticket window. Reeni turned to me and caustically asked: "Wanna go see?"

I'd acted deaf, pretended complete absorption in the apple I was eating . . .

I turned away from the window and dug around in Reeni's suitcase. I selected for her a western shirt with lariats on the pockets and mother-of-pearl cuff snaps, a white puckered bra with built-in tunneled falsies, a straight black wig and a turned-up rubber nose that was packed in an old Timex box. Safe clothes, safe looks for the flight home. I grabbed the blow dryer and carried everything into the bathroom.

"I want to ask you a question, Mr. Economical, Mr. Savings. Why'd you give that cabbie a thirty-buck tip?"

"He took us all the way out here to the airport, didn't he?"

"Oh, you're so right! He should be canonized maybe for not dumping us on the highway."

"Aw, come on, Reen. Break it off."

"No, I will not! The guy was a creep. His cab had a trunk, you know. There was no reason we had to sit under all our bags. I mean, was he charming? Did he even talk to us? I mean, please tell me how he earned that kind of tip. I'm interested."

"It's done," I said. "Maybe it was a little much, okay." I hadn't thought she'd noticed.

"Jesus God, you make me so mad, the way you worship the rest of the world!"

"What, worship? I gave the guy a goddamn tip. Sorry!"

And she said: "Right, a tip."

We found our baggage counter and joined the end of a short line. A lanky soldier turned around to gape. He was just a kid, and his sudden frown changed his loose pimpled forehead into fiery red pinwales. Then he smiled malignantly. The crimpled hair on the back of my neck all at once felt as humid and liquid as a marsh. Reeni didn't notice the vectored hostility. She said: "Weren't you gonna call Martin about picking us up?"

I gave a grunt and went and found a telephone booth. I fed it change and dialed a Jersey number.

Pigeon Mary answered. "Beef's not here, Grin. I haven't seen him more than once or twice in—what?—three weeks. He's rented."

"Where?"

"New York City. Some lady. But if he told you he'd pick you up at Newark I'm sure he won't forget."

"You sound funny, Pidge. Something wrong?"

"No. I got his number in New York. Want it?"

I said I might as well take it, then: "You really haven't seen him much?"

"No, but it's not only because of this Mrs. Sinakin person."

"Who?"

"Lady who rented him. No, he's got a thing going with some artist, too. Another female."

"Normal?"

"Right."

"He's got two rentals at once?"

"Not exactly. Hey, Grin, why don't you let him tell you about it?"

She read me Beef's telephone number and I coin-scratched it on the metal change apron. I told Pidge I'd see her soon, broke the connection, slotted some more quarters and redialed.

"Yes?" A woman.

"I'd like to speak to, um, Martin Stein, please."

"Who is this, who's calling?"

"Mrs. Sinakin? I'm on the extension," said Beef. "I'll take it."

"I'll answer the phone around here, if you don't mind."

"I'm sorry, Mrs. Sinakin. I won't talk long." He waited a beat, then: "Mrs. Sinakin?"

I said: "I think she's still on the line, Beef."

"That's all right, Grinno. Forget it. How was the tour?"

"Pretty good. We were wondering, hey Beefstone, if you could still meet us today."

"I'll try."

"You think?"

"I'll *try*."

I remembered that his renter was still on the line and "If you can't," I said, "it's okay. We'll get home, no sweat."

"Most likely I'll be there."

"Good enough." His nervousness was beginning to make me a little antsy.

"How'd you get this number anyways? Mary?"

"Yeah," I said. "You and her—?"

"*I'll try and meet youse*. Tell me what time."

Mrs. Sinakin cracked her receiver down. Beef sighed. "I really wish you hadn't called here, Grin . . ."

Reeni was standing alone in the boarding lounge with the tickets in her teeth and a hatbox in each hand. I took my box and we trudged down the accordion jetway. A stewardess, a slim girl with black ringlets like bubbling oil and a pronged pair of tits, saw us coming and took a giant sidestep, blocking the curtained doorway into the fuselage.

She was so pretty that I felt a sucking, tidal pain in my lower intestines.

She said: "I'm going to ask you to open those boxes."

"Masks," I told her. "We're entertainers!"

"She thinks we're smuggling caviar," Reeni said. "Isn't that what you think, lovely? Goldfish caviar?"

I felt like crumpling the side of her skull, I curled my toes till my arches, insteps and ankles cramped. With clumsy overeager fingers I worked the ribbon off my box lid and showed the stewardess my groomhead. She frowned at it, she frowned at me. I glanced away at paneling rivets.

"And now yours," she said to Reeni, who glared but complied, giving the stew a glimpse of the bridemask.

The girl thanked us, and I thanked her very much.

"She didn't check anybody else's."

"Don't be so touchy. I'm sure she did."

"She hasn't but. Not one single other person's bag."

"Just forget it."

"I been watching her, Miss Triangle Tits."

I shoveled potato chips into my mouth and, chewing, changed the subject: "It's not such a great idea, hon, taking off your glasses. Whyn't you put them back on? The lights are bright anyhow, no?"

Without an argument, she pushed her shades back onto her face—and the Chinese man sitting across the aisle lost interest in staring and finished his hard roll, sesame-seeded crumbs avalanching onto his paunch.

Once the plane was airborne, I hunched down and steepled my fingers at my lips. I tried to look contemplative. I counted heads, I studied Normal faces, hands, complexions, ear-shapes and haircuts:

An old person, sexless, traveling alone . . . faded blue eyes, liver-spotted temples . . . in a shiny black jump suit . . . smoking a filter cigarette with a slinky ash.

A fat lady in a purple caftan . . . tucking her meaty chin, swallowing belches. She had a roll of antacid tablets in one pudgy fist, a twisted facial tissue in the other.

Another woman, but slim and young—likely she was younger than me, still in her late teens—with short green hair greased to her skull, tiny features and thick orange eyebrows, moist mahogany skin. She was wearing a silver jacket whose upper right sleeve was taped over. I guessed there was a pornographic flicka-loop underneath, and guessed further that the airline had provided the tape. She wore polychromatic cord fashioned into a hangman's noose around her throat. I hoped Reeni was wrong. I hoped the stew had combed through *her* luggage, at least.

Most Antichrist Newsboys (or at least the ones who weren't being sought by the cops for planting bombs) wore nooses around their necks in public: their way of symbolizing their belief that the planet was under a sentence of death.

I finished my inventory:

Two men sitting together . . . one a business type with a rosy face, an expensive nonsynthetic flannel suit, slim mustache, white teeth, perfect bite . . . the other a Durham bull of a guy with greasy dark hair, a chin lunar with acne scars, a flattened nose, big dull eyes, and a long, crooked, unbroken eyebrow, like a Havana cigar.

A little later, the bullish guy stood up and came down the aisle, heading for the toilet. He passed us and stopped. I felt his gaze on the back of my neck. I wouldn't turn around. He didn't move, he cleared his throat. Reeni looked up from her newspaper, glanced over a shoulder. Her cheeks caved in. So I looked, too.

The guy was standing there grinning, and his grin was a deliberate forgery of mine.

I flipped through a copy of *Vogue*, fantasizing about a de-Freaked Reeni in some of those designer fashions. I pictured her depilated and pink, with flesh springy to the touch. I pictured her wart- and mole- and cyst-free. I pictured her with adorable five-toed feet, smooth calves and snowy thighs. I pictured her with clear golden-brown eyes, like the stewardess had. I closed the magazine. "Beef's going to see that Dr. Sleet soon," I said. "I told him whenever he did, we'd come along."

"Don't let's talk about operations again, okay?" She passed me her newspaper, folded so I should see a particular story.

COPS CRACK EGGHEAD PARTY

"Flour mentioned?"

"Why should he be? The story's about Cleveland, for Christ's sake."

"He's gonna get creamed," I said. "Flour."

"Don't talk bad luck! I don't wanna hear."

She couldn't stop me from wishing it, though.

Interlude: A Night
at the Sycorax Club
(July 14, 2009)

"He couldna been dead, not really," Beef said, shouting above the bar roar. "You and Flour made a mistake." He flipped his palm back and forth. "Weird, though," and smiled, and refilled his schooner from the ale pitcher, also refilled mine and Pigeon Mary's. Reeni, looking haggard and gloomy (her mother was failing), gave her head a stiff wag: *no more for me.*

I hunched over the table, and brushed away a few Spanish peanuts, a burnt match. "My cat was *dead*, Beefstone. As a doornail. No kidding."

He leaned back, his flat gristle-pale eyeballs rolling in their pink membrane pools. He smirked. "Goldfish."

"Grinner's telling you something, Martin," Reeni said and thumped the table. "You don't have to act like a friggen moron. Yeah, the goldfish, the goldfish *eggs!*"

"The asshole eggs?" Very lightly, he pressed the pale-blue chalk cap that was gummed to his left forefinger knuckle against the tip of his tongue. He squeezed his eyes closed for a long moment as the drug shiver tore through his bulk, all three hundred pounds of it. He was a sucker for all of the legal gimmick dopes; last year he'd gone around for a full month wearing buzz-candy braces on his front teeth.

I said: "Forget it, man," and half turned in my chair, scanned the club. It was packed with Normals, slobs and chichi both, locals and slummers, standing five deep at the short bar, crammed into cracked-leather booths, clustered around bistro tables. Saturday night. Blue smoke dizzied in the track lighting, layered and surged in the dimness. I felt jittery, wished Reeni and I were elsewhere. But I'd promised Beef and Pidge that we'd come to see their first rape gig.

I swung back around and dissolved a few salt pills in my ale. Pigeon Mary inclined her head, propped her chin in a feathered wrist: "So how's your cat now? Okay?"

"Fine." But he was jumpy and barely had an appetite any more. More likely, he was starving and just paranoid about food.

"I don't understand," she said, scratching her throat. Several creamy white hackles wafted to the tabletop. Beef picked one up and drove the down through his shirt collar: a boutonniere. Reeni scowled.

"What's to understand?" said Beef, by this time thoroughly bored with the whole subject. "He wasn't dead, stunned just."

"Nuh-uh, Beefstone," I said, "no matter what you say," and recalled pounding into the bedroom several nights ago and joining Flour, who was squatted and trailing a hand along Baudelaire's flank. My brother's eyes had flicked sideways, he'd bit his lip and said: "I'm real sorry about your cat, Grinny, but—Jesus!" There was a flood on the floor, there were atolls of wet gravel, chunks and diamondy chips of aquarium glass. Goldfish whumped and thrashed everywhere. God knows how, but Baudie had managed to tip the forty-gallon tank from its table base. Then he'd pinned one of the fish—one of the biggest—to the linoleum and mauled it open. It was still clamped in his jaws and drooling a paste of midget green eggs and unctuous black yolk. He was already cold and rigored—and less than a minute had passed since I'd heard the crash.

I helped Flour save his fish—we gathered up the school and tossed them into an emptied wastebasket, then we raced with it down the hall to the bathroom, where we filled and stocked the tub—and then he helped me take care of Baudelaire. We found a sheet and wrapped him. We fetched a shovel from the cellar and tramped out into the back yard and dug a hole. I picked up the bundle and made to nestle it down in the grave, and the bundle began to move in my hands. Paws patting and scratching at the sheet. Spooked, I let go, and Baudie wrestled free of his shroud, his fur stood up. He spat, first at me and then at Flour. He shook his head, he rolled on the ground, he crawled away crying . . .

"But how do you know," asked Pigeon Mary, "that it was the eggs? It could've been the fish."

"I know because my brother tried them both. The fish gave him, um, gas, and the eggs—he ate the yolk from two —killed him for an hour."

Beef's jaw dropped. "You din't tell us *that* before!"

"So what're you going to do now?" Pidge asked. "Tell the newspaper?"

"It's not my business, what to do. They're his fish."

"Yeah, but this is important. Isn't it?"—as though she weren't quite certain.

I shrugged. "Anyway, he moved all of them out of the house. Day before yesterday. I don't know where to."

Beef folded his arms like a djin across his chest. "Your brother's no dummy, he's thinking about bucks."

A bank of purple lights blazed on above the little stage in the corner, where two Freak bartenders were setting up a cot.

Beef looked up, pinched his lips, and "Wish it was us going on now," he said. "But we're next—the eleven-o'clock show."

At that reminder, Pigeon Mary scrunched down in her seat. She twisted her hands edgily in her lap, gaped up at a mock-splintery plastic crossbeam.

"This act's good, though," Beef continued, "this act coming on now. Give the Norms their money's worth." He chuckled, quaffed ale and sleeved his mouth. His lumpy face shone, juicy with sweat. His flesh was the same deep red as a bottom round styrene-trayed in a butcher's showcase. It was forked with gristle and white fat. His ears were as bantam as an ape's on a head as jumbo as a pumpkin. "They do a good rape." He licked his chalk again.

I reached out and squeezed Reeni's hand. She smiled wearily. She wanted to be home at her mother's bedside. Some kind of cancer. Cancer of this or of that. Leukemia? Terminal.

"I'll get you back by midnight," I told her. "Promise."

She kissed my scaly fingers.

Unannounced, they came out, in soiled and threadbare white cotton robes, from a little room at the back of the club. They weaved carefully between tables (a seated latino guy with a greasy pompadour dashed whiskey at them) and stepped up onto the stage. He was a foxface, she was a cyclops. They were both dwarfs, Negroes, and as thin as slats. They didn't acknowledge the audience, most of whom were busily collecting ice cubes and tavern nuts, bottlecaps and cardboard coasters to hurl later on. They unbelted and shrugged off their robes. They repositioned the cot, tightened some of its wing nuts and tested the canvas for give. Then Foxface cleared his throat, rolled back on his heels, rolled forward and smashed Cyclops in the nose, sent her reeling, staggering.

Beef leaned across the table, whispered: "He barely touched her. Fucken jigs got their timing down pat."

If the punch had been faked, the rape was genuine and brutal. And by the time it was done the Normals had run through all of their small-gauge ammunition and were chucking shot glasses and empties, they were lobbing stones from the chammy bagfuls sold at the door for a buck fifty.

Pigeon Mary asked: "Is it over?"

I told her it was.

"They offstage yet, they gone?" She spoke at the smudged grip of her schooner, as if it were a table mike. She'd kept her eyes lowered during the entire performance.

"They're going," Reeni said, and watched them both stagger through a gauntlet of swatting Normals toward the sanctuary of the back room. "They're gone."

There were semen worms and blood carnations staining the cot . . . a kid Freak with a veiny face and faceted insect eyes appeared with a janitor's push broom and started sweeping the stage . . . Normals stampeded the bar.

"Did they get hurt?"

"No," Reeni lied and took a swig of my ale. "I don't think."

Then Pidge glanced up, grinning self-consciously. She smoothed a wrinkle in the puffy sleeve of her green tissue blouse and blotted salt water from the corner of an eye with the side of a finger.

She'd only recently moved to Jersey City from Long Island, to be with her "people," as she often put it. She'd run away from Normal parents who'd kept her confined to their house, and practically to a single bedroom, for twenty-one years. A three-year-old kid, her chromosomes had been flummoxed when a fluke draft of Blofeld Street fallout came drifting over Bethpage. That made her twenty-four today. She looked fifteen: slight and hipless, with breasts like new potatoes. Beef had met her in late May, at Lincoln Park, where he was running and she was reading a book of collected Tennessee Williams plays on a hillside. She moved into his apartment the second week of June, and it took him a month to coax her into becoming his rape partner. They'd auditioned here at the Sycorax Club last Wednesday afternoon, and Ralph Studebaker, the owner, a Normal and a restaurateur from Maryland, hired them on the spot.

I didn't know how Pigeon Mary was going to find the strength to get up and perform. She was already trembling and there was still another hour, fifty minutes, until show time.

Beef was fidgeting, raring to go. Understand, he wasn't thrilled about the work, either. Like Pidge, he wanted to be a "real" actor. He was just itching to get his hands on some currency: the rate was ninety dollars split two ways for every hard-core rape.

He said: "Getting back to Flour for a second. You got any idea, Grin, what he's planning to do with them eggs?"

"Nope. But ask him yourself. He'll be here later."

"Here?" He laughed. "Din't think Flour'd be caught—excuse the expression—dead inside a rape bar. His brother don't approve," he explained to Pidge, and it was easy to read in the lazy nod of her feathered head that Flourface, sight unseen, had automatically scored some points with her. "His brother's also flat broke most of the time, so . . . Hey, Grinno, what's he coming by for?" Beef lit and toked a Salem mentholated joint.

"You can ask him that, too."

"What, don't youse guys ever talk?"

"Not much."

"He's gonna make bucks," Beef said. "Bucker-babies galore."

"Just keep it to yourself," Reeni said. "About the eggs. He'll do what he wants. In the meantime, Martin, he don't need it blabbed all over town." She and I had known Beef nearly all of our lives. The three of us, plus Flour, had gone through grammar and high schools together. He was my best friend and one of her least favorite people. She didn't trust him. Neither did Flourface.

She stood up from the table, turned and banged her hip. "I'm gonna call home."

So I rose, too; couldn't let her wander off alone, not in this bar. There was a pay phone on the stuccoed wall between the yellow doors of the two rest rooms. We squeezed our way over there and more than a few Normals must've figured we were the next act: I took some spittle on my cheek, Reeni got ear-stung with a chewed-wet stick of beef jerky. I stood sentry while she dialed and then spoke in a murmur to her father. A Normal guy in a butter-soft shovel hat, blue Levi's and an acetate shirt silk-screened with cocks-and-balls and multiple map-shapes of Texas came up and bumped me hard in the shoulder. I felt my sphincter unbind —but he staggered directly into the can.

I spotted Dinah Murphy waiting on tables, her four heavy breasts straining the front of her black-and-white uniform. She was wearing a wig of spun brass, a clunky play-gold chain around her neck, a little rouge. Her panty hose were zippered with runs. She deposited a round of brews on a table, was paid with a crumpled bill that caromed off her throat hollow.

I'd been startled earlier when I walked into the club and found Dinah working here, bustling about, smiling for tips and laughing loud between stained teeth at ugly insults. Amazing, because she hated Normals, had hated them ever since her globe-headed son Brainstorm's murder during the Bad Days in the spring of '05. He'd been ambushed by a squad of kids who'd driven up from the Jersey shore. Ambushed right on the corner of Bartholdi and the Boulevard, in broad daylight. They'd strangled him with his necktie, one of those wide navy-blue jobs that used to be sold as fund raisers by the Freak Pride Association, and that were stenciled: CALIBAN'S NIGHT *4/18/88 "You Shoulda Been There."*

Brainsy was fifteen when they got him. He'd been in a few of my sophomore classes at Snyder High. I'd known him slightly. Flour had known him well: they'd been friends.

Shortly after the killing, about fifty members of the FPA —including Dinah Murphy, who was then the organization's recording secretary—had bussed to the Paramus Mega-mall and firebombed a cinema that was showing *Freaks Amok.* Dinah got nine months for malicious mischief; the judge was lenient on a widow who'd just lost her only kid. Everybody else in the group pulled sentences of twenty years or more. Few of them survived at Trenton State Prison.

* * *

Reeni hung up and stood facing the wall for half a minute before she came over, red filaments rioting in her eyes.

"Any change?"

"She's sleeping. My father wants me to come home."

"We'll be going in a little while."

"All right . . . ," she said, then: "Grin, you shouldna told Martin about the eggs."

"Why not? It's not gonna stay secret too long."

"Flour asked you not to."

"Fuck him."

There was a low-built and stocky Normal straddling my chair at the table when we returned. He was flinging broad gestures left and right, talking fast and scowling. Beef was nodding like a dutiful son. Pigeon Mary sat rigidly, listening with her mouth open.

"Hey, Grinno, Reen," said Beef, ". . . want you to meet Mr. Ralph Studebaker."

Studebaker looked up, coolly measuring me first, then Reeni, then he allowed himself a brief smile. He didn't offer to shake hands. We didn't either.

He was in his late forties, I guessed, and was wearing a one-piece orange jumper zagged across the chest with a shiny black thunderbolt. He also wore a necklace and matching bracelets of dull-tipped pewter thorns. His face was the color of a manila folder and his features were mushy. He had a full new head of crinkly brown hair: you could see the peppercorn-size implantations that studded his crown.

Reeni slid into her chair and I was left standing.

Beef said, a little too brightly: "Mr. Studebaker was just telling us—"

Studebaker cut him off with a curt arcing chop of his pudgy hand. "I was just saying that I'm starting a new business. Actually, it's only a new wrinkle in this one—and I'm looking to hire talent. Are you looking for work, Mr., ah, Grinner?"

"Fistick," I said and rolled back my lips as far as they'd

go. "Always looking." Currently, I worked two afternoons a week at Lincoln Park, mowing grass and spiking litter—county charity. Occasionally, Beef and I would get a house-painting job, but there just weren't that many Freaks with loot enough to make property improvements. And forget about the local Normals: they wouldn't hire us.

"It's not club work," Studebaker continued. "It'll be a rental service. You know, serve drinks at parties, take coats. Maybe do some other things. Interested?"

"Very."

Studebaker handed me up one of his cards, a stiff gray square with raised black letters. A Manhattan address and telephone number.

I thanked him very much.

When he rose heavily, Beef pushed back his chair and got up, too: "And don't you worry about us tonight, Mr. S. We're gonna be great, just great."

"Don't spend too much time with the artsy mask stuff. Nobody's here for Greek tragedy."

"We just wanna be a little different."

"You're all different enough without masks," and Studebaker ambled away. There were two more thunderbolts, phalanxed, on the back of his jumper. There was a puffy storm cloud appliqued on each buttock. He wore high green leather spark-boots that spat red and yellow scintillas. The guy obviously had bucks galore.

I took my seat.

Beef toasted me with a half-filled glass of flat ale. "All *right*! Syntha-skin, here we come! All of us—yeah?"

I wished I could've pulled a regular-size smile of pleasure. I flashed, as second best, the okay sign.

Reeni was gnawing a mole on her thumb pad.

Pigeon Mary, eyes cast down again, was shredding a cock-tail napkin with print on it: LIVE FREAK SHOWS Fri. Sat. Sun. "Rapes 'n' Grilled Sandwiches"

* * *

"When youse were at the telephone," Beef said, "Di Murphy came over to say hello."

"Yeah, I seen she was here. Could hardly believe."

"Hardly believe what?"

"Waitress at a rape club?"

"Look, Grinno, we all got stomachs to feed. No but, I was talking to her—and wanna hear something funny? I asked if she still had her goldfish."

Reeni jerked electrically, her hand tumbling from her nibbling teeth.

"But she don't. 'Cause guess who bought 'em? *Yesterday?*"

"You shit," from Reeni, punctuated by a gust of breath.

Beef ignored her (animosity was mutual) and perched his chin on interlaced fingers. "What do you suppose he got in the works? Flour."

"I told you once already, I don't know."

"Beef," said Pidge in a solemn church voice, "I think it's time."

They had their masks in supermarket sacks underneath the table. Beef grabbed both sacks, pretend-punched Pigeon Mary on the shoulder, then pulled her to her feet. Eyes bright, she looked back at Reeni and me—we were the chaplain and the good screw, she was on her way to the gas chamber.

They disappeared into the back room.

Before Reeni could say anything, I apologized. "You were right. I shouldna said anything about the eggs."

"Maybe you'll believe me now. About him."

"Aw, Beef's all right."

"Grinner, I love you, but keen you're not when it comes to judging people. Believe me."

A few minutes later, Flour came into the Sycorax Club with Bobby Lumps and Dragon Luther. He stopped at the card table left of the door and bought a bag of stones, a bag of cinders and a bag of rock salt.

"What the hell does he think he's doing?"

Reeni didn't reply, just half stood and waved.

"I don't want him coming over here," I said.

"I waved just."

"I could see what you did, but you shouldn't encourage him."

"I *waved* just."

And he waved back. A large smile, ebony lips framing teeth like coffee-soaked sugar cubes.

"He best not come over here with those two bozos."

And he didn't: preceded by Lumps and the Dragon (the former a five-foot-nothing obese and ambulatory package of chunk-style cottage cheese and the latter a crest-headed seven-foot black giant), Flourface swaggered straight up to the bar, Western desperado style. Since the bar was all-Normal, I held my breath, expecting tumult. It almost happened, too. Some guy with a neck patched with Band-aid disks pushed Lumps and then tried to club him with a Rolling Rock bottle. The bottle wound up clattering onto the bar top, twisted from Band-aid's grip by a tall wedge-headed Normal in a black summer-weight suit.

Wedgehead whispered something to Band-aid, who stiffened, lost color and promptly apologized—*apologized!*—to Lumps. Then he made a beeline from the bar straight through the front door.

Flour moved from behind the Dragon and fell into an easy conversation with Wedgehead. He reached a hand into his jeans and pulled out a plastic rouge compact, which he tapped with a blanched tentacle-finger and then passed to the thin man in the black suit.

At that moment the purple stage lights bedazzled on again, and Beef and Pigeon Mary came filing—slowly and still in their street clothes—from the pokey back room, cumbrous papier-mâché masks concealing their heads and necks. The features had been brushed on with a mixture of model-airplane epoxy and food coloring (Beef had found the recipe in a library children's book called *Rainy Day Fun for Pre-teens*). The eyes and noses, the mouths, ears and "hair" were all shiny and lacquer-hard. The masks were supposed to typify the Homo sapiens' comeliness, but failed: facial proportions were all wrong, lines were ragged and impasto, there were dried paint spatters that registered as brown and blue and yellow zits.

The club crowd didn't know what to make of Beef and Pidge, and so, baffled, they lapsed into an uncharacteristic cough-silence. They swallowed the ginders they'd hawked to let fly (a roomful of bobbling throats), they swilled drinks but didn't fling them, they stood on tiptoes and craned. They jiggled peanuts, as if loose change, in open palms.

But as soon as the show got under way, the Normals turned loud and rowdy again; and grew louder and rowdier as it gradually dawned on them that the rape skit was a pared-down reenactment of a "classic" scene from the horror movie *Freaks Amok*, the scene where the pretty, uncontaminated housewife spurns her just-bizarred spouse:

Beef (sans mask) dropped to his knees and, flexing his fingers, pantomimed a plea for compassion . . . Pidge (still in her mask) stiffened her spine, hugged herself tightly and turned away . . . Beef pitched forward and mashed his face against the gritty stage floor, his legs kicking out in a tantrum . . . Pidge pretended she was packing a suitcase, emptying a closet . . .

Stones and cinders began to rain onto the stage. They plinked and ricocheted. They grazed Beef with welt-raising snaps. But nobody seemed to be taking deliberate aim at P.M.

. . . Unsteadily, Beef climbed to his feet. He whimpered, he rocked back and forth and thrust out his arms. He weaved his head in figure eights, and growled.

Pidge just packed, packed, packed her invisible clothes.

Then, swinging two pieces of make-believe luggage, she headed for the "door" (the tar-papered steps at the front of the stage). Beef yowled, stumbled, clutched her elbow . . .

Reeni cut her eyes away, she lit a cigarette and pulverized the charred match head between her fingertips, she blew lightly on the ash.

. . . The sound of fabric tearing, a choked-off cry, a crash . . .

And from that point on, the show was just another Freak rape. I watched a little bit of it. (I'd been morbidly curious about what Pigeon Mary looked like undressed: the insides of her stovepipe thighs were dark-gray unfeathered flesh, her organ hair was steelwool, her pearly nipples were dime-size. Then I shifted in my seat and scrutinized the fomented crowd—laughing, heckling, grimacing and squinting, hurling all sorts of crap. A girl Normal (radish-red hair banded by a coronet ziggy with alpha waves, a Greek nose, bull's-eyes on a holey shirt-jac) lunged from her chair at a nearby table and whipped back a forearm to sissy-chuck a spoiled mandarin orange. Then she noticed me and aped my grin, she changed her aim and popped the fruit in my direction; it struck the ashtray and flipped it over.

Reeni's hands flew up to her face like birds of omen, I froze for a moment like a deer caught in headlights. Then I picked up the orange, nodded at the girl who'd thrown it and flipped it back to her underhand. She caught it the same instant that a pellet of rock salt zinged her on the cheekbone. A moment later she was bombarded with more pellets, a regular sleet-storm of the stuff: Flour's entire bag's worth, flung from the club doorway. Laughing, my brother ducked outside, and so did Bobby Lumps and Dragon Luther. Wedgehead and a trio of hulking Normal cohorts leisurely followed.

The Coronet Girl was on her feet, fluffing rock salt from

her hair and swearing. Her table companions were glowering at me. One of them, an Indian with skin like cordovan, scraped his chair back ominously.

"Reeni—think we should wait for Beef and Pidge in the back room."

And so we did, with the door locked.

By ten of midnight, the four of us were out of the club, hurrying down West Side Avenue in the muggy dark. Beef had his car (an old gasoline Ford that he'd equipped with solar pie plates swiped from an auto-supply in Kearny) parked on a side street. We piled in and rolled south toward the Freaktown section of the city at forty kilometers, top speed.

Old Beefstone was ebullient: "We did good, no? Not bad for beginners, huh? And Studebaker was worried about the masks! They loved 'em! Those assholes."

Pigeon Mary looked at Beef, her almost-angry, almost-crying face greened in the dashlight. Then she went back to licking a deep gouge in her left palm. Her blouse was torn, ribboned.

Reeni drew a breath that seemed to inflate her shoulders, she let it out and slumped.

"Seen Flour," Beef said and walloped the horn to scare off a six-legged bulldog who was cantering down the middle of Mallory Avenue.

"And did you see the stunt he pulled—with the rock salt?" I asked.

"Nuh-uh, what?" (Of course he hadn't seen: by that time he'd been crashing up and down on top of Pidge.)

When I told him, he whistled and ticked his tongue on the backs of his upper teeth.

"That coulda got you guys smashed and carried off."

"The jerk!"

Reeni sat up and said she thought it was funny. In a scary sort of way. "I did, and I loved seeing that chick's face."

Pigeon Mary joined Reeni in a peal of tight laughter. I frowned at them both.

"That Flour's a wild man, no?" Beef grunted. "I've always liked him."

In fact, he'd always hated his guts.

"And hey—you guys catch who he was at the bar with?" Beef lifted a hand from the wheel, clenched and wagged it: all five knuckles were capped now with blue chalk. "Gabe Four-quarters—you heard of?"

"No," I said. "Four-quarters?"

"Big man in legit candy, but he also moves a lotta other junk not so legal. Everything from old-fashioned scag to bliss-beans. Din't I tell youse? Trucks o' bucks for brother Flour."

Pigeon pointed suddenly through the windshield: "Is that one of those space stations? Just under that cloud. See?"

"Nah," said Beef, "probably just some planet. I think it's Venus you can see in the summer. Am I right, Grinno— Venus?"

"Couldn't tell you."

"Venus," said Beef. "I'm sure of it."

He let us off at the corner of Seaview and the Boulevard. I linked arms with Reeni and we walked up the block. I said, "Poor Pidge," and she said: "Yeah."

We went into her building and she flicked through her keys, unlocked the lobby door. The hall, as it always did, smelled of Polish cooking, candle wax (a family on the first floor burned votive cups night and day) and lemon disinfectant. It was a clean place. We waited for the elevator.

I asked: "You think I should call Studebaker, don't you?"

"Don't have too much choice, do we? Sure, call him. I'd rather not do shows but."

"He said parties."

"Yeah, call him."

We stepped into the elevator and clinched, held one kiss until we stopped at the sixth floor.

* * *

"Daddy?"

Every single lamp in the parlor was burning, the windows were shut, the apartment was a steambox.

"Probably asleep," I said. There was a bottle of warm cherry soda standing on an end table. I helped myself to a swap and bounced onto the couch, I whacked the cushion. "Sit." I wanted to make out. With eyes closed, I was already focusing a mental picture of the redheaded Coronet Girl, stripped and with neat cupcake breasts. Then I wanted to fix something to eat. I was imagining the Coronet Girl, I was thinking about food and Ralph Studebaker. "Come sit," I told Reeni.

"Lemme go check on them first," as if she were the parent and they were the children.

I'd rasped my pants zipper halfway down when Reeni let out a slavered scream.

Zipped up . . . ran into the bedroom . . . bureau overturned . . . clothes strewn on the floor . . . lampshades askew . . . Reeni's mother sheeted on the bed.

"She can't be," but I looked and she was. Her eyes were closed but her lips were curled back over canine teeth and over black-red gums that were like wetted ash still bellied with embers. Dead. "Reeni . . . I'm sorry . . ."

I glanced down at the woman again and noticed that the case had been slipped from her pillow. It wasn't on the floor.

"Where's your father?"

Reeni was blubbering, staring blankly. "He *told* me to come home," and sniffled.

"She was all right when you called. You couldn't know."

"Where's my father?" she wailed, whipping her head around, eyes bulging at the room shambles. (Had she just noticed?) "Where's my *father?*"

We found him standing fully clothed in the bathtub. Skull Garden (a nickname—the top of his hairless head was like a truck farm yielding a bumper crop of cauliflower; actually, it was only a clotted blight of pale growths very similar to warts), Skull Garden had rolled up the missing daisied pillow case and noosed it around his scrawny neck (the harvest there resembled baby corn niblets). He was trying to knot both ends together around the shower head, but there wasn't enough slack: it was impossible.

He was crying and hyperventilating.

Reeni bolted across the floor. They embraced. I snatched the pillow case and shook it out and blotted my face with it. Then I left the two of them alone.

I got home about five, cottoned with exhaustion, nauseated from a headache. The only light on downstairs was the student lamp on Da's desk in the parlor. It cast a stark white parabola across pads, files, Polaroids, cassettes and my father's broad and sweaty naked back. He was conked. I snapped off the light, carefully stepped over his python arm and punched STOP on his fizzing machine: ". . . why the Blof—"

I went upstairs, considered waking Ma to tell her about Mrs. Stankunas, decided to wait. I wondered if Flour was home, slumped into the bedroom and discovered he wasn't. I took a shower, brushed and flossed and put on pajamas. I got into bed and smoked a last cigarette. Was stubbing it out when my brother came slamming into the bedroom with his white face and green shirt measled with blood. His hands were caked red.

He grabbed a newspaper from his night table, spread out sheets on the floor and stood on them. Emptied his pockets, tossing everything—rouge compacts, the bag of stones, the bag of cinders, house keys, coins and wallet—on top of the dresser. He stripped down. He loped for the door. "Stuff all that shit into my duffle," he called back. "*Every*thing, Grinner!" He pounded along the hall and jumped into the shower. I heard it siss on.

By the time he came back dripping I'd packed all of his

bloody clothes, plus the newspaper mat, and I'd cinched the bag and rolled it up. He grabbed it, slung it over a shoulder and clattered naked down the stairs. I tagged behind, thinking, *Christ, he's gonna wake up Ma, he'll wake Da for sure . . .*

But he didn't.

He charged through the kitchen door, vaulted the porch rail and located the filled-in grave we'd dug recently for Baudie. Dropped to his knees and pawed like a dog. He buried the bag, tamped the dirt with his fingers and drummed it with his palms.

"Okay, what?" I asked. "What happened?" I went and sat on the crumbly wall of the brick barbecue.

He looked shaky standing up. He looked like a vampire in the moonlight, so tall and gaunt and blanched. He gave a nervous laugh and walked over. A squirrel with a whippy rat's tail darted through the crabgrass behind him, ticked up the clothes pole and leaped onto the roof of Da's tool shed.

"This got to do with that Four-quarters guy?"

"He's dead," and Flour tightened his mouth. "I killed him, blew his head right off." He stretched out his left hand: the top joint of his middle finger was missing; no, not missing—

"I got eight of 'em, phony tips. Explosives. You can buy 'em cheap, if you know where. And Dragon does. In Passaic."

"You *killed* that guy?"

"Sssh, for God sake! I thought we were gonna make a deal—"

"About the eggs?"

He nodded. "But he wasn't gonna make any deal. He just wanted to know where we had the fish. Then they were gonna—" He snapped an imaginary twig. "You can't trust Normals. Just can't."

"I don't believe this!"

"I was real dumb. Dragon warned me not to trust those

guys. Wasn't for him I'd be swimming permanent right now for them lights I told you about."

"You still haven't told me what happened."

"Well . . . yesterday, me and Lumps went to Paterson to see this Four-quarters. We left him some eggs. Told him he should check 'em out and if he liked what he ate and figured there was a market, he should give me a call. We could talk. He called."

"And?"

"He was interested, but he wanted to see the goldfish for himself. I didn't think that was so strange, but Dragon did. 'Say no,' he says, so I said no. But Four-quarters goes, 'Without I see them, I don't buy no eggs.' Something like that."

"And you showed him?"

"Tonight, after we left the club."

"So where are they, the fish?"

"They're someplace." He stooped and picked up a stone, chucked it at the moon. "Head came apart like a friggen water balloon."

"And the other guys? That were with him?"

"Bobby and the Dragon took care of them."

"Christ, you know what kinda trouble—"

"Nobody's gonna find those guys. Never. It's all right."

"What're you trying to prove, asshole? You had to go out and sell the eggs? You couldna gave 'em to the cops? Or told the newspaper? Like Pigeon said. What, you want trouble, you gotta be strange?"

"*Pigeon* said? What's that mean, Pigeon said? I told you to keep quiet."

"I only told her and Beef."

"Son of a bitch!" and he took a poke. I jerked back and lost balance. I flailed and fell on top of the encrusted grill. Flour's arm flashed out, fingers squeezed my windpipe. I saw minuscule flak burst on a purple creped background. I nearly passed out. Then he stopped.

"I asked you to do one thing—*not* do one thing—and look!" Flourface said. "You're so untrustworthy, man, it's beyond belief."

"*I'm* untrustworthy! Me?" My voice sounded falsetto, as though I'd just finished sucking helium. "What about *you*— sneaking around after Reeni?"

"Who's sneaking?" he said. He turned and walked back toward the house.

Overhead, the squirrel went trotting along the telephone wire.

All I could think to call after Flour was: "Somebody's gonna find out about tonight. And you're gonna be creamed."

He stopped and slowly turned around. "You tell Beef about *this* and I'll clean you, I swear, like a fucken haddock." He went into the kitchen.

The squirrel, who was perched now on our chimney, bayed at the moon.

I didn't want to see Flour's ghoul face again, so I spent the remainder of the night sleeping in the bathtub, submerged in cool water that I'd laced with a cup of kitchen salt.

Ma was wearing her dark glasses—the wraparound kind with blind-man lenses—and a silver-blond wig, a long violet dressing gown geriatric with wrinkles. Her face and throat were mortared with makeup. Only her hands were exposed: yellow-green and scaly. She reached down a prescription vial from the medicine cabinet. She winced swallowing three gray-jacketed mild tranquilizers. The stronger ones, those were red, came later, usually at midday. Ma shot a look at herself in the mirror and pushed out her lips, which were painted a bright moist ceremonial crimson. She glanced over at me. "What do you think you're doing in the tub?"

She hated it when I used my gills.

I sat up, stirring wavelets. I told her about Reeni's mother.

"It's a mercy the woman's been released."

I stepped out and wrapped a towel around my waist.

"I hope," said Ma, "they make her look decent in the casket. Should I send over a wig? Do you think? Would Reeni like that?"

I kissed her good morning and she pulled another pill-taking face.

Flour, in his briefs only, was posing at the closet door mirror when I came into the bedroom. Legs spread into an A, fists balled, he was trying to look rocky. He often posed like that in the morning. Sometimes, he even practiced striding lionly across the floor, pretending that the rippling linoleum was a baking veldt. His conceit drove me crazy. We didn't speak. I dressed, putting on my only suit, fortunately a navy-blue one. Then I went downstairs for breakfast.

Da was at the table, left-handedly flicking through a sheaf of glossy photos. The top one was a picture of the Blofeld Hole choked to the brim with eccentric vegetation: licey brambles, fuzzy-sleeved yellow shoots, goitered gray trees foliated with bifurcated fungal sacs like stupendous scrotums. There was a plate of cold toast and a cup of black coffee set in front of Da. A greasy napkin, a vitamin pill. "Your mother just told me," he said. "About Mrs. Stankunas. I'm sorry to hear it."

I nodded, got out a box of salty wheat crackers and ate a handful between sips of orange drink.

"Were you both there when it happened?"

I shook my head. "We were at the Sycorax Club."

"Oh, that's lovely."

"Did I know she was gonna die?"

"What were you doing there?"

"Beef."

"So he really went ahead with it."

"Wasn't so bad."

Da narrowed his eyes critically.

"It wasn't! Ah, forget it."

He kept on staring, so I got up from the table. I filled the kettle and put it on to boil. I stood reading, for maybe the five hundredth time, the yellowed clipping from the *Jersey Journal* that Ma had Scotch-taped to one of the cabinet doors. It was two years old. It was about the first Freak, a woman named Armstrong, who'd been reupholstered with Syntha-skin. There was no postoperative picture (the shot printed showed a fortyish brunette whose face was a welter of rose thorns), but the article described her new looks as "scrubbed and glowing with health." (I'd often wondered if there were any Freaks on the newspaper's staff; I wondered again now, and doubted there were.) She'd paid for her freedom with state lottery winnings. The last sentence said she was planning to relocate to Paradise Valley, Arizona.

"Where's Mrs. Stankunas being waked?"

"Kessler and Kozakowski's."

"Your mother says she wants you to take a wig when you go over there later."

"Told me, too."

"You're not gonna, I hope."

The kettle started to whistle, the phone jangled in the parlor.

Da said: "Fix your coffee, I'll grab it." And lugged his arm out of the kitchen. A few moments later I heard him bellow upstairs to Flourface. Then he came back. "That's Reeni calling. Only she asked to talk to your brother."

Flour buttoned up his shirt, he crammed his wallet into a back pocket and scooped up rouge compacts from the dresser.

I stood blocking the bedroom doorway.

"Got my first customer," he said.

I wouldn't let him pass.

"Course," he said, "I won't charge him, him being kind

of a friend. Grinny, you don't mind, I wanna get through."

"What customer?"

"Skully wants to go try find his wife."

I put out a hand. "I'll take him the eggs."

"That's okay, I'll do it."

"Hell you will. Gimme."

"How 'bout we go together? I gotta pay my respects, don't I?"

I agreed, took a backstep into the hallway and bumped into Ma, who'd just stepped out of her room clutching a wig in each hand like human-hair pompons. She held up the blond one, she held up the brown one. "Which would suit her better? You help me decide, Charlie."

"Ma," I said, "I can't just—"

"Charlie," she insisted, "I want your opinion . . ."

So while I stood slouched at the head of the stairs glaring at Ma's wigs, Flour took his leave . . .

I rapped and rapped on Reeni's apartment door but got no answer. I went across the hall and knocked at Mrs. Scocco's. She opened up after I'd identified myself. She was a small, older woman with a rounded snout nose, a full beard of pig bristles and colossal hands at the ends of her spindly arms. Her glasses were smeared, her black hair was uncombed. She was still in pajamas and scuffs. She and Reeni's mom had always been close. "It's such a tragedy, Grinner," she moaned. "I'm so upset. She was such a lovely person."

I asked Mrs. Scocco if she still had the key to Reeni's door.

"Aren't they home?"

"They're home. Just don't hear me, I guess."

She disappeared into her apartment and returned shortly with a key on a chain of four trashbag twists. "You won't forget to return it?"

"No. Hey, Mrs. Scocco, could you use a wig?" I held up the pentagonal wig box that Ma had pressed into my hands as I was finally leaving the house.

"What color?" Mrs. Scocco said.

"Brown."

She took the box and looked in. "Oh, these curls are much too youthful. Thanks anyway."

Skull Garden was sitting bolt upright in a parlor wing chair. His eyes were closed. His hands rested on the padded chair arms. His fingers were spread and curled. They were oiled with black egg yolk. He wasn't breathing. There were green shell chips, a box of Ritz crackers and a heavy silver crucifix on a metal snack table.

The apartment was still airless.

I heard low talk coming from Reeni's bedroom.

I went and stood outside, my heart kicking.

I heard Flour tell Reeni about Gabe Four-quarters. She said nothing. I heard him say: "I already got six dozen goldies. I just knock on doors and if people got fish, I make 'em an offer. I say I'm gonna sell 'em by mail. Like they used to sell Blofeld flowers to the Japs."

Again Reeni said nothing, but her breathing was shallow and quick; anxious.

Heard Flour say: "I could make a lotta money, you know?"

And say: "You wouldn't have to worry about nothing. If we had lots of cash—right?"

"Don't," Reeni said. "Okay? Don't talk that kind of stuff any more. Please?"

"Okay, it's not the time. You're right. But would you do me one favor? Would you wait? Don't do anything in September. Wait a bit. Reen, you're gonna see that Grinner's got problems and he'll pass 'em all on to you. I'm warning."

"It was nice of you to come and say what you did about my mother, Flour. I appreciate that."

"Reen . . . he can't even look at himself in a goddamn

mirror. Reen, he crosses the street if he sees somebody with a straight nose. He'll make you crazy. He's a coward."

"So am I," she said.

"No you're not. You listen to me, you're not. And you're beautiful. Did *he* ever tell you that?"

"I got eyes, Flour, I can see."

"You don't but. You don't see, that's how come I have to—"

"You think?"

"What, I'd lie?"

"You wouldn't lie?"

"Not to you."

"Really?"

"Trust me."

I threw open the door and found my twin with his arms around Reeni. Her arms encircled his waist, her face was buried in his chest.

Seven of his false fingertips were ranged like whited thimbles along the top of Reeni's video player. On the screen a group of silhouetted red pandas licked their sores and a spectacular Hot Chinese sunset glowed purply-orange behind them.

"He was only trying to make me feel better," Reeni said.

"Can't *I* do that? Isn't that what I'm supposed to do?"

And Flourface just smiled his black smile and rolled his shoulders, prizefighter fashion.

At her mother's wake she apologized to me.

At the funeral she apologized.

After the burial she apologized.

I forgave her eventually and we were married as we'd planned, in late September.

Reeni was disappointed when Flour didn't show up at the reception. She stayed disappointed all evening long. Kept hoping he'd arrive shortly. "I don't want any hard feelings," she said. "We should all stay friends."

There was no honeymoon since we'd already started working for Ralph Studebaker's Rent-a-Freak service. The day after the wedding we drove to Connecticut and waited tables with half a dozen other Freaks at an American Legion banquet. As entertainment, a couple of Sycorax alumni staged a rape. Following that, there was a short film about last year's American invasion of Panama. When the lights came on again I started clearing dessert dishes. A legionnaire walked up and asked me if I spoke Spanish. I said no but still he jabbed my wrist with a cake fork thick with whipped cream.

Reeni was standing in back of us and she dropped her tray.

That night, she took her first egg. Reeni in the wing chair, Skully on the couch. So I did one myself.

My wrist got infected.

Part Two:
The Beefstone
(October-November, 2010)

5
Volts for Beefy

"Welcome back! Christ, but you guys look so Normal I nearly couldn't pick youse out. If it wasn't for them hatboxes . . ." Beef laughed and pummeled my arm muscle, he kissed Reeni on her putty nose and she winced, damn her face. He was wearing a glossy yellow poncho, patched jeans and bladder-green sewer boots. He grabbed Reeni's suitcase, and we followed him briskly across the Newark airline terminal and through the exit doors. Normal eyeballs dogged us, several handy Kodaks clicked our pictures.

It was raining, a vertical downpour from a churning, blurry sky. We bolted for the parking area. Sheet lightning klieged the air. We sprinted between long files of mostly compact cars. "Here," announced Beef, sliding a key from his slicker pocket. A gray Volvo 'lectric, with its toothy yellow trademark spitting across the doors. We clambered in, Beef and me up front in the lava buckets, Reeni in back.

"New car?" I asked.

"Brand," said Beef. "Not mine but." He shrugged his poncho off, balled it up and dunked it into the rear footwell. A gunmetal bracelet, busy with blinking studs and a series of small combination locks, was clamped over his left flannel shirt sleeve. I asked him what it was.

"It's your fault," but didn't elaborate. He started the car and backed carefully from his slot. "So how you guys been?"

I said we'd been great.

"Shows go all right?"

I said they'd gone fine.

Beef spotted a pair of enlisted spacers standing on the gravel skirt of the road about thirty meters in front of the Turnpike booths. Thumbs out, peacoat collars flipped up, damp duffels slung on their shoulders. The bags were stenciled with the name of their earth-orbiting bomber—*Binary Star I*—in cracked white paint. Beef pulled over, cranked down his window and angled the rearview to watch the spacers come splashing up. Then he stuck his huge meaty head through the window. "Where you guys going?"

They stopped when they saw him, twisted their mouths and waved us on, much to the Beefstone's glee. He put the car in gear and backed it up fast, nearly sideswiping the two guys. We roared off.

"Really funny," said Reeni. "A riot."

"I thought so," said Beef. He started to laugh, but all of a sudden his jaw locked open, he made a gargly noise and his eyes widened.

The blinking studs on his bracelet steadied for a long moment.

Beef sucked in, cursed out, stiffened.

I made a lunge for the steering wheel.

He whacked away my hand, "I'm all right, I'm okay," and pulled the car back into the lane.

The stud lights were dancing again.

Weak, static-frittered laughter issued from underneath a gray sweat shirt draped on the dashboard.

"What I'll do," said Beef, "for two hundred bucker-babies a day is amazing. Take a look." He yanked the sweat shirt away, revealing a little plastic statuette. At first glance it seemed to be just another of those patron-saint-of-the-road icons. But it wasn't. It was the image of a blubbery Normal woman, stark naked: a dissipated face, breasts like scale-model sandbags, a yeasted belly, an ecologically berserk pubic thatch. It laughed again: the sound was broadcast through a radio grid lodged in its mouth.

"Who's this supposed to be?" I asked Beef.

"Mrs. Sinakin. And a perfect likeness. This is her car."

Reeni asked him who was Mrs. Sinakin.

"One of Studebaker's clients. I been with her about three weeks now."

"Two hundred bucks?" I said. "A day?"

"Hey, Grinno, you think that's a lot? Considering what I put up with, man, she got me for dirt cheap, for pocket change." He tapped the bracelet. "I don't even wanna *know* what's inside her brain. See this bracelet—volts by remote control. Crazy old cee has a ball shocking me whenever she feels like it. So don't be too jealous, Grin. I ain't gettin' away with murder."

"You're nuts," said Reeni. "She could kill you."

Beef shook his head. "Nah, not with this bracelet she couldn't."

I covered the statuette again with the sweat shirt.

How could any Normal, I thought, let her body go to ruin like that? I asked: "Does she make you wear it all the time?"

"Oh, no, just when she wants to punish me."

Reeni leaned forward, folding her arms across my head-rest. "What's she punishing you now for?"

"I told her I'd be gone for most of the day 'cause I thought I had a fucken hernia, I wanted to see a doctor. Then Grinner called about picking youse up. She was on the line." He laughed. "I don't know why she bothered renting a Freak. I think she woulda got as many kicks outta being a foster parent. She only wants somebody to be witchy to, somebody who can't fight back."

"You don't exactly fit that description," Reeni pointed out.

"Sure, I could hurt her, but I ain't so dumb. I got a future to think about, Reenbo. Someday, don't forget, I plan to walk out of a hospital all Syntha-skinned up and looking like James Arness."

A few years ago, the Beefstone had purchased a bushel

basket full of old video cassettes at a garage sale. A lot of Disney crap and newsy crud, a few recent sitcoms, three or four feature-length blue movies and sixteen episodes of a mid-twentieth television program neither of us had ever heard of: *Gunsmoke.* The star was somebody called James Arness, and Beef quickly became a fan—mostly, I still think, because of the actor's height, which was towering. Beef had promptly decided to have his Syntha-skin face modeled after Big Jim's. "People will accept a giant," he'd say, "even a giant with a big head like mine, if—and this is crucial, Grinny—if the guy has rugged looks. Paul Bunyan, Paul fucken Bunyan—musta been rugged in the mutt. Right?"

Reeni said: "I still think you're stupid, Martin. This crazy lady could do a job on you."

"I didn't think you cared," and smirked, and sought her out in the rearview mirror.

"Personally, I don't," she snapped. "But you *are* a Freak —aren't you?—and so am I, and so there *is* a bond—isn't there? I probably wouldn't lend you a nickel, but that don't mean I wanna see you butchered."

"You sound just like Pidge."

Exactly what I was thinking. I was also thinking she sounded a lot like Flourface. I was annoyed. I changed the subject. "Speaking about Pigeon, she told me you had another rental going. With some artist?"

"Mmmm. Only it's not a rental-rental. I mean, Studebaker had nothing to do with it. I met this cee myself. All I do for her is pose for paintings."

"This in New York, too?"

"Yeah. Beefy's gonna be the next Mona Lisa. Take a look in the glove box."

"This?" A white business envelope.

"Yeah, that."

Inside the envelope there were close to twenty color prints. Photographs of pastel roughs and finished drawings.

Beef rendered photo-realistically, his bent-forward carriage projecting arrogance and menace. I handed the snapshots back to Reeni, who skimmed the bunch like some gambler checking a poker deck to find out whether the cards have been marked. She returned them without comment.

"What's her name?" I asked Beef.

"Cleo."

"Cleo what?"

"Nothing. With a capital. Cleo Nothing."

"Get out!"

"I'm not kidding. They don't all throw gravy bombs, y'know."

Nothing was the surname adopted by every Antichrist Newsboy.

"Reen-deen. Hey, Reen," Beef said after a while, "you wouldn't really refuse me a nickel if I asked, would you? Wouldn't you lend me a nickel? Reen . . . ?"

She didn't answer him. She was preoccupied—chipping roughly at her warted palm with a sheetmetal screw that she must've found on the car floor; chipping, and then sensually, like a fellatrice, lapping at her treacly brown blood.

Early in the nineties, the Greenville section of Jersey City became known as Freaktown once the Caliban's Night mutants started ghettoing there in greater and greater numbers for reasons of safety and group reinforcement. The Normals gradually, and grudgingly, moved away—to other parts of the city, the county, the state. By the turn of twenty-one, Freaktown was 99 percent homogeneous. A homogeneous slum, with chuckholed streets, jungly lots and buildings as bleak as the psyches of the terminally diseased. Fires were more regular than mail delivery. Property soon lost any value, and landlords stopped paying taxes. A week before our wedding, Reeni and I bought at auction a two-story house on Neptune Avenue, below Ocean, for $395. A real bargain. It was worth at least five times that much.

Beef helped us carry our things inside—and nearly had a foot severed at the ankle when some metal stripping across a doorsill sprang up suddenly like a guerrilla from his thicket. The sheets we'd draped on the furniture had been taken off, folded neatly and stacked on a table. "Guess your mother's been around," said Reeni. She unshouldered her paraphernalia bag and dropkicked her wig box across the floor and into a corner of the parlor.

Yeah, Ma had been over: there was no dust swirled around table legs, the rug had been vacuumed, the cafe curtains laundered. And there was a note from her sticking out of the toaster: "Brought cat back. Too much trouble. Feeding him here." Baudie's food and water bowls sat on a place mat on the kitchen floor.

I nosed around inside the refrigerator, which Ma had stocked weirdly with beer, frozen bagels and a bag of make-believe corn.

"I can't offer you much," I told Beef. Reeni had gone straight upstairs to unpack.

"That's okay. I'm gonna go see Mary anyhow."

I walked him back outside and we stood on the porch. It was still raining.

"You wouldn't believe what's happened around here since you left," he said.

"Like what?"

"No surprise, it's all on account of the eggs. They got county cops cruising the neighborhoods, stopping Freaks left and right. The old frisk-a-roon. I even heard they're traipsing right into people's houses. Looking for fish tanks."

"And what about Flour?"

Beef pursed his lips, he shoved off the balustrade and started to pace. He stopped at the end of the porch and watched a multiple-armed black kid, ten or eleven, come jogging around the corner from Garfield Avenue. "Flour? Who knows. Still scarce. What else he gonna do but hide? They're looking for him."

"Reeni probably knows where to find him."

"You think?"

"She dealt eggs for him during the tour. Must have ten thousand dollars in her suitcase. His money. I'm pretty sure she knows where to take it now."

He shrugged, cut his eyes to the street. "Hey, I gotta go." He didn't want to hear any woe stories about Reeni and Flour and me, stories to which he'd inevitably respond: "So let your brother have her. If she's such a cunt."

I asked: "You're really not living with Pidge any more?"

"I don't know if I am or not. Probably not."

"How come?"

"It's too boring to talk about. Hey, you're still coming with me next week, aren't you? To see that Dr. Sleet?"

"You got enough saved already? For the operation?" I felt a sirocco of panic and jealousy blow through my lungs.

"Not yet."

I was relieved. "I'll go with you, sure."

Beef started down the steps, I called after him: "Reeni wants out of the show."

He frowned, rain plinked off his scalp and runneled his cheeks. "I wouldn't worry about it. She's just tired."

"Not only that, Beefstone, she, um, she says she don't wanna go through with the operation."

"Tell you why?"

"She thinks she can be happy staying the way she looks. And living here. I don't know."

"Sounds like a crock."

"Sounds like Flour, is what I figure."

"So let your brother have her. If she's such a cunt." He gummed his lips and tramped back up on the porch, clipped me lightly on the arm. "Hey, don't get so down so fast. And don't *ever* listen to me! A few days back here and she'll snap out of it."

I said I guessed so.

Beef thumped me like a coach, he jerked his chin at a

house across the street. "I hear you got some Normal neighbors. Just moved in."

"What kind?"

"What kind do you think? Zombies. Pidge was saying they're coming over in packs. Coming straight to the egg source."

"How they getting along with everybody?"

"This I can't tell you, Grinno. But I can tell you something funny. I was talking, coupla weeks ago, with that kid Lazari who works in the bodega up Ocean? And he was saying how these crazy zoms are bringing tropical fish over here with them—like they figure the fish'll start dropping death eggs. Can you imagine how stupid?"

I laughed, I said I could imagine, then we shook hands and Beef loped for the Volvo.

I went back into the house and wandered through rooms, looking for Baudelaire. I found him crouched on the radiator in the downstairs bathroom. Without a hiss, he hurled himself at me, and I batted him in the flank. He howled, hit the floor with his legs churning, and scrambled away. The back of my left hand was left bleeding in three places.

I walked upstairs tissuing the wound.

Reeni was bathing.

6
Zombies at the Deli

Amid skirts and dresses, terry robes, sweaters and a variety of blouses, perfume atomizers, wired bras and beige hosiery, Reeni's father sat naked on his bedroom floor, weeping, swallowing hard, grinding his teeth as if against sudden strafes of hot pain. Reeni drew a short breath, moaned and moved swiftly across the unlit room. She hooked Skull Garden under his arms and lifted him to his feet. He paid her no attention. There was a pie of diarrhea where he'd been.

"What do you want me to do with these?" I asked Reeni, and pointed—that, that, that, that—to her dead mother's scattered belongings.

"Shove them anyplace. Out of his sight. Just use your head."

So I grabbed up a lidless clothes hamper and stuffed it full of my late mother-in-law's clothing and accessories. Good, expensive stuff. She'd been a Sears home-service operator, Skull had burgled freight cars. I set the hamper outside the bedroom door.

"Whyn't you maybe go make him something to eat, Reen? I'll get him dressed."

"Give him a bath first?"

"I'll help him find the tub."

She nodded, leaned forward and kissed her father's broad encysted fingers, then pivoted away, got up and went out.

"Okay, Skully," I said. "Bath time."

He said gibberish. He'd lost his voice after Caliban's

Night. Look down his throat, and it was a metastasized city of white corn.

I made him sit on the toilet while I closed the tub drain and started the water running. I crossed my arms and leaned against the wall. "Did you find her today, Skully? Did you reach the lights?"

He shook his head.

"I'm sorry. Honest."

He looked up, gazing at some mold that speckled the white plaster wall. Tears quivered like quicksilver on the rims of his eyes.

The rain had slackened to a drizzle, the streetlights had vapored on, it was almost full dark. With my hands jammed in my pockets, I walked to the A&P at a stickup man's getaway clip. I passed a little Oriental girl with cauled ears, lips pudgy as breakfast links. She was crouched in her muddy front yard soberly scorching a doll's face with a July Fourth sparkler. I passed a fat lady who was using her forehead fingers to give street directions to a gangly kid whose cheeks were mailed with interlocking eyeteeth. And I spotted a few Normals—young shuffling zoms with penitentiary complexions, all bundled up like polar colonists. They ignored me. Nevertheless, I steeled myself, I crossed the street twice and cut through a gooey lot, just as precaution.

Six zombies were congregated in front of the food market. Two of them—a guy and a girl in wet blue parkas—followed me inside but didn't take carts, just headed at a stagger up the fruit-and-vegetable aisle. I checked Reeni's shopping lists (one for us, the other for Skully) and went and got powdered milk, spring water and toaster muffins, a pound of chopped "miracle chuck" (I supposed that meant it was all grains and chemicals) and a bagful of chicken legs whose puckered skins shone with a sort of gasoline rainbow—the anticarcinogenic prebaste demanded by the

FDA. I got toilet paper and dish detergent, a dozen cans of soup, "chocolat-esque" grahams and a tub of instant potatoes. I got rice, lentil beans, pinto beans and kidney beans. I got ugly oranges at a discount.

At the deli counter I ran into the zombie couple again. They were pointing fingers at the glass-fronted refrigerator.

On chipped porcelain shelves there were trays of knishes, coleslaw and rice pudding, whiting that resembled chunks of bomb shrapnel; Italian, macaroni, health and egg salads.

"Half . . . a kilo," said the she-zom, now rapping gloved knuckles against the glass. "Egg sal . . ."

Big Dinah Murphy, standing behind the counter in a pleated mustard-yellow smock, smiled thinly as she half filled a white cardboard container with salad. "And what else?" she asked.

"And . . . six," said the he-zom, drawing three folded hundred-dollar bills from his parka jacket.

"If you want six," Dinah said, "you best find three more of those."

The zoms turned and looked at each other. They shrugged. "Just three . . . then," said the girl.

Dinah reached over and took the cash, squeezed it into a cup of her top brassiere. She grabbed up a margarine tub from the meat-slicer table, thumbed it open and picked out three death eggs, which she popped into the egg salad container. She filled up the rest of the container with salad, closed it and scribbled a four-dollar price on its side with a grease crayon. She passed it to the zombies. They galumphed off toward the check-out.

I watched them go, then asked Dinah: "Kinda risky, isn't it?"

"Some risky," she answered, pressing the lid back on the margarine tub. "But there's a girl at the cash register can warn me with a buzz if the cops show. So. What can I do you for?"

While she wrapped up cold-cut ends, I scanned the

salads. There was a special on macaroni—$4.19 a quarter-kilo—so I asked Dinah to give me some of that. She did, and pinched in a death egg. I told her to take it out.

"On the house."

"Take it out anyway."

She left it. "For Skully."

"How long you been working here?"

"About a month." Dinah shrugged. All four mammary glands rose and fell. "With the sideline, I make more than I did at Sycorax. And I like it a helluva lot better."

Both the Sycorax Club and its sister rape bar, Sun Demon's, had burned to the ground within a week of one another last May. Studebaker had decided eventually against reopening them someplace else. Rent-a-Freak and the road shows turned more of a profit, and with less aggravation.

"Di . . . you seen Flour?"

"In the recent past, do you mean?"

I let my grin hit its zenith and nadir. "Uh-huh. The recent past."

"In the recent past, no."

She had to be lying her tits off.

Twenty minutes later I was bagging it up Seaview Avenue in the dark when a car pulled over and honked. The front passenger's window zipped down and a male voice called: "Say, could you help us out? How do we find Winfield?"

I started to walk over, and stopped.

It was the Durham bull I'd seen on the plane, the guy who'd stopped to grin at me. His flight companion was behind the wheel and there was a third guy shadowed in the back.

I hurried up the block and into Skully's building.

With her sleeves rolled back to expose her furry arms, Reeni was damp-mopping the kitchen floor. She'd already

straightened up the parlor. Some of Skully's sweaters were
soaking in the sink.

"Where is he?" I asked her.

"Sleeping."

"What're we gonna do about him, Reen?"

"Why do we have to do anything? He misses her just. So
do I."

"Someday he's gonna skip the eggs and make himself another noose. You can't see it coming?"

"What'd I tell you this morning about talking bad luck?"

"All right, I'll shut up." I folded a bag and saved it for a
garbage-pail liner.

"Why should he skip the eggs? As long as they keep on
being available? Why *should* he?"

"I said all right, didn't I? *All right!*" And showed her the
egg in the macaroni salad. "So let's just figure they'll keep
on coming."

"Where'd you get that?"

"Dinah Murphy. She's selling them at the freaken A&P."

Reeni smiled. "And you bought?"

"A free sample for Skully."

"How nice of her." She handed me the mop. "Go rinse
this, will you, in the bathtub?"

7
The Nuclear Family

Pantyhose—navy blue, beige, lemon-yellow and black—floating in my mother's kitchen sink. Clay pots full of crispy brown wandering Jews hanging by leather thongs in the window, stiff shirt cardboard taped into a lower left pane. Combs standing in glasses of ammonia water ranged along the scabby sill. I spread home-cooked strawberry jelly on a heel of hard bread and peeked through the window. Da was in the back yard, talking with a stranger. They were sitting on the brick barbecue, facing each other across the grill. With his good hand, Da tinkered with the old recording machine that was balanced on his knees. Jabbing buttons, ejecting the cassette, blowing softly into the mike.

The stranger was a colored man with skin as bloody brown as calf's liver. He wore bib overalls and had long crinkly silver hair that fanned pyramidally across his broad shoulders. Pouched gray eyes, and a thick bottom lip that grew off into his cheeks then forked and meandered over his face like the decorative tooling of some leather craftsman.

Ma was still talking on the phone: ". . . *Electric Love* magazine is—now, just let me finish—is offering a special rate for this month only. Twelve issues for $28.80. That's a savings of $21.20 off the regular subscription price. Well . . . all right. Perhaps your husband would be more interested in *New Century,* which we can—"

Ma hung up and struck a pencil line through another name on her computer print-out. She sighed and fed herself a macaroon.

I sat down at the table. "Who's that with Da?"

"Some bird from Pearsall Avenue," she said, straightening her Goldilocks wig with two hands. "Claims he used to live near Blofeld Street time of the accident. My foot, if you want my feelings." Her pupils were gumdrops.

"Da paying him?"

"What do you think?" Abruptly, she held up one hand— stop everything—and tilted her head back, dabbing at her nostrils with two cotton balls. She took them away, bloodied, frowned over them, deposited them into her teacup.

"Anybody buying?" I asked her.

"Two subs so far, outta thirty-seven tries."

"Not so good, huh?"

"About on a par," she said, "with Willy Loman."

I considered asking her who was Willy Loman, but I let it pass. (Was he the Freak she knew from Danforth Avenue who'd once tried to sell authentic Jersey City cockroach powder as an aphrodisiac?)

She sat there shaking her head.

On top of the ironing board, next to the measuring cup, the dented funnel and the steam iron, there was a bulky black-and-white marbled accordion file. I got up and brought it back to the table, untied the ribbon, looked in. It was crammed with photos, dozens of them, each one dated, of the Blofeld Hole. Also: Baggies of soil samples and charred stones and plant cuttings, pieces of burnt wood, a few cassettes tagged with adhesive tape and numbered, scraps of paper with jottings on them in Da's scrawl.

I picked out two sheets of finely wrinkled onionskin. The four sides were covered with tiny backhand writing, heavy cross-outs and colored-in valentine hearts.

"Twenty bucks he paid for that," Ma said. "A love letter from some nobody nurse who can't even spell. Good money for rubbish." She reached out and whacked the letter with the back of her hand. "The his*tor*ian!"

It was dated April 2, 1988, and it began: "Dear, dear, dear Tony."

"How'd he get this?"

"Do I ask?"

I started to read.

Ma said: "Don't bother, you'll ruin your eyes. I'll tell you what's in it that's worth twenty dollars. Nurse lived on Blofeld—you start to wonder after a while who *didn't*— and she's writing to her boy friend who's at school. Okay? So she mentions—in a P.S. no less!—that her dog got tumors all of a sudden and died inside of a week. Now, Charlie, in all honesty, wouldn't you agree that's a clue worth twenty dollars?" She filled her cheeks and blew on her folded hands.

I shrugged and slipped the letter back into the file.

Ma spit on a cotton ball and cleaned her nostrils.

I knocked back a half dozen salt pills and drank a glass of water.

"Thanks again," I said finally, "for keeping an eye on the house. And feeding Baudie."

"That cat oughta be destroyed. I could show you scratches. It's a maniac."

"Yeah, well. You can't blame him for that, can you?" Then I remembered the main reason I'd gone over there and took out a bulky business envelope. I shoved it across the table. "There's five hundred dollars inside."

She looked at it but didn't take it. "This money you made with your show?"

"What else would it be?"

Carefully, with six fingertips, she pushed the envelope back toward me. "Can't take it, honey," she said. "As much as I appreciate the thought. Your father says I'm to refuse, and I'm not itching for a battle royal. I can get along nicely without lumps, thank you. Speaking of maniacs."

"What do you mean, can't take? Since when?" I'd an-

ticipated this: the day before we'd gone on tour, Da came to
see me. When he spotted the tuxedoes and the wedding
gowns hooked on the parlor traverse rods and the masks
propped on the couch, he pitched a fit. He called me im-
moral and practically disowned me. He felt I'd betrayed
him, that I'd warped his personal history into cheap por-
nography. And I suppose he had a good case, though I
really hadn't created the show to ridicule him. When I'd
conceived it (Studebaker and I hashed it out together, over
the telephone, shortly after Beef and Pigeon Mary quit the
circuit following their beatings in New Hampshire), a honeymoon rape seemed like an interesting skit, a commercial
idea, and nothing else. I'd realized—sure I had—what the
raw material was—my father's old bedtime story—but the
finished product was intended to be something anonymous,
something new. Da saw things differently. He screamed at
me that morning until the tears came and flooded his vision,
he shook his fist like somebody biblical, he spat a ginder
on the groomhead. "I'm not a monster," he said.

I said now to Ma: "Take the money. Just don't tell him."

She wagged her head, smiled, showed me lime-green
teeth.

"So you're mad at me, too?"

"Not at all. I know you do it for a good cause. Maybe
I'm not thrilled to death with the show, but I understand.
No, if I took it, he'd find out. Charlie, your father hated
it even when you and Reeni were just serving drinks to
Normals on Park Avenue, so—"

"But we make five times as much now."

"Like I said. I understand."

I picked up the envelope and put it back down. "And
where's your money gonna come from now? Strictly from
selling magazine subscriptions?"

"Charlie, sweetheart, don't get so excited. Please." She
stoppered her nose again with cotton and flopped her head
over the back of the chair. Her wig fell off. The plugs turned
sopping red in her nostrils.

I watched her tiny throat gills ripple and crack her makeup.

I waited for the bleeding to stop. I spread open the file again and filched out a Polaroid picture of Flour and me as little boys—the date faintly penciled along the shiny border read *Labor Day, 1995*—standing by the edge of the botanically weird Blofeld Hole, the pair of us wearing short pants and dark polo shirts. Flour's blanched arm is snaked around my shoulder, the tip of his tongue pokes slyly from one side of his black mouth. Naturally, I'm grinning. But, look, I'm also stiff as a goddamn board.

Ma's nosebleed ended and she said: "Don't raise stinks about this, as a favor? Your father and me are okay, moneywise . . . and you can take this cash and put it toward the operation. Did Martin go for his yet?"

"Ma. Is Flour supporting you now? Is that it?"

"Let's not talk about Alan." She rolled her head in a figure eight. She still hadn't picked up her wig and I wondered if she even realized she'd lost it. "We've had police here. More than once. With warrants, going through the house."

"I'm not surprised."

"You're not surprised and I'm not pleased. All of a sudden, his picture's in the paper and police are ringing my bell. How'd everybody find out?"

"Do you know where he is?"

"I got no idea, thank God. I just hope he got sense enough to stay far away from here."

"And I just hope Reeni got sense enough to stay away from him." I took back the money. "She's quitting the show," I said. "And that's final, she goes. She's even soured on the operation. All of a sudden."

Ma tipped her chair back, gazed up at the buckled tile ceiling and then glanced back at me. "Let me talk to her. You wouldn't mind that, would you?"

"Mind? I was hoping."

"I can't promise you nothing about the show, but she'll

have the surgery, if I got any leverage with her."

"You don't understand. No shows, Ma, no operations."

She ignored that, just sealed her painted lips and squinted. "And if Reeni keeps on saying beans, well, you can give me her share of the money and I'll come get skinned with you."

I knew she meant it.

Bright stringy blood bubbled again from her nose, streamed across her mouth, beaded her chin. "Oh, damn this!" And she wiped it with her sleeve.

She made sandwiches for lunch and we ate them with Sedata-Cola, the only soft drink she had on hand.

Afterward, she was getting down her bottle of red tranks (it was aligned between the turmeric and the dill weed in the spice rack) when she heard Da—*thump-thump*—coming toward the house. She bit her lip and pocketed the capsules, she gathered up the computer print-outs from the table and a pile of unpaired laundered socks from the seat of a chair. Without speaking another word to me, she hurried upstairs. Still bald-headed. I took a store babka from the refrigerator, was cutting a slice when Da walked in. He stopped. "How long you been here?"

"Just a bit, Da."

"What do you want?"

I didn't feel like arguing about the money, so I told him: "Nothing special. I'm visiting."

He breathed at me, then shuffled across the kitchen, his long, swollen, unserviceable right arm dragging heavily behind him. It was wrapped in knotted dish towels and dustrags cinched with coarse twine. The hand was mittened in a tough vacuum-cleaner bag. The bag was polished shiny with dirt.

Same as Ma, I'd always wondered how come he refused to have that arm amputated. Unlike her, I'd never called him the world's biggest fool for keeping it on. But I thought it.

With his left hand he yanked open the refrigerator and

squatted, began poking around on the shelves. He brought
out an orange plastic leftovers container sealed with aluminum foil. He stood up. He pinned the plastic bowl in
his left armpit, grabbed a gallon of red wine and started
for the back door.

"You need glasses?"

"I'll come back."

I got two glasses and followed him outside.

I decided, as I watched Da go thudding down the steps
and into the yard, that if Reeni actually went ahead and
scuttled the show I'd apologize to him about the wedding
playlet and buy him some nice gift, like aftershave or even
a disk recorder for his interviews. But it didn't make any
sense to say I was sorry as long as I continued to perform
the rapes.

I had to introduce myself to the stranger.

"Curtis Daudet," he said and his grip was meaty and
muscular, as dry as talc. When he smiled the lip surfeit on
his cheeks tautened and twitched. "You the son that's the
eggman?"

I handed him a wineglass.

"Naw," said Daudet, answering his own question, "he'd
be crazy be here. So that makes you the dancer." He cut his
bloated eyes to my crotch. "You dance and it dance, mmm?"
I felt hostility, as subtly lethal as isotopes, pulsing through
his good humor.

Da shot me a get-the-hell-out-of-here look and turned on
his machine.

I filled Daudet's glass.

"We were talking," said Da, "about your little salvaging
expeditions around the Blofeld area."

Very coolly, Daudet replied: "We were talking, Mr.
Fistick, about"—clearing his throat, dredging phlegm, firing
a green bullet at the dirt—"about overtime compensation.
I already gave you an hour of my life. You know?" He took

a sip of wine and set the glass down on the mortared bar-
beque ledge.

Da looked too embarrassed too quickly to be convincing.
"Well, Mr. Daudet, to be frank, I'm a little short on cash.
At the moment. So I was thinking . . ." He peeled the foil
off the bowl. "Fair exchange?" With his left thumb and
index finger, Da held up a death egg that was unusually
large and yet still no bigger than a sweet pea.

Daudet's lips slid off his front teeth, sending his facial
whorls into shivering convulsions. "You 'spect me to want
that shit? Man, I don't eat that shit nohow!"

"Not for yourself, of course," Da said and coughed, becoming genuinely mortified. "I thought you might want to
sell it, though, and make yourself a handsome prof—"

"You want what I got to say, you best got the cash!"

Keeping his eyes lowered, Da turned over his cassette
machine and thumbed open the battery hatch. He took out
three tens and passed them to Curtis Daudet.

I started back for the house. Behind me, I heard Daudet
saying: ". . . used to garbage-pick four, five days every
week, son and me together. And outside that house what
blew up, one time we found two of them ovens, you know
them ovens I mean—they heat real fast. Microwave, they
call 'em. Only they didn't work. They was burnt inside.
Both of 'em."

I stopped as though quick-frozen. I called to Da: "You
ever hear of a guy named Sam LaPilusa?"

"I'm busy, do you mind?" he answered.

So fuck him.

I went into Ma and Da's bedroom. The bed was unmade,
all the walls were lined with three-drawer steel filing cabinets, there were out-of-date physics books stacked on the
piecrust table. Wigs everywhere. I found the Sears catalog
on the vanity.

"Don't you worry about Reeni. I'll talk to her."

Ma was standing in the doorway. She'd put on a fresh tumbled blond wig.

"That'd be good," I said and held up the catalog. "Mind if I borrow this for a coupla days?"

"Go ahead." She smiled a lunatic rictus, a trank rictus. She girlishly patted a kielbasy curl. Then, clutching the banister like the poisoned heroine in some gothic tale, she crept downstairs "to make more phone calls, for what it's worth."

Before I left I did two things: clipped the five one-hundred-dollar bills with a bobby pin and stuffed them into Ma's teak jewelry box; checked to see if my parents' wedding album was still cached in the bureau. It was, so I flipped through it, as I'd done so often and leisurely as a child, studying the tall, wavy-haired groom with the cleft chin, the redheaded bride with rounded breasts and crimson bubble lips.

I snitched a few pictures, tucked them into the Sears book and walked home.

Reeni was still out. Over at Skully's again.

Tomorrow was November.

8
Little Suicides

"So, Fishy, you won't forget that date."

"Hardly, Ralph. But I'm writing it down."

"And I should know about the Canada thing by the time you come see me next week. It looks good, though. It looks real good."

"Ralph . . ." I threw a nervous glance over my shoulder at Reeni, who sat hunched forward on the couch watching video. Giraffes trampled sere grass as they loped across the screen.

"What?"

"Nothing," I lied.

"No, come on. You sound like you got some problem. You got some problem, Fishdick?"

"Nuh-uh," I said, and moved the receiver from one ear to the other. In a whisper so Reeni couldn't hear: "Everything's okay, we're just resting up. I'm gonna start making those new masks I told you about."

"Think you'll have them done by the Carnegie Hall date?"

"No problem."

He grunted and broke the connection. I shrugged and hung up.

"Well? Did you tell him?" Reeni looked at me through narrowed lids. Pink filaments lazied through her eye whites. Her knees were clasped in her arms.

I gave her maximum grin, acting the dolt. "Tell him?"

"You didn't, did you? Tell him we quit."

I crunched a few salt pills between bicuspids, swallowed

and slid into a chair. "Reen. Just listen for one second. Okay?"

Angrily, she whacked off the video player. "What do I gotta hear, for Christ's sake? I told you, Grinner, in Toledo—"

"Studebaker booked us into Carnegie Hall. One show only, and we make almost half what we made on the whole five-week tour. One show. How could I refuse?"

"Easy. You coulda said no."

"You'll do it but. Won't you? For me?" I slid down in my seat, tilted my chin and let my eyes wander like a war orphan's. It worked: Reeni pushed out her mouth and sagged.

"All right, the one show. But you promise me it's the last. I want you to promise."

I promised, I sprang up to embrace her, I sucked beesting hickeys all around her throat. I unbuttoned her blouse and nuzzled her furry chest—but I quit that when her muskiness suddenly queered my stomach. Funny, her scent never bothered me before. Goddamn zoo, goddamn monkey house.

Reeni was kissing me back. I wished I hadn't started this.

"You'll keep your promise, won't you, Grinny?"

"A promise," I said, "is a promise."

There was still plenty of time, I thought, to coax her about the short Canadian tour. No sense mentioning it tonight and making her mad. I'd wait until Studebaker had all the details and the dates. Over the phone just now he'd told me that Ontario was the perfect place for some rape gigs, what with all those French nuclear space stations hovering overhead . . .

We were in bed.

"Don't you want to do anything?"

"Sure I do," I said. "Go ahead."

"What's the matter?"

"Nothing. Just do it, make me hard."

She frowned, she rolled onto her side and shimmied south on the mattress, and sucked me.

Nothing. Except that I got that queasiness again. I half sat, pressed down on Reeni's head and squeezed her neck. I dug my nails into her throat.

She broke away, red-faced and coughing. Her eyes were glassy. She flung herself off the bed and "Get stiff your goddamn self!" Puffed out the water candles, stormed into the bathroom and slammed the door.

I lay on my back. My fingertips throbbed as though bantam hearts were beating inside each pad. I made fists then lost the urge to strike myself. What the hell was wrong with me? Why'd I try to hurt her? Christ! I got up and knocked at the bathroom. "I'm sorry."

"What do you think, you're back on stage?"

I tried the knob, she'd locked the door. I slipped the lock with a book of matches. Reeni was crumpled naked on the toilet. Her closed eyelids were percolating. Black yolk on her cheek. Egg shells were sprinkled between her six-toed feet. She was still alive, so I tried to keep her that way, tried sticking two fingers down her throat to make her vomit. It didn't work. I lifted her up and laid her flat in the tub, I turned on the shower.

Finally, she began to choke and to spit runny bile, she leaned forward and rocked slowly on her coccyx.

I gripped one of her hands and told her I loved her. I swore I was sorry. She went palsied with the hiccups. She fingered kelpy clumps of dark fur from her eyes, and stammered:

"Nnnn-ow you sssee hoo-why I wa-wanna quit?"

The shower blasted down, I stroked Reeni's shoulder and combed my fingers through its drenched fur.

She dipped her shoulder to shake my touch. Her eyes teemed with red strings, a riot of mercury. "Yoooo hay-*hate* me. Nnnn-*ormal!*" She jerked, gave a rattle and went limp. I caught her before she whacked her skull on the bathtub fixtures. I left her there in a few centimeters of draining water, after blanketing her with towels.

It was a long night.

I smoked, and drank brandy from a juice glass. I read some of the Chamber of Commerce booklets that I'd picked up during the tour. Resettle in Chicago after the surgery? Columbus, Ohio, looked good, too—particularly its university. Ma always said I should go to college. *Your brain at least*, she'd say, *at least your brain is just as good as anybody else's.*

I called my father at 1:30 A.M. I knew he'd be up. He answered midway through the second ring.

I said: "You didn't have to be so snotty when I asked you about that Sam LaPilusa guy."

"What LaPilusa?" I could hear another voice droning behind Da's: a taped one.

I told him about the murder I'd heard about in Toledo, Ohio. About the home-built reactor, the microwave ovens. I told him Sam LaPilusa had worn a neck brace, that the cops had discovered his body decapitated. Da started breathing sexually, I heard him scratching down notes. I said: "And you were so snotty."

"I didn't see it in the papers," he said.

"It was Ohio."

He wrote some more.

"Good stuff?" I asked. I wanted him to thank me. "Don't you think it sounds a lot like Blofeld?" I wanted him to apologize.

Da said: "For this I'm gonna give you fifty bucks."

"I'm not taking any money from you. What do you think I am?"

"I pay for my information. No exceptions. Fifty bucks."

I clubbed down the receiver and the cradle dinged.

I sat on the toilet, keeping Reeni's cadaver company, feeling lonesome as an exile on a sandbar. With my toes I crushed the eggshells that were strewn on the tiles. I got up and searched through the medicine cabinet, found where she kept her supply of death eggs: in a dental floss cylinder. I shook out two. Cracked them against the sink, let the yolk drizzle into my cupped hand.

I looked at Reeni, at the dents my fingernails had made in her neck.

Guilty and confused, I licked all of the egg.

There were six of them, glittering blue-white points up ahead. Impossible to tell how far away. Nothing to match them against. Was Reeni nearby? Were there a thousand zombies ghosting past? Maybe she was, maybe they were, but I couldn't know. All I saw were those lights. Time, but not clock time, passed.

Gradually, I became aware of that dull general pressure which signaled the start of resurrection. And, just as I'd remembered, there was an emotional ache, too. A reluctance to return to the body. The blackness started to gray, the godlights to smear. And—*what the hell is that?*—I glimpsed a long tubular thing, a greasy blur of green and silver, spinning like a rifle cartridge through eternity. Only a glimpse, and then I was gone, thrust back into my body, which immediately started to shiver. There was vomit in my throat. I'd soiled the fluffy yellow toilet seat cover.

Reeni was not in the tub.

She was on the telephone.

I heard her tell somebody: "Tomorrow." Then, shuddering and turning blue, I went and dragged my winter coat from mothballs and slept in it. Darkness and no dreams. I woke twice with a parched throat, with a headache, and with a mind full of clay and furry greenmold: fear and despair.

"I'm sorry, Reeni," I muttered—but I was too sapped to tell whether or not she was in the bed with me.

9
A Feathered Chauffeur

I spent the next morning down in the cellar leafing through Ma's Sears catalog and making check marks with a red pencil next to promising photographs. Finally, extra carefully, I went back over all the possibilities and selected two. I tore the pages from the catalog and pinned them to the corkboard behind my workbench. Then I studied them:

A blond girl with a pale narrow face and arched brows, a full-lipped mouth and green eyes—she was modeling a white bra patterned with inky-black fingerprints and a matching crotch delta . . . A brown-haired guy, clean-shaven, with squinty eyes and chiseled facial planes—he was modeling a corduroy bathrobe with squiggling neon wales.

On my table were three corked vials of different chemicals: pink, clear, pale brown with heavy sediment. An atomizer, a bunch of long-bristle brushes and a few tubes of pigment. Also: a brick of modeling clay, a dozen thin shingles of flesh-tone rubber, a can of liquid adhesive. A pad of bristol board and a coming-apart book called *Tricks of the Great Hollywood Makeup Men*. It was opened to a chapter called "From the Planet of the Apes to the Federation Outpost." It told you how to make a man look like a monster; I'd just have to adapt all the tips to my reverse purpose.

I studied the photographs again, made a few sketches in my pad, did some more reading and took a gang of notes.

I tore off a hunk of clay and tried to sculpt a Normal nose, just to get a feel for the material . . .

Reeni came down at lunchtime to say she was going out.

"Seeing your father again?"

"Yeah." Cold. "Do you mind?" Glacial.

"You're still mad."

"I still got the marks, don't I?" She fingered aside her blouse collar. "So why shouldn't I still be mad?"

"I didn't mean anything."

She looked at me.

"I didn't!" Squeezing the clay nose into a squash ball, flattening it into a pancake.

"What's that?"

"This?" I peeled the clay from the tabletop, chafed it between my hands and made a wurst. "Fooling around just. It's clay."

"No kidding!" Then she spotted the Sears pictures and the how-to book. "You're making new masks."

I shrugged.

"Awful lotta work, isn't it? Just for one performance?" She narrowed her eyes suspiciously.

"I guess. But I felt like making them. It's not like I'm doing anything else these days."

"Well, you might *think* about doing something else."

"What's that supposed to mean—I should go back to the county park?"

"I'm only saying you should think." She clumped back up the cellar steps. I followed her, she carried her Schwinn from the front porch outside.

"Forget last night—please? I'm really sorry."

"Why'd you take the eggs?"

"I was feeling real low. I didn't mean to hurt you. Swear." Stiffly, she moved her head: down and up. "Forgotten."

"I love you, Reen."

"Yeah," she said. "Like a Bantu loves his chimp."

She pedaled off, and I thought: Let's hope she's not such a wise guy after the surgery.

*   *   *

Flour's egg money was gone from the dresser drawer where
Reeni had hidden it.

My bicycle still needed a back wheel.

I made a phone call.

Pigeon Mary was playing at steering the old Ford. Down-
shifting, pumping the accelerator pedal, gripping the wheel
in both feathered hands, going: "Vroom!" Then: "How
long are we going to wait here? I was just wondering."

We were parked across the street and up the block from
Skully's apartment house.

"I told you when I asked for the car. It might take a few
hours. You shouldna come, you shoulda listened to me. I
know how to drive."

"Phew, are you finished?"

"Sorry."

"You sure she's still in there? Reeni?"

"She's in there."

"Okay," and Pigeon Mary poked a cigarette between her
lips, lit it and hunched back over the wheel. Made believe she
was taking a dangerous corner on two wheels: "Screeee!"
Then she "braked," jerked in her bucket, slumped and
brushed ash from her blouse. She looked at me sideways.
"Don't you feel creepy doing this, Grinner? Spying?"

I didn't reply.

We sat in silence, five, ten minutes. Sunlight and branch
shadows rubbed the windshield. Dead leaves somersaulted
across the hood, the solar pans gleamed.

"When's he going for his operation? Beef, I'm talking
about."

"Nothing definite," I said. "But why ask me? You should
know more about it."

"Believe me, I don't." She lightly shined the wheel horn
with the side of a fist. "And you guys? You and Reeni?"

"Whenever we get the money."

"What are you going to do afterward? You can't do the show. Nobody will even rent you." She smiled.

"I haven't thought. Something. When I look different, I'll find something."

A gang of Normal zombies came slouching up the sidewalk just then, all of them wearing gloves and heavy jackets and scarves in the warm sun. Mumbling, they passed by—except for one of them, a young kid. He squinted through the car windshield. Our eyes met. His widened while mine turned to dashes.

He mouthed: *Eggs?*

I mouthed: *Sorry*, and he drove his middle finger up in front of his face, then stumbled away.

Pidge said: "What gets me," and trailed off.

"Yeah?"

"About those eggs. What gets me is how come so many people want them. Jesus, Grinny, I don't want to die—even if the world *is* scary. Even if there *is* another life. If you can call six light bulbs in a dark room another life."

As far as I knew, she'd never egged down.

"Aren't you afraid of dying?" she asked.

I thought for a moment. "No. It's spooky but it's not frightening. It's boring but it's not so bad. No, I'm afraid of living more. Like I am, like I look right this minute. Living like this I'm stuck. It's worse than six light bulbs in a dark room. It's no light bulbs."

"Poor Grinner."

I let that pass.

"Well," said Pidge, "*I'm* afraid. Which, I guess, is why I'm glad Beef's not living with me any more." She scratched the bridge of her nose and a minuscule critter leapt free of the feathers. "He's gotten strange, Grinner. He does crazy things for no reason. Mostly to me. Crazy things that hurt. Some nights I had to leave the house. I got afraid that he'd kill me."

"Beef isn't like that."

"You're trying to tell me what Beef isn't like? I have to tell you, you don't know. Getting beaten for money is one thing. It's bad enough but it's still money. Offstage and unsalaried—Grinner, I don't need it. I'm glad to be alone. I'm just sorry that he changed."

I flipped the glove box closed, shifted in my seat and showed her my back.

"Sulk if you want, Grinner, but it's the truth. Look, I loved him, too."

"You broke up," I said. "Okay, I understand that. But do you have to go around bad-mouthing him now?"

She let her fingertips dribble down the arc of the steering wheel.

"Hey, Pidge . . ."

"Hey, Grin . . ."

We both smiled—she with her lips, me with my eyes.

I grubbed one of her mentholated cigarettes. She lit it for me. Then I said: "What, did he hit you a coupla times?"

Pigeon Mary made a face, and "Aw, come on. I can see we can't talk about Beef. So let's don't."

The car filled up with scribbles of blue smoke.

"He's a good guy," I said.

Pidge shook her head. "You don't know."

"I know." I glanced down the street. Reeni's bike was still leaning against the front of the apartment house.

"Grinner, did you ever wonder . . ."

"Wonder what?"

"Forget it."

"No. Wonder what?"

"Okay. Did you ever wonder how your brother got tagged as the eggman? You ever wonder who told the cops? Or, better, who *sold* it to the cops?"

I nearly slapped her. I didn't only because it was her car and I needed it. "God," I said, "I can't believe you're so vindictive! You're really something. That's ridiculous."

She threw up her hands and a few short feathers glided to her lap. "Bucks," she said, using Beef's jargon and trying to imitate his gravelly voice. "Bucker-babies . . ."

Reeni squatted and unchained her gold Schwinn. Straddled it and pedaled off the curb and into the crumbly street. She deranged a game of crate-slat hockey and was pelted with a pink ball pitched by a little brown-skinned boy with basset ears.

Pigeon Mary switched the engine on.

"Let her get a little ways ahead—okay? Before you go."

With lips ferociously tucked, Pidge turned the wheel hard to the right, she kept her foot down on the brake and "I've seen enough old flicks to know what I'm doing," she said.

Reeni shot up the Boulevard, then cut west on Danforth, then north on West Side Avenue.

"This is nuts stuff, following your own lady," Pigeon said. "If you want my opinion."

"You wanna get out here and I'll bring the car back later?"

"I was only saying. What's this all about, Grinny?"

I leaned forward, folded my arms on the dashboard: I'd seen enough flicks myself.

Reeni bounced onto the sidewalk, braked in front of an out-of-business shoe store, chained her bike to a headless parking meter. She tapped on the soaped-over door, it opened a body width, and she slipped inside.

"Well," said Pidge, "now you know where she's going. Do you want to wait again?"

"No. You can take off. I'm getting out here. I'll see you."

"You're welcome," said Pigeon Mary.

I cupped my hands and peered through a gap in the swirled soap on the store's plate window. Empty shoe pedestals and curling Miles posters still on display. I swallowed poisonous saliva and tried the door. It was open. A cashier's station, two rows of plastic chairs arranged back to back, shelving units along two baize walls. Shoe boxes and loose lids: some on the floor, some on the shelves. Inside one box was the iridescent head of a mutant goldfish. Nobody. Then somebody: two somebodies: a fox-faced dwarf and a guy with ropy red hair and a gulch where his nose should've been. They stepped through the curtain at the rear of the store. "How the fuck did you get in here?" demanded Gulch-face.

I told him: I'd just walked in, the door was open.

Foxface tapped his sternum with the cut-down handle of a snow shovel. "Don't look at me, man," he told Gulchface. "I didn't leave it unlocked. Bobby let her in. Blame Bobby."

Gulchface turned back to me. "What are you doing here?"

"I'm looking," I said, "for her. That Bobby let in."

Gulchface called over his shoulder, "Get Bobby," to a kid who'd just appeared. The kid had green filament hair and epicanthic eyes situated at the same facial latitude as his earlobes.

Bobby, I'd figured as much, turned out to be fat Bobby Lumps. When he saw me, he said: "Asshole." He was wearing positive-negative pants (the legs pulsing black, then white, black, then white . . .), a holstered revolver and a wash-faded Freak Pride T-shirt—a red-outlined explosion cloud on its front served as the word-balloon for *What a Difference a Day Makes*, in white script. He was barefoot. "What do you got for brains, Grinner? Bread?"

"Come on, Lumps, don't fool. Where's Reeni?"

"So long, Grinner. Okay?"

The Freaks moved aside to let me through. I started for the door and a lady's glitter-boot whizzed by my ear, a polio shoe caught me square on the hip, a galosh wobbled past my head. Foxface guffawed and bowled a clog. "Bye-bye, Grinner," he said.

The kid with the low-down eyes opened the door.

"Wait up," and Lumps stepped outside behind me. "Don't be so stupid again, yeah?"

"Is Flour here?"

Lumps squeezed his eyes shut, feigning cancer pain.

"Like I said, don't be so stupid again."

"Bobby . . . just tell me something. No, hold on, before you do—" I grabbed my wallet, took out a twenty-dollar bill. "Just tell me if they got something going—those two."

He took the money. "Those two?"

"Shit. You know what I'm talking about."

His fist, with the currency inside, chopped down on my shoulder, falling harder than a simple take-it-easy clip. He turned to reenter the store.

"Hey, fuckit, Lumps—if you won't tell me nothing, give me the goddamn money back at least."

He smiled and closed the door.

Reeni's bike was gone.

I found a pharmacy, bought a bottle of salt pills and walked home.

10
Dolphin in the Bathtub

As I came scuffing down Neptune, I spotted Ma standing on my front porch. I waved and walked through the gate.

"You coming or going?"

"Going."

I looked past her and there was Reeni's bike dumped on the porch. "Did you talk to her?"

"We talked," nodding and gumming her lips—a pale pink color. Her cheeks were shiny with a much deeper pink cosmetic, applied as thickly as stucco. A bowl-cut russet-colored wig today, an acetate scarf looped around her neck, black funeral gloves.

"And?"

"I tried, Charlie, like I told you I would. Really. She says she don't wanna be Normal. She says she wouldn't do it even if Syntha-skin cost a buck forty-nine."

"I don't understand."

"She goes, 'Why should I spend all my money just so I can throw some bottles myself?' I swear, that's what she went. I think the tour got to her."

"You wanna know what *I* think got to her?"

"I asked her about that. About Alan."

I looked up. There was some dried blood, like flaky boathouse paint, below Ma's nostrils. Her pupils for a change weren't dilated. I said: "Yeah? So?"

"So nothing. They're just friends, like they always been friends. Did you know she sold eggs for him during your tour?"

"I know."

"She didn't want to but he asked her. As a favor. And did you know she earned a thousand bucks? I wouldn't believe Irene could be so nervy. There's nothing between them, Charles."

"You believe her?"

"I believe her."

"Well, if she's telling you the truth, then crap, Ma, I really *don't* know what's with her."

"Maybe, like she says, she made up her own mind."

"Aw, Ma, gimme a break."

Reeni was watching a program on television. It was a rerun—I'd seen it last year—about dolphins, about how they'd turned misanthropic, were refusing to share any more of their myths, their math or their semisacred medical arts. Running along the bottom of the screen was some late-breaking news in luminous green caps. It was about Belgium; who cared about Belgium, so I didn't bother reading it. Reeni read it, though, as carefully as a recipe. She was playing ultrapreoccupied. That way she didn't have to notice me. Finally she looked up with counterfeit surprise.

"Aren't you cute?" I said. "The egg lady."

And Reeni was suddenly on her feet, hands curled into fists, the whites of her eyes moiled with blood. "Why the hell did you go following me? It's none of your business!"

"It's not, huh? Was Flour there?"

"No, Flour was *not* there. I haven't seen him and that's the truth. I'm getting pretty tired of all this, Grinner. Think anything you like, but I haven't seen him."

On the TV, a man in a white smock was cutting up a dolphin brain on a stainless steel table with a knife and a fork.

"Okay," I said, "you haven't seen him. But would you answer something? Before we did the tour, why didn't you say you were gonna be selling his eggs?"

"I wasn't *selling* them. I was *distributing* them to different people. *They* sold them."

"Same difference. Why didn't you tell me?"

" 'Cause you woulda said no, I couldn't."

"You're right."

"So there."

"You shoulda been honest with me, Reeni."

She threw me a scowl, closed an eye, folded her arms. "Like you're honest with me."

"I am."

I didn't like the way she laughed, it was a growl, a grunt. She said: "I talked to Studebaker."

"What do you mean, talked?"

"Words. You know? Talked. Sentences? He called about half an hour ago. Just after I got in. Just before your mother showed up. He wanted to let us know Toronto's all set for late January."

"Oh."

"Oh, he says! You didn't say nothing to me about Toronto, Mr. Honest."

"I was waiting for the right time."

"Why won't you listen to me, Grinner? Why can't you respect me that much? I don't wanna do any more shows, I wanna—"

"What? Do you wanna walk around looking like a goddamn cavewoman for the rest of your life?"

Her mouth dropped open, her jaw hung slack. She gaped at me as if I were a prowler. I pivoted (thinking, You should apologize for *that*) and stormed out into the foyer. I took the stairs up, two at a time, sawdust puffing from termite holes.

"Grinner." Soft.

"Grinner!" Sharp.

"Grinner!" Shrill.

I came back down, slowly.

Her shoulders were slumped, her stained teeth glistened. Looking at her, I got the feeling there was some confession—but of what?—loitering fidgety just in back of her tonsils, like a troupe of acrobats, whippy with adrenaline, about to hit the trampolines. I waited. (Apologize, Grin, make everything all right.) And waited. She glanced off into the parlor. I glanced there, too. Dolphins thrashing in their tanks, sudsing the water.

I drummed my fingertips on the banister.

"I'm sorry," I said. "For yelling."

She waved that away. "Would you listen to me for just a minute. That's all."

"I always listen," I said.

She stood at the foot of the stairs, looking up. "Grinner. For five weeks, honest, all I thought about was coming back. She's crazy, you're thinking. But that's all I thought."

"Even when you were selling eggs?"

"That's all I thought," she said. "Coming home. When I left here it seemed like a prison. When I was away but, it seemed like the only sanctuary in the whole world. Didn't you ever get that feeling?"

"No," I said.

"Grinner, it started with the rentals but it didn't hit me so hard until the tour. Grinny, those faces I seen in every city that we played, those Normal ones I always wished were mine. No distinguishing marks, like it says in the post office. But nothing, only panic, in their eyes. Didn't you *see?*"

"How many eyes you actually see close up? Come on, Reen, don't exaggerate."

"I seen."

"Okay," I said. "So what?"

"Grinner, we're safer here than we could ever be anyplace else. I believe that now. I know, you're going, She's really crazy. But we are, I think."

I said nothing.

"Grinner, they got the same poison meats in Kansas, they got the same cancer rains in Illinois. It don't make sense any more to get skins. Unless they're armored. So we might as well stay here."

"Might as well stay here," I said. "Fishdick and Ugly Irene." I stamped back upstairs and went straight into the bathroom. I turned on the bath water. Stripped and glared at myself in the medicine-cabinet mirror. The green face, the tumbled hair, the bladder-green gums, the stupid involuntary grin. I grabbed my jeans from the toilet seat and flung them. The zipper ticked against the glass and my loose salt pills—all flecked with lint particles—flew from the pocket and ricocheted off the pebbled window, the black-enameled radiator, the yellowed porcelain sink.

I heard Reeni coming upstairs and stood holding my breath. She paused on the landing, then passed the bathroom. She called as she walked: "Your mother's not gonna make me change my mind, either."

When the tub was two-thirds filled with cool water, I closed the spigots tightly and sprinkled in sea salt from the tube that I kept in a moistureproof zip-bag in the shower caddy. I climbed in and sat down. My nose plugs and athletic mouth guard were inside a plastic box on the slimy soap dish. I took out the plugs and worked them far up into my nostrils. I slipped the mouthpiece into place and bit down. Then I submerged until only my knees stuck out. Operculums, they were between my ribs, unclosed. Gills drank, rakers strained, filaments extracted oxygen.

It took some time before my heart quit hammering, before my anger drowned. But finally, and with a feeling of weightlessness, I relaxed and then napped. Amazingly, I didn't dream about Reeni. I didn't dream about Flour. I didn't dream about Reeni and Flour.

I dreamed I was surrounded by bottle-nosed dolphins in a huge tank of green seawater. There's been some horrible mistake. Let me out!

Part Three:
The Antichrist Newsgirl
(Mid-November, 2010)

11
Sharkey and Laudermilch

I'd almost finished work on the new superrealistic groom-head. Sure, why not—I'd done practically nothing else but sweat, blink and grouch to myself over the latex bastard (actually, it was a beauty, it was Lancelot) for nearly a full week. Beef had telephoned to cancel our trip to Dr. Sleet's office—Mrs. Sinakin was taking him with her down to Palm Beach, Florida, for a couple of days. And Reeni, Reeni was still spending most of her time over at Skully's (she said), watching him drink eggs, bathing him after he'd resurrect and consoling him when he dumbly sang the blues for his lost spouse—those godlights remained as unreachable as ever. From the way she dressed lately—more sweaters than a Klondiker, quilted slacks and thermal knee socks, and that was how she dressed *indoors*—I knew she'd been join-ing her old man on some death trips. But about that, even though it made me anxious and a little guilty, I'd said noth-ing. I'd put myself on a no-quarrels regimen, for peace of mind. Reeni, apparently, had done the same thing—wearing a crushed smile all of the time and speaking only of vege-tables, the laundromat, and furniture sales. Nights we slept as chastely as a couple on the downhill side of their diamond jubilee.

My brain felt clayed.

I was stitching individual sable hairs above the groom-head's left glass eye when I heard the cellar door open. A shadow skimmed over the brick stair wall. "Reen?" I called, just as a gray suede shoe and a black trouser cuff flashed down a riser. More shadow ballooned ahead, ruptured against a beam. A leather-gloved hand squeezing the banister, a leather jacket sleeve. Then a profile, then a full-face: the Normal from the airplane, the car on Seaview, the Durham bull, the guy who'd mocked my grin. He stopped and called back upstairs: "He's here, Sharks, come on down."

I sat mutely at the workbench but I measured how far a reach it was for my X-acto blade. It was a short reach.

I recognized the man called Sharks, too. He'd also been on the Toledo–Newark flight—the natty exec with the perfect skin and the trimmed pale mustache. Glen plaid today, and a pair of black perforated shoes that gleamed like obsidian. He came trotting down the cellar stairs and pulled a patty-wallet from his hip pocket. He thumbed it open and showed me his silver shield and laminated ident card with its bleached-out photograph, its official seal (a humpbacked monkey lined up in a calibrated rifle sight) and its motto in Latin. He was with BORD, the Bureau of Restricted Drugs, and his name was Niles Sharkey. And "Jack Laudermilch," he said, indicating his companion.

I got the brachiated willies.

"You can probably guess," said Sharkey as he put his hands in his pockets, "why we're here."

I said, "No, why?" and then was distracted by Laudermilch, who'd begun to wander around the cellar peering into storage boxes, fingering tools that hung on pegboard.

"We'd like to talk to you about your brother. Just for a few minutes."

"There's no point," I told him. "I really don't—I'd like it if you didn't touch those, okay?" To Laudermilch, who was now shaking one of the mask boxes that I'd left on a stack of old screen windows.

Snap, the handle twine broke, and Laudermilch chucked away the lid. He lifted out the papier-mâché groomhead. "Would you mind doing me a little favor?" He put the mask down in front of me. "Would you mind wearing this while we talk?"

Sharkey sighed faintly. "My friend," he said, "is being very silly—but what can we do? He's got a very limited aesthetic sense. Put on the mask. It'll speed things up, Mr. Fistick."

I didn't like his tone so I did as he said. Then: "Listen, would youse listen? I got nothing to do with my brother, I don't"—and broke off to watch Laudermilch unscrew a light bulb from the ceiling socket. Clutching it by the threads like an ice-cream cone, he walked up to me and shattered it against the groomhead.

Sharkey rolled a cardboard rag drum out from underneath the stairs. He walloped the lid a few times to gauge its strength, then hoisted himself up and sat down. "Okay. Where's he breeding those fish?"

I moved my head, off balance from the mask, from side to side.

Laudermilch unscrewed another bulb and dropped it. It burst into a billion frosted splinters. With the edge of his shoe, he swept away the glass.

Sharkey lit a cigarette. "Let me tell you something, Mr. Fistick. For the last few weeks of your . . . tour, we watched you. We'd decided you and your wife were involved in this business."

"I guess you were disappointed." My heart had shrunk to a painful nubbin.

"Not exactly," he said, then nodded to Laudermilch, who reached into his jacket and took out a small deck of photographs. He spilled them on the workbench.

"You'll recognize," said Sharkey, "the woman."

Reeni, standing outside the University of Michigan gymnasium, passing a shoe box to a gaunt, crewcut Normal wearing reflector sunglasses and holding a bulky refrigeration bag . . . Reeni, in her bathrobe and slippers, leaning against a cracked wall in a hotel corridor, balancing a campanile of three relish jars in one hand, accepting cash in a bank wrapper from a shadowy figure . . . Reeni with the she-zom who'd followed us in Toledo; you can just barely make me out in the background, in my wig, my cap, my shades and safety makeup . . . Reeni knocking at the Miles shoe store.

The last picture in the batch was of me standing slope-shouldered in front of the same store thrusting a twenty-dollar bill into Bobby Lump's hand.

"Come on, these don't prove anything," I said. "Except maybe that she sells hot dog relish. And shoes."

Laudermilch pulverized another bulb in his gloved fist. The only light left burning now was the one in my gooseneck table lamp.

"All we want," said Sharkey, "are your brother's goldfish. We don't want to hurt you. Or anybody, for that matter. We just want the fish."

"So go find them. I don't care."

"It's not that easy. Which is why we need you. You're going to help us."

"I don't think so," I said.

"I do," he said.

I took off the mask and set it down. I picked up the lamp and offered it to Laudermilch. "You want the bulb? Go ahead, take the bulb. Just, I don't wanna hear any more of this crap."

Laudermilch glared as he brushed glass splinters from his glove fingers onto a trouser leg. He lunged for the lamp and light went swiveling.

"*Jack!* Jack," said Sharkey, "do me a favor. Go upstairs and go on outside and wait in the car."

"Hey—"

"Thank you very much, Jack."

Laudermilch slammed down the lamp base, swung his

eyes to mine and squeezed a lot of muscle into his wince.
Then, leaden-footed, he climbed to the kitchen.

Sharkey came and stood opposite me at the table. He
picked up the new almost-done groomhead and turned it in
his hands. He was wearing a fat gold pinky ring. "Nice piece
of work," and laid down the mask. Sucked on his front teeth,
shrugged. "I don't think your brother understands what
he's selling," he said.

"Oh, I think he does, Mr. Sharkey."

"He doesn't. Believe me."

Sharkey watched me thumb open a bottle of salt pills and
swallow five. He craned a yellow eyebrow.

"A mild high," I explained. "Unfortunately for you, Mr.
Sharkey, salt's legal."

"Cheap, too."

"And I'm the only fucker in the world gets off on it. A
fringe benefit."

"I understand you've been making plans to—how's the
best way to put this?—join us?"

It was my turn to raise an eyebrow.

"Well, it's no big secret, is it? Aren't you? Making some
plans?"

"What of it?"

"Nothing, nothing." He smiled a huge one. "Do you have
the money?"

"I'm getting there, Mr. Sharkey. I'm also getting your drift.
Tell me if I'm wrong, but you're gonna offer me an op in
exchange for my brother."

"Almost," he said. "I'm offering you *two* operations and
a promise that your wife won't be indicted because of these
photographs."

"They don't prove shit. I thought we decided that."

"*You* decided it, Mr. Fistick. But say I brought them to
a prosecutor. I think *he'd* use them. I hate to sound like a
Normal . . . but I *am* one and so's the Hudson County

prosecutor. So's the judge. And your Maureen's a Freak."

"Irene."

"Irene, Maureen, she's a Freak."

"We'll take our chances," I said. "If you didn't arrest her when she had the stuff—*if* she had it—then you blew your case."

Sharkey checked his wristwatch, pushed a hand through his hair. He leaned down, flicking through the snapshots. He scraped one up: Reeni arriving at the shoe store. "You talk about cases," he said. "See this? We know the shop's a distribution point. We also know we can bust at least a dozen Freaks there anytime we want. Mr. Fistick, the fact is I really *don't* give a shit about a case. Or your brother. I'm interested only in the fish."

"So, like I said, go find them."

"If I could do that I wouldn't bother with you." He bent and braced his hands flat on the workbench. "We can help each other. Nobody has to know."

"I don't need your money," I said. "I'll get my own. We're in demand, Mr. Sharkey. Could work every day of the year, if we wanted."

"Demand," Sharkey said. "There's a thousand Freaks can do what you do." He smiled and collected his snapshots.

I glanced at his pinky ring. It was minted with the spacers' insignia: a spoked orbiter with an encapsulated American eagle plummeting from its bomb bay.

"I thought you were supposed to be a narc."

"I'll talk to you again in a few days," he said.

12
Grinner Rebuffed

Tears ran down Reeni's face. There was a tea-colored bruise on her cheek. I stood in front of her, shaking. I broke out in a sweat. Enraged, I'd squeezed her flesh as soon as she'd walked in, I'd torn the sleeve from her blouse, I'd struck her and screamed in her face—*You see, you see, you see—they'll put you in goddamn jail for helping him, stupid ape!*

I cracked her again with an open hand. She recoiled, spun away and touched her cheek. Then she smiled, her eyes berserk with blood filaments. She *smiled*!

She dabbed at her swollen cheek with a face cloth knobby with ice cubes.

"How many times do you want me to apologize?" I said. "Okay. I apologize again. I'm sorry. I didn't mean to hit you."

She lifted her eyes and lowered them. "And you don't even know you've changed," she said. "That's the sad part."

"I haven't changed. Not me. You."

"I've changed my mind, but that's all." She dumped the cubes into the sink and went upstairs.

Much later, when I came to bed, I pressed myself against her, murmuring further apologies. I begged her to forgive me, I swore I loved her, I squeezed her breasts. She grabbed my wrist and slammed my fingers against the cold bedroom wall.

13
"Wash Your Face, Monster!"

Eyes flickering, Beef sat hunched forward on the couch. He sighed, his nostrils shook. Green and red lights glimmered on his heavy metal chastening bracelet. A fuzzy valentine of caked blood was centered on a raft of gauze taped across his slaughterhouse forehead. Reeni brought him a glass of orange juice and a bottle of aspirin. "What was it?" she asked him. "A wrench?"

He tackled a smile. "Would you believe a little ceramic angel? It broke."

Reeni shook her head. "That woman's gonna kill you one of these days, that crazy lady."

"Won't get that chance, Reenbo. 'Cause today I tell her to shove it. Take this fucker off my arm, Mrs. Sinakin, and shove it."

I let go a blast of canned bug spray and a golden palomino cockroach the size of a megavitamin lost traction on the radiator valve and plummeted to the floor. I murdered it with a claw hammer. Beef flinched at the bang, then checked his watch. He asked Reeni if she was coming with us. She wasn't.

"Should. Be real interesting."

"I'm sure," and she smiled vaguely. "But Grinny can tell me all about it in glowing detail."

I zipped my parka, filled a pocket with salt pills, grabbed my gloves from the TV. "It's not like you're doing anything special today," I said. "Change your mind, Reen."

"Have fun. And give my regards to Dr. Frankenstein."

Beef didn't think that was so funny. "What's with the mock? I can remember a certain, um, woolly female friend sitting on this couch here watching an old flick on the tube and telling us how she was gonna order some looks along the lines of, of—what's her name? That singer with the tin man. Garfield."

"Garland," Reeni corrected, and "Well, that certain female friend said it before she went out and spent some time in Judy Garland's world—all right?"

"Ain't no Judy Garland's world outside. She's dead. It's our world. Could be. Why d'you have to act so difficult, Reen? You got worms or something?"

Reeni smiled in spite of herself. Beef shot me a frown, I tilted my head and blew a gust. Then I checked myself in the hall mirror: my wig was on straight, my flesh was evenly pinked. My glossed-over scales looked like killer zits smeared with acne cream. Well, better they should think in New York that I was some kid with a shitty complexion . . .

We left and I scanned the street for the gray Volvo 'lectric but couldn't find it.

"We're right here," Beef said, nodding at a VW Screamer that was stripped of all its lacquer. Its hood, roof and door panels were scabby with brilliant rust. The car couldn't have been older than two years: it had those new kind of red-chrome grimace fenders. Screamers had the reputation for being a good car for vehicular homicides. Still banned in some states, they were cheap, fast, ugly and morbid. Naturally, the Newsboys loved them.

"I guess this belongs to that painter, huh? Cleo?"

"Uh-huh."

The seats were upholstered in burlap, the ceiling was glued with pads of rubber gag vomit, there were snapshots of morgue corpses straight-pinned to the sun visors.

"Cheery," I said.

"Ain't it." Beef let the motor idle while he fished out a pouch of dried banana slices from his coat pocket. He ate a few, and I almost grubbed some. Then I noticed their light coat of brown hypno-glitter.

"How can you afford that stuff, Beefstone, and still save?"

"Gotta have a little fun, don't I? I'll get the money for the op, don't you fret." He drove south for a block on Garfield then cut up to the Boulevard. "We have to get Cleo before we go on over New York."

"She's here?"

"I dropped her off on the way to your house. She wanted to take some pictures."

"So I'll meet her."

"Big thrill."

"Strange?"

"I'm telling you." He tried to beat a red light then had to slam on the brakes to avoid plowing into a woman who was halfway across the intersection in back of a baby carriage. She swung her face around to glare at us: skeins of deep-red capillaries and snow-blue veins, in bas-relief. Submissively, Beef lifted both hands from the wheel. She pushed the carriage to the curb. Beef gave her the finger and screeched away, not bothering to wait for green.

"You haven't told me much about Florida. What'd you do down there?"

"Aw, you know," he said. "Just a bunch of old Normals like Mrs. Sinakin. Actually but, it wasn't too bad—she showed me off and I stood around at her parties looking ugly. It was kinda like the first months we did rentals. Soft stuff. Like, one night this old Cuban geezer showed up with a print of *Freaks Amok*. They ran it and then afterward I had all these ancient assholes ask me if it *really* had been like that—if the Freaks had gone certifiable after Caliban's and beat the living shit outta one another. If they *really* screwed with their fists."

"What'd you tell them?"

"I told 'em sure—what else was I gonna say? It was their party." He smirked. "And I got laid down there, Grinny. A Normal."

"No kidding! Old?"

"Not too. She fainted."

"Get out!"

"I swear! Right in the middle, she passes out. Would you believe?"

"What'd it feel like but? Before she fainted."

"It was all right. Not bad."

"You son of a bitch."

"Ain't that something? And she paid, too."

"Now I don't believe."

"My old man woulda bust a kidney, wouldn't he? If he'd seen the Beefstone putting the blocks to a Norm?"

"I guess he woulda."

"Poor fucker," said Beef. "I miss him."

Beef's father had been stabbed to death in a Trenton hotel room by a beautician he'd picked up at a smoke bar. He'd seemed perfectly Normal until he undressed and revealed his chestload of coppery female nipples. The girl had gone wild, dug shears from her bag . . . and Mr. Stein ended up perforated with seventeen holes on a vibrating mattress. That had been five years ago. Beef's mother died some years earlier: she went into Medical Center to have an abortion and left on a mortician's stretcher. Blood poisoning, it said on the death certificate.

"You ever do it with a Normal?" Beef asked.

"Me? Get out. Never. Just Reeni."

"Just Reeni," he said. "Just Reeni, who don't give a good shit about Judy Garland's face any more."

"That's enough, Beef. Okay?"

He bellied out his underlip and shrugged, then: "When you seen Pidge, did you notice anything different?"

"How?"

"Guess you din't. She's pregnant."

"No fooling. Yours?"

"Don't be wise. Whose else?" I could hear his teeth squeaking, grinding. "And she's gonna have it, too. That's the pisser. You think she'd have more goddamn common sense. You're lucky, Grinner."

"Lucky?"

"You never have to worry. I mean, din't you tell me once?"

"Yeah, I told you."

"We should all be. What's the point of making any more of us? I told her to get rid of it, it's free, it takes ten minutes. She won't, so I wash my hands. I could beat the crap out of her but, for keeping it."

"She told me you already started doing that."

"She's a pasture, man, she's full of it."

"I figured as much."

"Sure, you'd figure. You know me. Grinner and the Beefstone, two peas in a pod."

Cleo Nothing—short green-dyed hair, linty gray flannel pajamas, black basketball sneakers—lowered the camera from her face and turned when Beef blasted the horn. Her lips curled back over yellow teeth, she held up a finger: *Be right with you.* She crouched again, refocused her lens and snapped the Freak—a fat gray-headed guy with huge facial pores—who was posed standing sentry on an apartment house stoop with a sawed-off tree limb for a cudgel. Then she clapped on the lens cover and pulled a wallet from her flicka-bag. An animated cartoon played across the bag's beige fabric: an army of red amoebas devouring a tribe of ciliated green foodstuffs. She offered money to her model. He shook his head in refusal. She didn't press him.

"I think I seen her before," I told Beef. "She been on television?"

"I doubt it."

"Real familiar."

By the time Cleo climbed into the back seat, the amoebas were being swallowed by a horde of corkscrew critters. She had a permanent crease between her eyes, spittle balls at the corners of her mouth. Calluses and nicks and puffy scars on her palms. I gave her a nod, she gave me one back. She wet

a thumb and brushed it across my cheek. "What're you wearing makeup for, monster?"

Beef laughed. "Don't take offense, Grinno. She calls me
that, too. She's just being affectionate—aren't you, Cleo?"

"Affectionate," she said tonelessly and stuffed her camera
into her bag. Schools of little fish were chewing at the cork-
screws.

"Get any good pictures?" Beef asked her.

"A roll." She was squinting at me now, studying me—
spooky eyes, varnished as if illness were either coming or
leaving. I looked away, saw a Normal he-zom braced against
a tree, dry heaving.

"Anybody give you any trouble, Clee?"

"No." She kept her influenzan gaze fastened on my face.

Beef snorted, glancing sideways. "She thinks Freaks are
great. She thinks we're the greatest things since gravy bombs.
She keeps hoping we're gonna take over the world or something. I keep telling her she's a friggen loose-screw Newsboy.
But she's cute, ain't she?"

"She's staring," I said.

"Yeah, she does that. Just tell her to stop. She won't blow
you up. Cleo, quit staring at my friend. By the way, this is
Grinner."

Cleo said: "Wash your face, monster."

"Din't I tell you she was a barrel of fun? Hey, Cleo, you
got three bucker-babies for the toll?"

She handed three singles up front. On each bill Washington's eyes had been whited out with correction fluid; it made
him look pathological, which was the whole point, I supposed. Fucken pro nihilists could be as cutesy sometimes as
those sheiks who wore bubble rings filled with crude oil.
Beef crunched up the bills in his fist and lobbed the ball at
the Normal tolltaker. Then we rode through the Lincoln
Tunnel behind a fuming Chrysler Marin whose rear bumper
was plastered with stickers that urged NO WHEAT FOR SWIT-
ZERLAND, U.S. ANNEX HOT CHINA NOW, HACKENSACK CASINOS
—YES!

14
Nuts in a Blender

Dr. Sleet ran through the combination on his vault refrigerator. A solid click, and he pulled the door open. He lifted out a chem beaker filled with pale-brown fluid and some floating things that resembled worms and lumps of bubble gum. He set it down on his cleared desk blotter. "You gentlemen are both, you should by rights be—Caucasoid?" Sleet was himself Negroid, thin and bony, fifty possibly, without a wrinkle on his face.

Beef cleared his throat into a fist. "You mean white? Yeah, that's correct." And laughed, and looked over at me.

Sleet nodded sliding open a desk drawer, fetching out a long silver implement with a hooked end like a dental curette. With it, he fished from the beaker a long strip of pink flesh. He laid the flesh on a paper towel and offered it to me. He could've been a deli man tendering a free sample of Gouda. "Go ahead and touch it if you'd like."

I decided only to look and to say: "It sure seems real." What else could I've said?

"For all practical purposes it is. Another Du Pont miracle."

"Those fuckers at Du Pont, boy," said Beef. "Always busy."

"It was originally developed for grafting severe burns and for minor cosmetic surgery. But I've adapted it—as you know. And successfully, too. In the past year I've resurfaced eleven of your . . . compatriots." Sleet grinned. Was he mocking me? No, he wasn't even looking at us. He was staring over our heads.

Beef said: "Me and Grinner are lucky, I guess. Not to have dead wings or anything really wild. That stuff must be a bitch, huh, Doc?"

"They're more difficult, but not hopeless. Would you like to see some pictures?" He stood and yanked open a filing-case drawer, picked through color-coded folder tabs.

Beef and I turned in our seats and looked at each other. He smiled, then his face drained and his eyes seemed to leap—more random volts from the bracelet.

Sleet spread half a dozen folders across the front of his desk, then sank back into his chair. I picked one up. Beef walked his chair over and plopped it down next to mine. His breath was hot and moist on my shirt sleeve. It reeked of banana.

The top picture inside the folder showed a woman, about forty, in a three-piece swimsuit. Her skin looked like a cob of corn after the kernels have been scarfed. The remaining photos showed the same lady clear-skinned, the new flesh luminous and taut.

Beef couldn't have been more impressed: he giggled. "And this Syntha-stuff"—pointing at the little swatch drying on the paper towel—"I mean, does it bleed when you cut it, or what?"

"It bleeds." Sleet rolled his tongue around his mouth and I got the feeling he was putting Beef down, which nearly made me scrap my own question. But I asked it anyway:

"No scars?" I wouldn't pay for scars. Scarred was only one rank up from deformed, and being deformed was just an atom more tolerable than being a mutant. As far as Normals were concerned. Long ago I'd figured out all the ranks, the degrees.

"No stitches," said Sleet. "The flesh is heat-sealed."

"My eyes," I said.

"You pick the color and I'll take care of the rest. They'll be real, of course. From a bank. If you must have eyes with perfect vision, we can provide them—but there'll be an added charge for a search fee."

I knew I wouldn't bother with that. Most Normals wore glasses, of some kind, for some purpose. There was no stigma. Besides, I was already nearsighted.

Sleet pinched the skin strip between his thumb and first finger and dropped it back into the beaker. When it hit the fluid it appeared to wriggle; it reminded me of a minnow.

I took out the prints I'd swiped from my parents' wedding album. I bit my lip and passed them to Sleet. "You told us there'd be no, um, problem with a new"—I touched my cheek, ran fingers lightly over cool nubs—"face."

"Certainly to have a photograph I can model from is a good idea, but I can't promise an exact duplication."

"No, I don't want it *exact*." Sleet still hadn't glanced at the pictures so I nodded at them. He finally looked.

"I gather you want me to use the man as the model." With a little smile.

"Not exactly," I said, then spread my hands and brought them back together. "If you could take some of the features from both, from the man *and* the woman. Do you see what I'm saying?"

"I'm not quite sure."

"I want to look"—and felt a wet heat seethe through my skin, all over—"like I might've."

He raised his eyebrows.

"Now. Important. Very. I'd like to know when you gentlemen, and *Mrs.* Fistick, might be ready for your operations. There's considerable scheduling to be done. And then I'd like to explain—"

"How much?" Beef interrupted.

"All right, let's talk about that," Sleet said.

Beef gripped the arms of his chair as though he were a spacer in a G-force simulation chamber. I clenched my teeth and took a deep breath. As it turned out, our melodramatics were in order . . .

"Nothing," finished Dr. Sleet, "ever gets less expensive. Does it?" He tried hard to sound wistful.

* * *

The corridor walls outside Dr. Sleet's office were covered with carroty fakefur. I pulled at tufts, I stood with Beef and waited for the elevator. The doors sucked open and the car was crowded with Normals heading for lunch. I tugged on Beef's sleeve. The elevator descended without us. We started walking down. It was ten flights. Beef got another jolt on the seventh-floor landing. He slumped against the wall, his chest swelling like a bellows. Then he was okay.

"So what do you think?" I asked him.

"About the operation?"

"The cost."

"Well . . . it's about eleven thousand more than I got right now. You? You have that much?"

"What are you, kidding? Three more tours, at least. I guess you'll have to stay with Mrs. Sinakin now, huh?"

"I'm not changing my plans."

"So what're you gonna do?"

"Cleo has bucks. Her father left her a pile. She offered me a job. I'll say yes."

"More posing?"

He laughed. "Eleven thousand bucks worth of posing? No, Grinner, not posing."

"What, then?"

"A little business, that's all."

"You're not gonna tell me."

"Guess not."

"Does it have to do with Newsboys? Something illegal?"

"Nothing to do with Newsboys. Just forget I said anything, will you? I'll get the cash for Sleet."

"You told him January. You serious, Beefstone?"

"Matt Dillon," he said. "Matt fucken Dillon by February."

Then he got hit with another shock and his scream echoed down the stairwell.

When we got back to the car, Cleo had claimed the driver's seat. She had a newsprint pad propped against the wheel. With a stick of charcoal she'd already filled a page with nine or ten renderings of my grin, disembodied. They gave me the heebie-jeebies.

Her bag was looped on the passenger's visor: cartoon dogs swarmed over the carcass of a horse.

I climbed into the back, Beef sat shotgun, Cleo ditched her charcoal through the window. She dusted off her hands and shelved her pad on the dashboard. Started the car. "Where to now, monsters?"

"Park and Thirty-sixth," Beef said. "I gotta get this thing off before my arm withers." He grabbed up the pad and flipped it open to the grins. "She'll be wanting you to pose pretty soon, pal."

Cleo was making no attempt to pull from the parking space. Transmission in neutral, she tapped on the gas pedal and stared transfixed through the windshield at a scabby and pyorrhetic bag-hag who was trying to keep her footing on the Fifth Avenue slidewalk. With a twine-and-foil filled Macy's sack clutched in her arms, the hag lurched, staggered and fell. She was carried a short distance along the uptown strip conveyer. She got up again, swollen kneecaps cross-hatched and bloody, tongue spastic. And went down again. She threw herself on her bag like a hero soldier smothering a hand grenade. The slidestrians around her acted sensorially deprived.

Beef said: "Come on already, Cleo, kill them compassionate eyes. That shit don't flush. Come on, ghoul, I got a special appointment."

She nodded and threw the Screamer into reverse, backed it up and twisted the wheel savagely to the right—at the same moment a red Solaris drew up to us parallel and braked. Its grayed driver's window lowered. Sharkey's smiling face. "You've been to see Dr. Sleet, Grinner?"

I cranked down my window. "You wanna move so we can get outta here?" Laudermilch was in the back seat with an older man, maybe fifty, dark-haired, who squinted straight ahead, who was bundled in a heavy overcoat and a thick woolen scarf that came up to his lips. "Do you mind? You're blocking us."

"He's the guy I had in mind myself. Sleet. To send you to."

Beef was swiveling puzzled glances from me to Sharkey, from Sharkey back to me. His mouth hung open and his brow was corrugated sirloin.

"Piss off, Sharkey," I said.

"Expensive, isn't he? But as they say, if you want something badly enough—"

"That's right, you'll find the money. And I will. Myself."

"Might be harder than you think." The window hummed up and he drove off.

"What was *that* all about?"

"Never mind, Beef."

"Who was that guy, hey Grin?"

Cleo said: "His name is Niles Sharkey. He's a spacer. A colonel or something."

Beef and I turned to look at her.

I asked her how she knew that.

"Hey, Grinno—this ghoul's not your run-of-the-mill gravy chucker," said Beef. "She was born on an orbiter. Lived on the friggen moon till she was ten or eleven—ain't that right, Clee?"

"Thirteen," she said.

"Till she was thirteen, there you go. See, she knows these guys. What I wanna know is how *you* do. What's up?"

I leaned my head back and stared at the vomit on the ceiling. I took out my salt. "Nothing. Leave me alone."

Beef said: "Nice friend. You'd think I was asking him to tell me the secret of life or something."

He was still peeved when we stopped in front of Mrs. Sinakin's apartment house, a yellow bricker with a scalloped canopy and a wrinkled doorman in crisp livery. He promised Cleo to call her later then vaulted from the car with only the barest nod at me. The doorman saw Beef coming and developed a riveting interest in the wood chips that filled a cement jardiniere. Beef let himself into the lobby.

"I can take you back to Jersey City if you want, monster."

"Fifty-fourth and Broadway is good enough."

"Sure, monster."

"Christ, you don't have to call me that. I got a name."

"Why don't you," she asked, "wash your face? So I can see what you look like?"

Without further conversation she drove me up to Ralph Studebaker's office: Bonaparte Caterers, Realty Associates, Rent-a-Freak, Inc.

I sat in the waiting room with a waterhead dwarf who kept sneaking scowls at me, enough of them to corroborate my suspicion that he was a Natural Fluke and not a Caliban's mutant. The Flukes had an even stronger animosity toward Freaks than Normals did. We were the new kids on the block, the foreign whores, the black sheep, the heteroclitic Mafia. We stood, chemical pretenders, outside of history and legend and art, we had no overtones and lit no votives to the memory of General Tom Thumb.

I asked the dwarf: "You do a show?"

He said: "Screw you, I'm a licensed realtor—and unless you want three bedrooms, a full bath and a sunporch, shut your mouth!"

I shrugged and spread my legs and read some old news: the couch I was sitting on was upholstered with plasticized newspaper clippings, three-column leads as well as squibs and one-panel cartoons. I read a war dispatch with a Calgary dateline. I read about the accidental vaporization of an entire shift of workers at a commercial bakery in Connecticut (they blamed it on the food chemists). I read about a lost kitten named Shamus who traveled across four states and the Mississippi River to find his master. Read a garbled account of some bloody uprising in Nicosia tagged the Cold Beverage Riots, and glanced at an editorial cartoon titled A SOLUTION TO POLLUTED COWS??? It showed a breasty woman suckling a newborn and her swollen-bellied husband. MISTRESS BLINDS ARGENTINE STRONGMAN IN SAN JUAN CASINO. IRON ENGLISH?

BLIMEY, THEY'RE JUST REG'LAR MATES (about the rise in beer consumption since fascism). EGGS NOT KILLERS, SAYS DOC (yet another attempt—this one dated October 14, 2009 —to squelch the then-new death-egg hullaballoo; the "doc" said the eggs simply put a body "on hold," whatever that meant).

And I read about the launch, in midwinter, 2002, of the *Everlasting Streak*, a giant American silver-and-green rocket that had been programmed to blur through the galaxy and interstellar space, exploring for extraterrestrial life and habitable worlds.

You never heard about the *Streak* any more. I wondered if it was still functioning.

"Grinner?"

I glanced up and Studebaker was standing in the inner-office doorway. He was wearing a red leotard with a yellow thunderbolt appliquéd across his titty chest, gray sneakers that puffed fog around his ankles, and harridan-length narcotic fingernails—some nibbled shorter than others. He waved me over with a few brusque semaphores, he told the dwarf: "No, I'll need more time." I followed Studebaker down a long perfumed hallway. "I'm running late, Grinner, so—"

"Well, you said you might have the contracts for me—"

"—I hope we can wrap this up pretty quick."

"—to sign."

"Take a seat." We'd gone into his office, a suite as cluttered and commodious as a furniture showroom: two desks and a jumble of tables, couches, video players, cabinets, bookcases. A life-size holographic little boy in a foil toga and reflector sunglasses—Studebaker's son—bounced a ball on a low felt-topped pedestal.

Studebaker closed the door and drew the blinds. He walked around behind one of his desks—a blond-wood landing strip with two telephones, four metal trays, a clock-radio, and a stuffed diamondback rattler, curled as if for a strike, which had pens and pencils slotted into drilled holes along its hide.

He stood there chewing his lip. "I said maybe I'd have the contracts, plural. Scratch that. What I've got for you is a contract, singular. For Carnegie Hall. And I want you to hurry up and sign it, don't read it even. I want your signature pronto, otherwise"—his tongue burst from his mouth like a man on fire—"something might go wrong."

I signed the blue papers, I frowned, I squinted, I said I didn't understand—huh?—what was the matter?

Studebaker flopped into his chair, lit a cigarette and dragged on it. The burning paper sounded like drizzle on crisp leaves. "I have to give the Canadian tour to somebody else."

"But—"

"And the spring tour and the summer circuit." He trayed his smoke and wobbled his hands like tambourines. "Very spooky stuff going on here."

I pushed fingertips into my eye sockets: purple scintillas and yellow whorls gushed through the darkness. "Sharkey," I said. I let my hands drop, blinked a few times. Studebaker's head looked wavy behind blue smoke. "He can't make you—"

"Stop right there, Grinner." He reached down into the desk well and brought out a black metal wastebasket, tipped it so I could look inside: a used condom, a cardboard coffee container, lots of charred paper. "Some of my old tax returns, plus a recommendation for a fraud indictment. He *can* make me." He smiled, heavy red lips shadowing snowy teeth. "I told him that Carnegie Hall was already definite, I told him you'd already signed, I did you that favor."

"I need the money, Ralph."

"Grinner, what can I say? He's got my nuts in a blender, he's IRS."

"What?"

"I said he's IRS."

"Ralph, he is not, he's a narc . . . or a spacer."

"Or a *spacer*?"

"Something's very weird. I don't understand what's going on."

"He had IRS credentials and he had the goods. He was nice enough to burn them."

"He had BORD credentials when I seen him."

"A deal's a deal. And he *did* burn them."

"Ralph . . . what about plain rentals, parties, some photo sessions? I need the money."

"Grinner, whatever the man wants from you, do it. I'll put you on the road again as soon as he gives me the word. Look, it's not as if I don't *want* you to work—"

"Some rentals—"

"I can't." He stamped out his cigarette on the side of a work tray, coals sprinkled over the snake. "But speaking of rentals, I just had a very disturbing phone call from—"

"Ralph, this isn't fair!"

"—from Mrs. Livy Sinakin. Do you know who she is?"

"Ralph, I'm pleading here—"

"She's the widow of that congressman, the one who changed his sex? She was complaining about our mutual friend Mr. Stein. He—"

"I've been dependable!"

"—just quit on her, no warning, no notice. And not just quit, he had to go and piss on her rug. Now, can you imagine this woman's state of mind? He's finished, that kid's burnt toast as far as I'm concerned. I always liked the girl with the feathers, but him, that Beef—"

"You have to admit I've been dependable!"

Studebaker closed his eyes, pinched the bridge of his nose. "Grinner. I'm sorry." And picked up the blue contract, leafed through it. "You missed one place. And these boxes get your initials."

I crossed my legs, I smoothed the contract on my thigh and clicked the pen.

"Did you say something, Grinner?"

I looked up. "I said, I'll kill him."

"Sharkey? I wouldn't advise."

I snorted, then signed my name, initialed boxes.

15
Veiled Elements

With a head that felt packed with clay, I came outside and it was dark. The first snow flurries of winter were doing their imitation of moths in the streetlights. Normals were rushing along the sidewalk, cars were snarled on Broadway. Traffic cops, aloft in lucent orange hover-buckets, were tooting whistles. I pushed up my collar and tugged down my wig, I copped my reflection in a camera-store window: I looked part fish, part wild-eyed sniper.

"You don't look happy, monster," from alongside me.

"What do you think you're doing here?"

Cleo rolled her shoulders. "My car's over there."

"You been waiting all this time?"

"Hey, do you want a ride? A drink?"

I said I'd take both.

"What were you doing in Toledo last month?" We were stopped for a red light on Ninth Avenue and some Puerto Rican kids had clustered, hunkered, in front of the Screamer to mimic its sardonic fender. They were good at it, facile. They looked murderous.

"How'd you know I was there?"

"Before. When you said you knew Sharkey, I remembered. You were on the same plane back as me."

"I don't remember seeing you. Maybe you had different cosmetics." The light changed and the kids scattered.

"I asked you why you were in Toledo."

"I was taking pictures of a body." She removed a hand

from the wheel to point at the cadaver snapshots pinned to the visors. "Like those. I'm painting dead bodies lately."

"I thought you were painting Freaks."

"I'm painting both. You'll see."

"I'll see?"

"I'm taking you down to my studio."

"I thought you were taking me home."

"I thought you wanted a drink."

I unpinned one of the snaps, a sheeted woman on an autopsy table, scalp removed, big toe tagged like an appliance. On the flip side were some details in ballpoint pen: Boston, multiple rape, suicide. I told Cleo she was sick, and she asked me: "Who's well?"

"You went all the way to Ohio for a corpse? There's not enough here?"

"Yeah, but this one was special. Somebody killed him and cut off his head and one of his hands."

"Sam LaPilusa."

"Right! Shit, monster, all of a sudden we got a lot in common. You know about him too, huh?" She gave a short laugh.

"Not much. You tell me."

"I only went for the pictures. But you heard about the ovens and the reactor? Sounds like just another guy trying to build a mind rocket. Don't ask me why 'cause I don't care, but they always seem to base their schemes on microwaves. You'd think they'd use longer waves—but then what do I know from waves?"

"What do you mean, *another* guy?"

"You'll pose for me if I tell you?"

"I'll pose for you." Suddenly I felt like Da, bartering for answers. "Tell."

"The spacers been trying to make a mind rocket for years. My father was involved. So was Sharkey. And that other one, Laudermilch. They all worked on it for some general. There were lots of people. It was a big deal."

"What was this general's name? It wasn't Poole, was it?"

"No. It was German but he wasn't German. Tumpel, I think. Or close to that."

"I don't understand, mind rocket."

"The spacers," she said, "are about as pessimistic as the Newsboys."

I fumbled the top off my bottle of salt and started popping pills carelessly, three at a time, four. "What's that mean?"

"It means they don't expect the planet to last very much longer, either. And they're looking for another earth to murder. Remember the *Everlasting Streak*? Only that's one ship and it's too slow. The spacers want to send minds into the galaxy, thousands of them. As scouts. Now, I figure you owe me three hours in the nude."

I said: "Nothing's gonna happen to this planet."

She said: "Poor monster, he wants his piece of the world —only when he gets it, likely it'll be an asteroid."

"I told you once already, don't call me that. Monster."

Cleo said nothing, just smiled.

"I got a coupla more questions."

"You willing to pose a couple of more hours?"

"This guy LaPilusa. Was he a spacer?"

"I don't know who's one and who's not any more. I left the *Eisenhower*, I don't live on the moon."

"Okay. That general with the German name. Did you see him in the car today with Sharkey? Was he the second guy in the back seat?"

"I didn't see."

"Tell me what he looks like."

"Ordinary. Older."

"He don't wear anything . . . unusual?"

She glanced at me, glanced back at the street and made a left-hand turn on Fourteenth. "How'd you know?"

"He does, doesn't he?"

"Wear a thing on his neck, a brace? Yeah, but how'd you know?

I swallowed more salt, giggled, was stoned.

* * *

Spring Stret. Parked, walked a block, turned into an old graystone building with a buckled metal door, into a freight elevator with a caged blue bulb, a rusty throttle, a kitten napping, or dead, in a corner on a pallet of soggy newspapers and torn-up art postcards.

On Cleo's bag: a lizard on a flat stone watched a fly bathe in a water droplet, then pounced.

Loft painted flat black, a warped and pitted floor speckled with pigments. Turp jars and stretcher strips, canvas scraps. Empty plastic pouches, the sort Newboys fill with explosive brown gravy to lob at random targets—a travelers' information kiosk, a stripped car in a vacant lot, a state senator on a walking tour, a junkie in his cups.

Current oscillated and crackled through fluorescent tubing.

The place smelled like there'd been a fire recently. I stumbled, sniffled, rubbed at stinging eyes and asked for cold water to sober up. I got it and sipped at it and wandered around, coming slowly unmuddled. A stripped mattress spotted with dark menstrual stains, sprinkled with cake crumbs and strewn with clothing . . . seven wire-mesh windows in a row . . . movie and still cameras jumbled on an aquamarine plastic couch.

And then there were the paintings.

A bunch of small canvases were stacked on the floor, their pictures slashed by a knife and scorched black. Others, the larger, unruined ones, leaned on French easels or hung on walls. Each picture was divided in half by a thick and raggedy black vertical. In the left-hand panels: dead Normals, bloodlessly nude or fully dressed, laid out on porcelain slabs or propped up like statues. In the right-hand panels: Freaks (mostly male and mostly Beef; two or three m&f Sycorax artistes; some perfect copies of photos that had been published in Ralph Studebaker's short-lived porno magazine, *Caliban Contempo*) done impasto, described in naked states of genital excitement.

"So what do you think of them, monster?"

"I think you're a ghoul, like Beef said. Plus, I think you're a fucking romantic. All wrapped up. No offense."

She frowned and squinted. The skin around her eyesockets and across her cheekbones drew taut. "You know where the word 'monster' comes from?"

I only wished I could've flashed her a contemptuous smile. "Listen to the Newsgirl, would you? With her Latin roots."

"From 'warning.' "

"Shit." And me completely out of salt.

"Like, they show up, monsters I'm talking about, when there's death coming. And disaster. Before annihilation. Perfect."

"I'm gonna use your telephone," I said.

I got no answer at the house. I dialed Skully's and let it ring twenty times. Called Ralph Studebaker and left a message on his recorder: "Book us with different names. Could you do that? I've never given you trouble, I deserve some favor."

Cleo was walking around clinking a wineglass against her teeth. Light split, and split again, on the dark Valpolicella. Her bag hung on a hat rack constructed of narrow-gauge pipes: a pen-and-ink nursing infant chewed on its mother's nipple, then swallowed the breast whole, swallowed a shoulder, an ear, a cheek. Then nose, lips, chin . . .

"Cleo," I said, "you got any salt? Just a teaspoon."

I stripped and washed at the sink. Cleo spread a comforter over a splintery skid. I stood on top. She made a few quick sketches in a pad, took some pictures of me with an instant camera. Took some more with a good reflex. Then she decided to draw directly on a stretched gray canvas whose left half was filled by a charcoal prelim of a headless cadaver wound in a shroud and hovering in midair.

Even salted up again, I stayed anxious, upset—a sort of unfocused anger. I said: "I'm not a monster," and cleared my throat.

Cleo shut one eye, taffied a kneaded eraser. "Why deny it? You should declare it. You're lucky, you're new."

"Forget it."

"Don't you see? Such perfect timing—the change of the millennium, the *change,* the—" She broke off to sweep an arm toward her finished paintings. "You're the new race. You're going to replace the rot. Me. Us."

"Go finish your drawing," I said. "What do you think I am, anyway—from outer space? Me, the Beefstone, all of us—chippie, the only difference between you and us, it's this!" With a fist I struck my hip, my sternum, my lips.

"Move your hand back to your breastbone," she said, "and keep that pose." She rubbed out what she'd already drawn. "And can you get an erection?"

"I'm not about to try."

"Want help?"

"Stay right the hell over there."

She unbuttoned her pajama top and shrugged it off her shoulders. Her breasts were small and hard, tipped with crinkled brown nipples. "Does this help?"

It helped but again I told her to stay on her side of the loft.

"Don't worry, monster. I'm asexual."

"You give me the creeps."

"I should give you more than that. If you had any consciousness, you'd kill me."

"Who burned those paintings over there?"

"I did."

"And cut them? They weren't any good?"

"Yeah, they were good."

"But . . . ?"

"No but. I just destroyed them. There's enough clutter, there'll be enough artifacts without those."

I hated the silence, the scratch-scratch, it was making me nuts. I was tired of standing, I'd sweated out most of the salt. All I could think of, think over and over of, was

Studebaker, Studebaker and Reeni, and where was *she*?

And so Sharkey was a spacer. What did *that* mean? Eggs and Sharkey. Eggs and Flour. Eggs and sausage. Nothing gelled. And Cleo drew. With her tongue mumping her cheek she drew as if she really cared about it. But she didn't, really —did she?

The silence was making me crazy, so I broke it: "I hear they got some beaut plutonium warpies over in Hot China. Not as glamorous, maybe, as us mystery Freaks, but still. If you're so stuck on monsters you should take a trip."

Cleo said: "I've already been to Hot China."

Hot China, Spain, South Africa, France and Argentina, in the company of her father three years ago. That revealed, and without my prompting her, she went ahead and told me her life story. As soon as she began, I stopped fidgeting. Sure, that was her primary objective, but eventually I began to think she also hoped to convince me of the logic of her negativity. She didn't, but her story was entertaining.

Cleo's mother was a Portuguese artisan who'd emigrated from the Douro valley in 1993 following the execution of her co-husbands by the monarchist puritans during the counterrevolution.

This snippet of world history was news to me: I wasn't aware there'd even been a revolution, much less a counter-revolution, in Portugal in the nineties. I interrupted Cleo to ask if these puritan guys had won. She said, "You never heard of the Iberian Hostilities?" and when I admitted, "No," she just closed her eyes.

Cleo's mother stayed briefly in Civitavecchia, Italy, with a Canadian arms dealer who'd done business with one of her husbands.

Cleo's mother left the Canadian to fly to Paris with an aging German radical, the Lone Ranger of the famous Baader-Meinhofs, who was carrying enough vials of meta-strep germs in his false jowls to wither every larynx on the European continent.

She betrayed him to an Israeli agent and with the bounty

she earned from that she purchased a whore's franchise on the seven-thousand-man American orbiter *David Eisenhower.*

"That's where she met my father. He liked her, he had the money, so he offered her a contract. One year. With an option for renewal. She signed and moved into his quarters. Then she got pregnant. As a hunk of jelly I almost got flushed into space. But then my father decided to let her keep the embryo. He'd never slept with a breeding woman before. So I got born."

"You're lucky," I said.

"Don't joke," and rubbed her drawing with the pad of a thumb.

After the year was up, Cleo's father, a nonmilitary spacer, a physicist named Follet, declined to renew the contract, and her mother, with no hard feelings and having been delivered of the child, returned to the whores' bay. Cleo spent the first months of life in the orbiter's small nursery. Then she was taken by shuttle to the American moon colony, a small bubbled port city christened Markham but called Graytown. There, Cleo was raised in a special compound with a few dozen other so-called spacer orphans. Follet visited her three or four times a year.

She said: "I remember one of his visits. I'd just turned nine, but he came about three weeks *after* my birthday. Big deal, I didn't care he missed it. He comes busting into my cube, he looks at his watch and says we have to hurry. Why we do, he doesn't say. We take one of the ups-and-downs to the top of the dome, to where we can see the earth best. He says, 'Now watch,' and what I see in a couple of minutes is a puff, then another puff, then two more. Follet says, 'That's China.' Before I'd even been down to earth, I had the privilege of seeing part of it blow."

I'd done some calculating, I said: "How old are you, Cleo?" China went hot in '03, she was nine . . .

"Sixteen."

"I don't believe it."

"Do I care?"

Occasionally, Follet allowed—but never invited—Cleo to shuttle up to see him.

By this time—we're talking now about five years into twenty-one—Cleo's mother had moved her bed and business to an armed Kuwaiti barge anchored in the outer Van Allen. She was never heard from again.

During her vacations on the *Eisenhower,* Cleo was left, more often than not, to amuse herself at the cinemas and arcades. Her father was too busy with his project to play daddy and she was forbidden access to the testing center. But when she did see Follet, she'd ask him: "What are you making?"

A mind rocket.

"How do you make one?"

He wished that he knew.

"But what are you *doing*?"

And he'd tell his eleven-year-old: "We're mixing microwaves and alpha waves, proteins, electricity, hot sauce, and volunteers."

Hot sauce?

"Sssh," he'd say. "Top secret. *Hot* hot sauce."

Cleo would laugh: she thought it was funny, Follet using such a juvenile euphemism for radiation.

"Yes, but what *kind* of hot sauce, Father?"

"From-beyond-the-rainbow hot sauce."

After receiving these sorts of Golden Book nonanswers to her questions, Cleo stopped inquiring altogether about Follet's secret project. If he wouldn't, or couldn't, acknowledge and respect her precocity, then screw him.

I asked Cleo: "But what'd he mean, beyond the rainbow?"

"I always figured he was talking about the Veiled Elements."

I told her I didn't know what those were.

"Veiled Elements? From Venus? The Sergio Probe of 1986? You never heard, really?"

"Just tell me, okay?"

"Six brand-new elements with major, fissionable isotopes."

She could've said, Nine superducks with shiny flammable armor: I would've looked at her just as blankly and shrugged the same shrug.

I said: "This probe was—when?—1986? That brought these veiled thingies back?"

She nodded: 1986.

Two years before Caliban's Night.

Eggs and sausage and superducks with shiny armor.

I called for more salt and was spoon-fed.

Cleo was thirteen when finally her father took her down to visit the earth.

In Peking, Hot China, Follet passed a week at Occupation Headquarters briefing a fraternity of U.S. military physicists while she, bundled up in an antiradiation ensemble, was taken sight-seeing by a stout Ukrainian woman who spoke colloquial American English and loved the surreal sunsets, the sudden and violent hailstorms, the phosphorescent rubble and the gypseian sight of sparking campfires at evening.

Cleo saw no bomb mutants—a big surprise to me, I'd always thought the place teemed with them. Beef owned a thirty-minute video cassette of a dubbed Soviet-made film called *It Can't Be . . . But It Is,* and I was sure there'd been Hot Chinese mutants in it. I clearly remembered a band of yellow blob-heads shitting on the Great Wall as the narrator spoke of "the majesty and bravery that once had been."

Cleo saw only ribby survivors who walked slowly and hardly ever lifted their sloe eyes, and whose blisters and sores were dressed with clean white gauze pads and star-spangled (or red-sickled) adhesive tape which only made their gray cassocks (of Russian manufacture) look even filthier.

In Pretoria, South Africa, Follet took Cleo to a cryogenics sleeperie. They lunched with the black director and later were escorted to a vast and chilled underground room where

hundreds of human brains housed in bell jars were connected by spaghetti wires and BX cable to a bank of television monitors. The pictures on most screens were snowy
but on a few there played blurry and fleeting dream images.

I interrupted Cleo: "They can really do that? That's
amazing!"

Cleo raised her crescent eyebrows. "Sure. But do you
know where the brains came from? Keep that fist on your
chest! Do you? From the bodies in the sleeperie. From the
assholes who thought they were going to be revived some
day, cancer-free."

"They can't do *that*! Come on, Cleo, gimme a break!"

She smiled. "Follet bought a dozen. And had them
shipped to the *Eisenhower*. His volunteers."

"Gimme," I said again, "a break," and snorted.

Then I asked: "Really?"

Cleo and her father went next to Bilbao, Spain, where she
celebrated her fourteenth birthday by watching the corpses
flow in the Nervion River while he attended to some business at a chemical factory.

I said: "Watching corpses? What do you mean, *corpses*?"

She said: "Bilbao?"—as if that should've explained it all.
"Two years ago?"

"I'm sorry," I said, "I don't know."

"And you say you don't belong to a new race! My death!"

"Look, I just don't follow the news too close. I guess
I heard of Bilbao. I think I remember now."

They flew to Paris, where Follet, his schedule free and
clear for several days, took his daughter to the opera twice,
to Napoleon's tomb and to a *son-et-lumiere* held in honor
of the birthday of some patriotic French writer named
Céline. They were still there on the morning when the
Rouen nuclear reactor melted down and leaked a fudge of
uranium and plutonium.

I said: "I remember *that*. You were there?"

"We didn't stay," she said, "for the casualty bulletins. We flew straight to Argentina."

In Bahía Blanca, Cleo had her first encounter with organized nihilism.

While on a visit by herself to the Bernardino Rivadavia library (Follet had gone to interview a woman who'd gained local celebrity as an astral projectionist), Cleo spotted a young man ahead of her in a corridor with a hangman's noose cinched around his neck.

She followed the young man until finally he drew from his raincoat a small liquid-filled sack which resembled those one-serving bags of turkey and gravy that you boil in water for dinner.

He glanced over his shoulder, saw Cleo and grinned.

Then, throwing underhand as if pitching a horseshoe, the young man sent his bag flying down the hallway. It slammed into a glass display case and exploded.

For a long moment the corridor was flooded with light— melted margarine. The shock lifted Cleo up, fricasseed one side of her face, singed her eyebrows and slammed her hard against the wall.

She remembered seeing the young man sprawled on the floor and frowning at his shoed left foot which he held in his bloodied right hand like an indecisive shopper mulling over a new species of styling comb. And then she was arrested.

"Hold it," I said. "What was so special in the showcase that he wanted to blow up?"

Cleo sighed heavily: "I'm sure he didn't have the slightest idea. Destruction *qua* destruction. Anything and everything." *Qua*? And she was sixteen? They must have *some* schools, I thought, up there on the moon.

"Okay, okay—so you got arrested . . ."

"Skip it. Follet straightened things out. And we flew to California to meet Sharkey and some other spacers. But we didn't. Then we were supposed to go to Houston and shuttle back up. But we didn't. And then I joined the Newsboys just after the purge of the Dead Christian Kids, when it was strictly secular *nada*. Seattle, Chicago, Albany—but don't ask me why—and New York. Here. And now."

"But what happened to your father?"

"He died."

"How?"

"He died. I'm done. You can put your things back on."

I stepped off the pallet, did some deep knee bends and collected my clothes. Cleo brought me another soup spoon of salt, but I didn't take it. I got dressed. I said: "I'd like to travel myself some day. After the op."

Just to let her know I couldn't be downed so easily. Maybe it's not a wonderful world, I thought. Okay, so maybe it's not so wonderful. But it's all right. It's all right. Gotta be.

Cleo laughed and tipped the spoon, she ground the salt into the wood floor with the soles of her bare feet.

"You taking me home?"

"Yeah, I'll drive you." She hunted up her sneakers and a linty peacoat. "Well, aren't you going to look at what I've drawn?" She was annoyed, crabby: I hadn't gone straight to the easel.

She cared. She didn't care. Who knew which? (And who cared?)

So I walked over there and looked and, yeah, it was good, it looked just like me. Me and my hard-on. Next to a levitated and headless Sam LaPilusa.

But then suddenly I was more interested in watching the animation strip playing on Cleo's flicka-bag as she slung it on a shoulder.

A cartoon Beef was bludgeoning a cartoon Cleo to her knees.

He laid it on and laid it on and the film at last ran completely out. Empty beige vinyl screen.

16
Lover Boy Supreme

Cleo ("Take care, monster, stay new") dropped me at the house in Jersey City around midnight. Nobody was home except Baudelaire. I went down the cellar and tried to do a little work on the new bridemask. No go. I botched the delicate paring of a latex nostril and sliced my thumb with the razor blade. Then I took out the finished new groomhead and put it on. And stared into the oval magnifying mirror. I looked exactly—*exactly!*—like a Sears, Roebuck lover boy supreme.

But you couldn't wear a mask all of the time.

Upstairs, the telephone started ringing.

It was the Beefstone.

"So," he said, "you were over to Cleo's. Dismal place, no?"

"You there now?"

"Nah, I'm at Mary's. But I just hung up this second with our moon girl."

"I heard what you done at that lady's apartment. Dumb, Stones. How you gonna work now?"

"I told you. I'm finished with all that horseshit."

There was a long pause.

"I'm still hurt, Grinny. I ask you a simple question—what'd those guys in the Solaris want?—and you treat me like a dog."

"It's none of your business, Beef. Honest. It's not even any of mine."

"I mean, I'm your friend, aren't I?"

He was right. He was my friend, the best. So I told him what he wanted to know, in digest form: they were cops, they were squeezing me to help them run Flour down, they'd pay for the operations if I did.

"Cleo said they were spacers but," Beef said.

"It's not what they say. I don't know."

Beef clucked his tongue. "But you're gonna. Do it. What they want."

"No, Beefy, I'm not."

"You might but. You're considering it."

"I already considered it. This afternoon. But I can't."

"After what Flour's done? Sneaking around after Reeni, and all. I were you, I wouldn't forget that."

"I'm not forgetting anything," I said. "Look, Beef—is there something else you wanted? I'm tired."

"But say you really knew where Flour was—*then* you'd help those guys. Right?"

"Beef, you drunk?" I said. "You eating candy?"

"Bullshit!"

"All right, then. Shut up."

"You *can't* turn down a free op, Grinner. That'd be nuts."

"Fucken Beefstone, you're going on and on, and I'm getting a headache here. Just cut it. Anyhow—where do you get off, so offended when I don't tell you something? I asked *you* what kind of deal you made with Cleo. But did you answer me?"

"It's not important." Then, after a beat: "She didn't say anything to *you* about it, did she?"

"No."

"It's not important."

"Okay, so it's not. But I gotta hang up now. I hear Reeni coming."

"Where she been?"

"No place. She just went out for a walk. Around the block."

"All right, let you go. And Grinner? Good luck Flour-hunting."

The bastard broke the connection before I could swear at him.

I tried to call him right back but Pigeon's line was already engaged.

And it wasn't Reeni I'd heard, it was only a Normal she-zom who'd hunkered down on my front porch with a can of cola and some death eggs in a Baggie. I chased her away before she could die.

Reeni came home a little before three. She pulled off her gloves and opened her coat clips and stood there gazing at the wall behind me. She said: "Maybe I'm in the wrong house?"

"Funny," I said.

I was still wearing the groomhead. I pushed fingers through its wavy hair. "Have a good time?"

"Work's work," she said. "But not bad." She tossed her coat on the table. "And you? How was Dr. Sleet? Come on out in the kitchen, I'll make tea. Or do you want coffee?"

She filled the kettle and put it on a front burner.

I dropped into a chair, told Reeni that Studebaker had cut us loose. "Because," I lied, "of Flour's reputation. He has to protect himself."

"And all those arguments we had. For nothing. You feel bad?"

"What do you think?"

"I'm sorry, Grinny. Well, I'm not, but I am." She smiled weakly. "Coffee?"

"Tea's all right."

"Whyn't you take off that mask?"

She sighed when I didn't, she got milk from the refrigerator. "We'll be fine, Grin. Really." And when I didn't say anything, she asked: "Can't you be satisfied? Can't you try?"

"You'll notice," I said, "that I haven't asked where you've been until almost four o'clock in the morning."

"Don't exaggerate. It's only three—"

"Only."

"—and, yeah, I noticed." She took cups from a shelf and put them on the table. "I been with the Dragon. We drove up to Hasbrouck Heights."

I looked at her.

"I made five hundred dollars, Grinner."

"Your cut?"

She nodded. "Look, I know I said I wouldn't . . . but, Grinner, you haven't come up with any profitable ideas. And I don't mean to sound critical, honestly. But. It's income."

"Reen, those eggs, I think—"

"Okay, so it's not rice for the Swedes, but there's a market."

"That's not what I was gonna say. Listen. Somebody told me something before and I been thinking about it. And I think maybe those eggs aren't—" I broke off when Reeni jumped up to snatch the kettle off the flame.

"I'm listening. What?"

"Do you remember those two guys that came here? Those two narcs?"

"How could I forget?"—splashing hot water into my cup, her cup. "They made such an impression on you. Sugar? There's the milk. And you turned around and made some impressions on me. They were purple, I think."

"Reen, I don't think they're narcs. They're spacers."

She thumbed her tea bag against the bowl of her spoon. "Spacers. As in *outer*-spacers?" And threw me a quizzical squint: *what's the joke?* And *how much salt have* you *had tonight?* "Come on! What do they care about eggs? Aren't they too busy polishing bombs?"

I sat back rubbing a smooth cheek then tapping latex lips. "But they *are*."

"And who told you?"

"That girl Cleo."

"Beef's Newsboy?" She rolled her eyes.

"You don't understand. She knows."

"Grinner: would you please take off that mask? You don't know how stupid you look! And for God's sake, it's like talking to a stranger. Please, would you?"

I stirred my tea. "Cleo knows," I said. "And those guys *are* spacers. And I don't want you or me involved. At all."

"Grinner, it's like I said. It's income. Something you don't wanna think about. Unless it's from a rape show."

"Don't worry," I said, "about income. Don't worry your furry little head."

The mask lips were terrific: I curled them back into precisely the sort of smile I wanted: a thin one, possibly affectionate, possibly not.

Reeni blinked.

On my way through the parlor I grabbed Reeni's coat to hang it in the hall closet. One pocket was smeared with a soft fawn-brown pulp. I scraped some off, rubbed it between my fingers: it was friable.

It was mushroom.

Reeni came in from the kitchen and we went upstairs together.

When I turned off the lights, a thumb and two fingers—the same ones that had crumbled the mushroom—glowed in the dark. A weak pearly beige. I climbed into bed.

Reeni reached out but as soon as her hands touched my face, they dropped. Lead ingots.

"I suppose you're gonna sleep with that on?"

"Haven't told you about Dr. Sleet yet, have I? Keeps samples in a beaker. Honest to God. In a beaker. Reen? Reeni . . . ?"

Part Four:
The Eggman

(Late November, 2010)

17
Da Declines

I found Da at the Ocean Taproom sitting alone at a gimpy table blowing smoke into an empty beer glass.

"I seen."

He glanced up. Frowning, his brow clots pinked. "So you been up the house? What's your mother doing?"

"She was on the phone," and sat and moved a bowl candle, leaned on folded arms. "We didn't talk. What *happened*?"

I'd poked through the barbecue pit in the back yard with a stick, I'd poked just enough to know that all of Da's tapes, photographs, copy books and transcripts were carbonized. Twenty years' worth of curiosity reduced to powder and ash.

And Ma, cupping the telephone mouthpiece, had said: "Ask your father." Both of her eyes were moused, her lip was gashed, her makeup smeared, her neck scales were torn.

Da shook his head. "She did it while I was out this morning. And, hand it to her, she got practically everything. All the good stuff."

"Why but?"

"Why else? She was tired of it. And can I blame her? I can't." He struck a book match with his left hand and lit up a fresh cigarette. The old one, just its filtertip, was sizzling in his glass.

"If you can't blame her, how come you— She looks awful. If you can't blame her."

Da said: "I'm sitting here sick, Grinner. I'm sitting here sick."

"But Ma shouldna done that. I mean, that's your life she burnt."

Da smiled a sour one. "Exactly."

"Well, never mind all that stuff," I said. "You don't need it. 'Cause I got something to tell you."

"All these years she's been scared of me, I think she's lunatic, I leave her alone. And now she finds out she wasn't wrong to be scared. Today I find out, too. I'm sitting here sick, a shitfaced monster. I thought I knew Joe Fistick—what he could do, what he couldn't. Scratch I knew."

I got up and went over to the bar. A cheap little hologram of a baseball player hopping off a dusty bag and then hopping back again to touch it with his cleats flickered perpetually in a gap on the liquor shelves. The bartender was a poxy freak with a fearsome palsy. A lemony glaze leaked from the corners of his eyes. He was dabbing a wet rag at the ooze, and shivering. Finally he got around to drawing me two beers.

On the TV was a pregame locker-room interview with a Jersey Giant linebacker who blinked sheepishly at his kneeguards, whose skin was pale, whose shoulders were draped with a fur coat. He muttered, he chewed on his upper lip.

"Now ain't he some specimen," said Lemon-eye, drawing himself a short beer. "They gonna let a zombie like him play ball against the fuggen Delaware Vandals? Now, this oughta be a game and a half!" His head snapped suddenly, involuntarily, to one side and his mouth sagged open, spilling its coated tongue.

I carried the beers back to Da's table.

"What's happened to this place? Nobody here on Sunday. Where's all the neighborhood guys?"

"Nobody," said Da, "likes to look at the new bartender. All that drip-drip."

"So why don't the owner sack him?"

"Because he *is* the owner. Just bought it. I feel sorry for the guy."

I looked over a shoulder. The guy was swiping his cheek

with his apron. "Yeah. But it *is* a little disgusting."

Da sipped. "That's my arm you're stepping on."

"Sorry."

"Just so you'll know. She was on the telephone you said? Your mother? I should go home."

"Would you just wait a bit? I wanna talk to you."

"I never *once* did that before. She mighta *said* I did, but I never did. What happens when you're so goddamned wrapped up in your own business. You get funny and you don't even know it."

"Da, would you just apologize when you see her again? That's all you gotta do—and now listen up to me."

"I suppose you came for your fifty bucks."

"Not exactly."

Da pushed his wallet across the table. "Help yourself. And there's a clipping there you might wanna read, but I don't know." He bent his head and textured beer foam between his fingers.

I took out five tens and the newspaper cutting. From the *Toledo Blade* and dated five days earlier. "How'd you get this?"

"I sent them a check for ten bucks and asked them to mail me everything they ran on that murder you heard about. LaPilusa."

The headline read: "MOM ARRESTED IN SLAYING OF SCIENTIST SON! 'I Did It to Save His Soul!' She Weeps."

"That's another thing," said Da. "All the money I've shelled out over the years! She's probably still on the phone . . ."

There was a picture of a fat white-haired woman with zealot eyes pinioned between two scowling plainclothes detectives.

I skimmed the story and got the gist:

LaPilusa's mother lived on a holy-farm (bees, apples and topiaries of the saints) in upstate New York with a few dozen other fifty- and sixty-year-old Children of Christ, the Organic, a small, impoverished fundamentalist cult that had flourished briefly during the last quarter of the twentieth.

Last September, she took a bus to Ohio to visit her son Samuel, 43. He was a physicist (ultrasonics and thermodynamics) who'd recently been awarded a private research grant by—

"The spacers," I said. "Again."

Da said, "What?" Said, "It's not a question of a *simple* apology, it's not that simple." Said, "Spacers. Yes, peculiar. *Again?*"

The story didn't mention what Sam LaPilusa was researching, but it did say the police were still at a loss to explain the presence in the victim's cellar of a portable atomic reactor.

And it did say that the spacers assured investigators that *they* hadn't authorized it.

The reader was left to conclude that LaPilusa, a lapsed Organic Christian, was also a renegade researcher.

The renegade researcher had been murdered with the blunt edge of a door panel unbolted from an Amana "Breath-Touch" Radar-range 190-M-4.

His head and left hand then had been cleaved off with a chef's knife, with some assistance from a hacksaw.

When the police arrested LaPilusa's mother at the holy-farm, the woman promptly declared her guilt and loudly praised the Lord God of Bran and Herbs.

She was questioned repeatedly and her story never varied: because her son had made a pact with the devil, she'd been forced to take drastic action to liberate his soul before it could be "fatted."

She had no doubt that a pact had been made—how else explain the cluster of blind red eyeballs on her son's neck, or his withered and animal-furred left hand? He'd tried to keep those "marks of Beelzebub" concealed, but his mother had seen.

Had seen, had chopped, had burnt.

However, she denied having ransacked her son's house.

The demons (she said) in their terrible frustration must've done that.

"Demons," I said, "with little insignia rings and smelly cigars." I passed the clipping back to Da, who was chewing on his gums and wagging his head.

"Da," I said, "I'm gonna tell you something that'll knock you down. So you listen." I reached over and rapped his fingers. "Listen!"

He looked up with lips out.

"What would you say. If I told you. That I know all about Caliban's Night. What would you say?"

"I should try to call your mother."

I stared, I slid down in my seat, I threw up my hands.

"Okay, okay—what would I say? I'd say, Tell me. What else would I say?"

"All right, good. And I *will* tell you—'cause I *do* know. I'm sure. I'm *pretty* sure. Close to certain. But you're gonna have to pay me. I gotta have an income."

"How much?"

"Da. A lot. But this is the whole story you're gonna get. And you'll be proud of me. A little information, a little thinking. And it's really simple, what happened."

"Oh, I was always sure it would be. Plus I was always sure it would be a disappointment. Have to be, after so long." He narrowed his eyes; little slits of yellow. "A lot. And where am I gonna get a lot?"

"From Flour. He's supporting you now. So let him finance this."

He shook his head. "I'm gonna go call your mother now."

I called to him as he stood dialing the phone: "You can't fool me! One fire's not gonna turn you around. You still wanna know. And I can *tell* you!"

Lemon-eye was staring at me.

I got up and started to leave. As I passed Da, I gave his snake arm a solid kick. He didn't notice, he didn't feel anything, it was dead meat.

He was saying into the phone: "It's all my fault. Don't you think I know that? I'm sorry. I'm selfish. Yes, I am . . ."

18
Abducted!

Outside the Taproom, Dragon Luther was leaning against a parking meter, tossing up a furry blue crab apple and catching it. He tossed it to me, but I let it fall. It burst on the sidewalk, releasing a gang of accordion-bodied slugs that crept from the juicy ruins.

"Grinner! How you doing?" He came over and watched the slugs disperse, smiling down at them as if they were squalling infants at baptism. "Need a lift home, babes?"

"It's just a few blocks. No, thanks."

"You gonna *walk*? In this weather? In this snow?"

It wasn't snowing.

The Dragon took my arm. "Give you a lift." And hustled me around the corner, to where Big Dinah, with knees bent, stood on the curb talking to Bobby Lumps, who was scrunched behind the wheel of an old glitter-gray gasoline Mercury Dallas. Motor idling, windows fogged.

Dinah yanked open the back door and Luther shoved me in.

"I seen this," I told Bobby, "on some gangster cassette," and reached to open the street-side door to hop right out again. "And I seen this, too." There was no lock button and the button screw was mounded over with criss-crossed masking tape. Bobby smiled, tremoring his curdled face. Dragon Luther jumped in after me, Dinah waved, and off we went. Me asking: "Okay, what? What's this? What's the fun?"

I got no answers, naturally got jumpy.

We changed cars on Audubon Avenue, north of Freaktown, switching to a solar Eclipse. And were glowered at by a couple of Normals, a man and a woman, who were outside unstapling cardboard Pilgrims, turkeys, maize and cornucopias from their front door.

"Okay, okay—come on, you guys! What's up?"

The Dragon leaned over and drew a long, curling blue-black claw down the side of my neck, from earlobe to hollow.

I said: "Hey, Lumps, this your car? Smells new."

In silence, we drove around the city until the moon came out.

Then Bobby took us up to Blofeld Street.

To where the blast had been.

19
Fish to the Slaughter

Blofeld was a dead end, a steep incline. The top of the
street, where it intersected with the North Boulevard, was
fenced across with chain-link five, maybe six, meters high.
But there were several gaps. Some had been clipped, others
stoned, open.

We squeezed through one of the gaps—first Bobby, then
me, then the Dragon.

A few standing houses, gothic with dilapidation . . . but
as you walked down the chunked street, the structures turned
fragmentary—here a swayback porch and some wall, over
there the crenellated yellow brick front of an apartment
house.

We passed three rotting and roofless ticket booths, their
windows shattered, their paint scabby, their turnstiles rusty
asterisks.

The short-lived stab at tourism in the mid-nineties (sponsored by the Freak Pride Association with the grudging ap-
proval of the Parks Department) had been a genuine fiasco.
Except for occasional clumps of Japanese tourists, the Normals never came—they were still afraid, even then, of "con-
tracting the Fallout Flu." There were enough contaminants
already in their Idaho spuds; no sense risking any more.

My father had manned one of those booths on Sunday
afternoons, while Flour and me and some other friends—
the Beefstone always, Reeni sometimes—roamed around and
concealed ourselves down in the Hole building a shack, play-

ing guns, playing tag. ("Grinny's It, Grinny's the Normal—
run! run!")

Bobby stopped to flick on his long-barrel flashlight.

"Is my brother," I asked him, "gonna be here? Is that
what this is all about?"

He gave a grunt.

We tramped down to the pearly glow, to the blast sight,
to the overgrown gully.

Bobby stopped again to graze his torch over the vegetation.

I hadn't been here in a long, long time. But nothing was
changed. It was still like seeing a few acres of another planet.
Behind a porous veil of sticky moss, goitered trees phospho-
resced, their limbs coiled tightly, their barks fleshy, their foliage as puffed as pastries. Mustard-yellow fruits shone from
inside snarly white thorn bushes—thorns like cones of green
incense. Tall furry shoots wobbled, and, growing low to the
ground, huge red cupola blossoms (pooling labial-pink
fluids) were supported by darker-red stalks even skinnier
than licorice whips. Mushrooms the size of bullfrogs, cheese
soufflés, Tiffany shades. The earth was marshy. The air was
hot and muggy.

Bobby's light picked out a cloud of raisiny mosquitoes.

He said: "You remember where the best paths are, don't
you, Grinner?"

(Oh, yes—and Lumps had played in those Sunday games,
too.)

"I'm not going down there. Let Flour come up."

But the Dragon convinced me to change my mind: a low
growl, the pressure of three sharp points just above the
crack in my ass.

The path was practically vertical but staired by shoe heels
and well trodden. Where the pit bottomed out it was swelter-
ing, plants dripped like midnight faucets, the muck turned
gelid. A mosquito syringed blood from my thumb knuckle.

"Here's good," said the Dragon.

"Good for what?" I said. "Where's Flour? Isn't he coming, isn't that—"

Bobby tipped his torch to show me his knife.

He said: "Flour says to tell you: he knows all about your little deal with Sharkey and Law, Law, Law-somebody. Oh, fuckit!"

His bladed hand jerked up, started down.

20
A Crushing Blow

"I really hope you've learned something from this shitty experience, Grinner. Like, for instance, who's got the more huggable personality. Me, by a kilometer."

"You son of a bitch!"

"Is that any way to talk about Ma? Now get up already. Wipe yourself off. Catch the old breath. Find yourself a comfortable mushroom and let's talk."

I was down on my knees in the black gelatin, down where the Dragon had shoved me.

Flourface stood over me, swacking the flashlight barrel against his open palm. Lumps and the Dragon had gone slogging off—I presumed they'd climbed out of the Hole but couldn't be sure.

I'd wet my goddamn pants, I had a mouth full of goo and a crazed heart.

"If I give you a hand, will you be tricky?"

"Give the hand," I said and took it when it came.

Flour blazed the light on a boulder-size fungus growing near the base of a tree that might've resembled a white birch if it hadn't been for its green-and-yellow mottling and its foamed-over branches. "Sit there."

I did.

He clicked off the flashlight. A bluish flame soared, went out, left an orange dot. The dot moved back and forth, across the clearing, then stopped. Smoke went tumbling. "What a sad, sad friggen state of affairs, hey, Grinner?"

I felt a salt pang, I said, "Lemme have one of your cigarettes." My ears were frying, my belly was cold. I could smell piss. It was making me sick.

"Smoke your own!" I heard him scratch a cheek. "You know, that's a historic toadstool you're sitting on. Guy named Four-quarters is buried right under it. Remember him? Guy's pushing up toadstools."

"Why'd you wanna kill me?"

"Who said I wanted? Naw, Fishy, I never wanted. I was tempted but—give you that. Compromised. A little scare, a little warning. Only the Dragon, he was all for spilling you. Bobby, eh—he's wishy-washy. He woulda gone either way. The question is: *Why* was I tempted? And the answer is: So you couldn't get the chance to do me first."

"That's crazy."

"Don't tick me, Grinner. I *know*! I mean, sure, there's no love lost—but to spill me for an operation? It's depressing."

"You're talking about those two guys."

"Kill me and they'll make you a mammal. And you said yes."

"I said no—and they never asked me to *kill* you. They want your fish. They don't even care about you."

Flour laughed. "And what kinda narcs are these—don't care about me?"

"Not any kind. They're spacers."

He came slopping over, switched his light back on, spotted himself: inky bladder lips, closed around a cigarette, thinning as they broke into a smile. He plucked away his smoke, it fizzed in some gully fluid. "I like this, I *like* the new Grinner. For once, crissake for once, you make a joke." Light off. "But you told them no. You say."

"I told the spacers no. That's right. No help."

"Cut with the spacers, Grinny. Ain't no spacers looking for me. They want my fish! For what, to put in orbit? Please, I got enough troubles." He splattered away. "So. To get back. Who am I gonna believe? You? Who says you're pure.

Or . . . somebody else? Who says you're not. Who says you made a deal."

"Are you talking about Reeni?"

Flour's flashlight, tomahawked, burst against the tree behind me.

"I didn't hear that," he said. "I musta heard wrong."

"I asked a question."

"You asked a question."

"I wanted to know."

"He wanted to know. He don't even trust his own lady. He thinks, what a prick, that she mighta sold him to me for three thousand dollars. For three thousand bucker-babies."

"Oh shit."

"A crushing blow for the fishman!"

"He lied," I said and stood up. I felt heavier, say by a quarter of a ton. "I didn't make any deal. Beef lied."

"Now you see how come I was only tempted? I been telling you about that boy for years. And years."

"Why'd you give him the money?"

"Maybe so I could say what I just did. And leave you without a floor to do a song and dance on. Maybe?"

A lemony-auraed mouse hurtled across the ooze, barely touching it.

Flour lit another cigarette. "Want one?" he said.

"I'm going," I said. "You don't mind."

"So go."

"You had to bust the flashlight."

"That's okay," he said. "I wasn't gonna loan you it anyhow."

"You're not coming?"

"With you? No. I think I'll walk around the botanical gardens for a while. I always liked the place. Find your way out okay?"

"Don't worry."

"Hey, Grinny? How come you haven't asked me?"

"About what?"

"Come on, you know what about. About Reeni. And me."

I pushed through some hedges that burned coldly with a glowering plummy light. Got lost. I patted for my matches and found them soaked. Popped a few salt tabs and shoved on, trampling tacky sedge. Shut my eyes and shouldered into a mass of spade-shaped blistered leaves, circumvented a curtain of red moss whose interstices were resilient membrane.

And then Flour was standing beside me crunching on an exaggerated pear that he held with two hands. "Having trouble?" he asked. "Guess it has been a long time, huh Grin? Since you were here."

"I'm tired," I said. "Where am I going, Flour? Back where I came? Down? Up? What?"

"You remember how Da used to take us up here—you, me, some of the guys? Reeni? Hey—you 'member how if she lost the tag choose, she'd make us do it over? She was a pain about that. Never wanted to be It, never wanted to take her turn playing Normal. She was a real pain in the nuts, wasn't she?"

"Am I going in circles? Where's the freaken path, Flour?"

"You 'member how she used to come out sometimes on Sundays with her fur all streaked different colors? How'd she do that? Was that food dye?"

"Am I gonna hit the path?"

"They used to look nice, them streaks. Was a shame when she stopped. Guess she got too self-conscious. Would you say that's what happened, Grinny? Did she get too self-conscious when somebody she liked started to criticize?"

"Bullshit, criticize. She grew up, Reeni grew up. Something you never done."

Flour tossed his pear core into some bushes, he kissed juice off his fingers, finger by finger, and very, very carefully. "Yeah, you keep going this way, you'll find a path up," he said. "But watch, there's a lotta crap can trip you."

Five minutes later I was lost again. Again, my brother

appeared, and this time he crouched to snap a bunch of creepers, spiny things, that had lashed themselves around my ankles and calves.

"You got some memory of this place," I said. "How you get around so easy?"

"Like you say, good memory. You shoulda wore heavier socks, man. You're bleeding."

"If I'd known I was coming, I woulda worn," I said.

He gave a short laugh and got to his feet. "Good memory, bad memory. You like that, too? Five years ago—sharp. This morning—a cloud. I wonder if we got at least that much in common."

"Flour, I wanna get the hell outta this pit. You mind helping me?"

"Like, I 'member the day Reeni's mother died, so clear. Bet you 'member that day, too. I 'member how you looked at me—like I had Reeni undressed or something. You know, you get points for being human to people when they're blown down."

"What, you want points?"

"Forget it, I got points. Grinny, I never touched her—I mean, touched her the way you got sick ideas I did. Never. I'm sorry to say."

"Now you want medals?"

"No, no medals. 'Cause I haven't won anything yet."

"But you're working on it."

"No," he said. "You're working on it. Come on, pathfinder, I'll show you how to get outta here."

Neither of us moved.

I was wondering if he still wore those artificial fingertips. I said: "Why don't you leave me and Reeni alone?"

"I am. I thought I just told you so."

"You're giving her money—that's leaving alone?"

"I'm not giving anything," he said. "She's doing a job for me. You want one, too?"

"Fuck yourself."

Flourface said: "No, I think I'll wait for a better deal."

I was still wondering if he wore those artificial fingertips.

I followed him through silky underbrush, through scored and silvery crabgrass, through a stand of sumo-squat and leafless trees whose sucker-bearing boles, catching the breeze just so, moaned. We hopped a percolating streamlet and chopped through hedges that were hoary with lice.

"And here's your path," said Flour. "Straight up, and I'll be seeing you, I guess."

"We have our lives planned," I said. "You got no rights."

Flour said nothing.

"I don't want Reeni selling your eggs any more."

Flour said nothing.

"Did you hear me?"

"You'd rather she go ahead being raped for a living?"

"I'd rather she kept performing with me—yeah, damn straight, I'd rather. But that's a little beside the point now. Because of you, Studebaker won't book us any more."

"She quit first. What I heard."

"She woulda changed her mind."

"For the man she loves. I get it."

"So you owe me something."

"How you figure that, Grinny?"

"It's your fault I got no career any more."

"Career, the fishman calls it."

"We could settle the debt simple," I said. "For the price of two Syntha-skin ops. You must have the money."

He laughed, sucked his cheeks, spat. "Against my religion. Couldn't conscience that, Grinny. All those lovely scales mummied over. I'd lose sleep."

"You owe me."

He moved his head. "All I owe you is an apology for tonight. I was wrong. I apologize."

I started to climb the steep-sheared path.

"If you wanna collect any debts," Flour called after me, "or any more apologies—go to Beef. I'd say he owes you three thousand bucks. And a bunch of I'm-sorries. At least."

I stopped, I spoke over a shoulder. "Don't you hurt him, Flour."

"I think I told you this once or twice before. But, Grinner. From the bottom of my heart. You make me sick."

I climbed the rest of the way out of the Blofeld Hole.

Bobby and the Dragon weren't waiting for me on the Boulevard, and neither was the Eclipse—so I called for a cab from a booth on the corner. The radio dispatcher asked me where I was going. I told him Freaktown. Eventually, I gave up waiting and walked.

Fortunately, it was late and the streets were dead. But it was cold, and my wet cuffs frosted. My shoes cheeped. And I moved like a cowboy, on account of a urine rash.

21
Betrayed by Mushrooms

I was sitting on Skull Garden's couch drinking hot salt water. Reeni, astraddle a hassock, was jabbing half moons into a cube of rosy process cheese with her big square thumbnail. She screwed up her mouth and shrugged to herself. She looked at me. She looked at the floor. She dropped her cheese into an ashtray.

I'd told her all about my trip down into the Blofeld Hole.

"This is a stupid mess," she said. "His fault, my fault, yours. Martin I'm not gonna mention—he's beneath contempt."

Almost everything: I'd skipped over my incontinence, my lost ramble.

She came and sat beside me. Took my hand and squeezed it, rubbed it. "You believe I love you, don't you? Shouldn't doubt that. You got a self-confidence problem, Grinny. Honest, you do. You should trust me more."

Skipped also mentioning why Flour had flown into a rage and shattered the only flashlight.

"Reen, *he* loves *you*. That's the stupid mess."

"He does. But it's no threat, I promise."

"No threat? What no threat? He thinks he's gonna take you. From me."

"No he don't."

"He said!"

"Even so, so what? I'm not, like, for the taking."

Skully sat lost in an armchair popping his lips, not hearing a syllable of any of this.

"Flour musta been out of his eyes to believe Martin,"
Reeni said. "*I* know you wouldn't help the police. I *know*
you're not like that."

And I agreed with her, a few times.

"I couldn't love anybody who was."

"Wouldn't expect you to," I said. "I told those guys no.
They tried to scare me, they broke light bulbs. No. Take
away my job. No. What's Flour think I am anyway? He
must be out of his eyes. Just like you said."

My grin matched my disposition perfectly: one of those
rare times.

Reeni kissed my knuckle, the swollen one that blazed
waxy red from the Blofeld mosquito bite.

"It was weird, hey Reeni," I said. "Being down in the
Hole again. At night, yet. And so hot it was Florida! I can't
remember when I was there last. Long. Years."

"Me, too," she said. "Long time."

Skully made a saliva sawing noise. He rose slowly and
glanced Reeni a fleeting smile—a measly watt of flickering
recognition—and shuffled toward his bedroom. We watched
him go. He closed the door.

"You gotta get him off those eggs, Reen. The man's a full-
fledged zombie."

She let go of my hand. "Maybe he'll find her. Maybe
he'll be happy. There's a chance."

"I don't think so," I said.

She ignored that. She frowned at her knees, at mine.
She jerked up her head at the sound of a crash, a heavy
toppling, in Skully's bedroom.

We found him on the floor. He must've stumbled against
the dresser and, falling, struck his ear on a fancy brass
drawer knob. He'd torn cartilage and some moles, and there
was blood on his throat. There were eggshells in his fist.
We dotted him with adhesive disks, we lifted him between
us and laid him into bed. I checked his heart, his wrist, I
glanced at Reeni, who thumbed closed his eyes.

"Maybe he'll find her," she said.

And that time, I said: "Maybe."

She stretched out alongside him and nuzzled her face against his ear and streaked her jaw fur red. He was still bleeding, a little, through Band-aid gauze and perforations. She closed his top coat button.

"You're not gonna . . . do any eggs yourself tonight, are you?" I asked.

She rolled onto her back and folded her arms behind her head, smiled up. "Not tonight. I don't think I need any. Do I?" And smiled wider; those king-size teeth. "Friends?"

I nodded, my grinning still completely legitimate.

"Let's stay here overnight," she suggested. "You can go pull out the couch now, if you'd like."

I nodded again, and flicked my eyes to Skully, who was turning rigid and seeping gas.

"In a way," Reeni said, "I'm glad what happened did. Almost. I got pains like I'd never felt when you told me about Bobby's knife. It was good to feel them."

I said: "Screw Bobby. And Flour, too. But yeah, I'd like to be friends again." I wished my brother could've been eavesdropping.

Going out to unfold the convertible couch, I wondered how Reeni would like her new bridemask, and wished that I'd got some response from Ralph Studebaker about my changed-names proposition: I could be billed as the Barracuda, instead of Fishdick, on theater posters, and Reeni—scrap the name Ugly Irene and just call her Cavewoman. I fantasized standing-room-only in Canadian halls, in the deep South, in the far West. I thought about my parents' wedding pictures, about Judy Garland's mouth.

I made up the bed and while Reeni showered I called Da. I figured he'd had enough time to think over my proposition, figured he would be ready to say yes to a cash deal.

My mother answered, with a tremolo in her voice—that

anticipation of tragic news. "What's the matter? What's wrong?"

"Nothing, nothing. Is Da around?"

"Around? He's in bed. He's been in bed for two hours, I've been in bed for two hours. Charles, don't you own a clock?"

Da had never gone to sleep before three. He'd always been too busy listening to tapes, transcribing, scribbling.

I guess I hadn't expected the barbecue fire to change anything very much. I was disappointed with him: if I'd been Da, I probably would've stayed up trying to recollect specific interviews or even doodling on empty pads, just to stay up. I would've apologized to Ma but then kept to familiar schedules. Stubbornly. If I'd been Da.

I asked Ma how she was feeling and if they'd patched up their quarrel.

"He shoveled all the ashes by himself," she said, "and dumped them into cans."

"But how are you?"

"I'm just fine," she said.

"Tell Da if he wants to call me tomorrow about anything, I'll be home. Would you do that?"

"I don't think he'll get the chance tomorrow, Charles. He's going to the doctor's."

"He sick?"

"No. He's going about his arm. He's finally gonna have it taken care of."

"Taken care how?"

"Taken care *off.*"

A kid, Flour used to walk Da's right arm as if it were the downside of a seesaw, his own arms teed for balance . . .

Reeni turned off the lights and we climbed into bed. Two minutes later, in the clinch, I was having difficulty: ornery blood continued its boycott of my sex organ.

"Cuddle just," she said finally. "I like that, too."

Not me, so I tried to sorcery-up some Judy mouths in the dark, for inspiration.

It used to work, now it didn't.

So I pretended I was Mr. Sears-Roebuck, and managed— although Reeni complained I was being too rough, then didn't climax. But she could've shammed it, I thought, if she'd really gotten those pains when I told her about Bobby Lump's knife charade.

She dozed off but I stayed awake, staring at several white patches that glowed faintly over by the kitchen doorway. That glowed just as my hands had glowed the other night after I'd swept off Reeni's soiled jacket.

I got up and switched on a light, I grabbed my jeans from the back of a chair over by the kitchen door. On their seat were clots and specks of mushroom, or toadstool.

. . . *That's a historic toadstool you're sitting on* . . .

Reeni had elbowed up, was blinking.

"I have to trust you," I said. "I have to *trust* you more."

She knuckled gumminess from the corners of her mouth. "What?"

"And you haven't been down in the Hole for years—huh? You were down there the other night, when you goddamn came home at four o'clock!"

"Grinner, lower your voice, you don't un—"

"What, you like the *botanical gardens,* too? What, you both take walks together?" I scraped away the fungus and flung it, mealy buckshot, across the parlor.

Red spots, red strings scrambled, tumbled, throughout Reeni's eyes.

"How romantic. Two Freaks down Blofeld," I said. "Hand in hand? And you tell me Hasbrouck Heights with the Dragon to sell eggs!"

"I was where I told you I was."

"How'd you get that crap on your coat, then?"

She wouldn't answer me.

"Where do you go, youse two, after you meet at the Hole?"

"I don't *meet* him anywhere!"

"Then why you been down there?"

"Lay off, Grinner, just lay the hell off! I done nothing wrong!"

"You go down the Hole to pick crab apples? For what then? Pears outta season?"

She glared, she geishaed herself in a blanket, she went and slept the rest of the night in bed with a dead man.

Part Five:
The Other Mr.
Sears-Roebuck

(December, 2010)

22
Surf and Turf

"Have any names picked out yet?"

Pigeon Mary half turned and peered down from the aluminum stepladder. "Way too early for that," she said. "When I have the kid safe in a blanket, then I'll think up something." Carefully, she draped more tinsel on the Christmas tree, looped a styrene ball over a branch, reached up and straightened the crowning angel—its red and green lights strobed across her feathered cheek. She stepped down. Her belly was only beginning to bulge. "Another drink?"

"I still got some left." And took a bite of a homemade butter cookie faced with colored dough: three blue eyes, yellow smiling mouth.

"Where's Reeni?" She rummaged through the ornament box, came up with a batch of pinecones and a tiny ceramic booted dwarf.

"At her father's." At least, that's where she'd claimed she was going. Blunt exchanges of simple information: we were back to that.

"Speaking of fathers," and scissored off a branch tip, hung the dwarf. "Speaking of fathers," Pidge said, "I saw yours.
"Emergency, or what? His arm."

"He decided to have it cut, that's all."

I'd seen him myself last week, I'd waited for him to mention our bar conversation, I'd expected to negotiate. Instead, he'd demonstrated how simple it was to pluck a juice glass from a shelf with his new stainless steel fingers, how simple to fill that same glass with red punch and deliver it to my mother.

He'd been wearing makeup.

"Got your tree yet?" Pigeon unraveled a long silver garland.

"No, we're not gonna bother." I walked over to the window. Its pane corners were triangled with aerosol snow. "When's he supposed to come?"

She squinted at her watch ring. "He should be here. You two really haven't talked since you went to New York? What's the matter? On the outs?"

"There's never any answer at Cleo's."

"I know."

"When did he call?"

"Just this morning."

"Thanks for telling me."

"You asked."

"Won't stay long," I promised. "I just wanna see him for a coupla minutes."

"You really on the outs?"

"He told you January third? That's definite?"

"He'll be in the hospital till the twenty-fourth."

"No car," I said.

"What?"

"I said, I wonder how come he doesn't have a car. Beef."

"He's here?"

"He's coming. But he's walking."

Wearing a parka with the hood flipped up and his old yellow sewer boots, the Beefstone came stamping down the street, followed by a gaggle of begging zoms. He stopped and shoved one of them and the rest dispersed, trickling across Cator Avenue, then coalescing around a barrel fire in a vacant corner lot.

Beef pounded his feet on the rubber porch mat.

Pigeon Mary met him at the door. He picked her up to kiss her, looked past her ear and spotted me. I raised my cup in a salute. He let Pidge drop, tried hard to slice a grin through his lips. "Hey."

"Hey," I said.

He tore off his gloves, unzipped his coat and shrugged it into Pigeon Mary's arms. Wiggled his shoulders and blew on cupped hands. "Nice surprise. How you been, Grinny?"

"Not so wonderful. I had a little—"

"Hey, Pidge-o, don't hang up the coat, there's something in it for you." From the pocket he pulled out a package, thick and lumpy and gift-wrapped. "Merry. A little early."

She turned it around in her hands, she moved across the parlor and snatched up a flat and square gift of her own (parcel-papered, fancied with hand-drawn and crayoned bells and four-armed Shiva-Santas) from underneath the evergreen tree. "Well, since we're exchanging . . ."

Even though it was obviously secondhand, Pigeon Mary made a big grateful deal about her Christmas present: Cleo Nothing's canvas shoulder bag, minus its flicka-screen.

And Beef said, after tearing open his gift and whacking away the paper, after groaning: "Aw God, are you *serious*?"

Pidge looked puzzled, then stricken, then her whole face collapsed. She'd given him a large velvet-finish photograph, in a gilt frame and under nonreflecting glass. A picture of Beef and herself standing arm in arm next to their pie-plated gasoline Ford.

I recognized the picture: I'd taken it for them. You couldn't see it because the background was sun-bleared—but the Sycorax Club was across the street.

"I'm starting a whole new life," Beef growled, "and I want this? For what? My wall? So people can ask who's that ugly red slab?"

Without expression, without tone, Pigeon told him: "So throw it out. You might save the frame, though. It's pretty good."

"Oh, the frame's good. Wonderful." He looked at it, he tapped it, he passed it back. "Very thoughtful. Did you get a chance to look for those cassettes I asked you about?"

He wanted all of his *Gunsmokes*.

Pigeon Mary scratched at the back of her hand; a few short pinfeathers dropped off. She nodded and bit her lip. "I put them all in an old camera case," excused herself and vanished down the hall with the rejected photograph.

"I tried to call you, Beef."

"Moved outta Cleo's." He wouldn't look at me. He seemed to be tallying tree ornaments.

"How come she didn't answer?"

"Aw . . . she's off somewhere."

"How about your deal? You make that deal with her?"

Beef's eyes climbed the tree, they locked on the angel beacon. "Bought that for Pidge last December," he said. "We were up in Boston, doing shows." He reached and tried to straighten it, only made it crooked. Left it crooked. "We were stuck in the city over the holidays. No performances from, like, the twenty-third till, like, two, three days after the Big Birthday. So I picked that up in the hotel lobby. For the room. We didn't have no tree, but she was happy. Cost an arm, a leg, a fucken torso it cost. It's got an eternal battery, they call it, and all them lights." He stuffed his hands in his pockets. "Turned out to be a nice Christmas." He took a breath. "I don't know why I did what I just done. That was a really shitty thing."

"There's something else I don't know why you done."

He squeezed a knob of dark-red cheek and turned slowly around. His eyes prowled for mine, then skittered off. "I'm glad nothing happened to you."

"Makes two of us."

He dropped into a chair, toed giftwrap. "I was short, Grinner. You can understand that."

"Short. Even after what Cleo gave you?"

"Short."

"Jesus Christ, Beef!"

"I knew they wouldn't hurt you. Not really."

"How'd you know where to find Flour?"

"Me? I didn't know. Dinah Murphy did everything. I called her up and told her what you told me—"

"I didn't tell you I was gonna kill Flour!"

"I know, look, I know. What do you want me to say, Charlie? You want me to say I'm sorry? I'm sorry."

"I want the money. You don't think you owe me that?"

"Be glad to give you. Only it's spent. Every dime."

I'd expected more to happen. I'd even brought a razor blade sheathed in cardboard just in case. But nothing more happened. I just stood there, he just sat there. And he didn't apologize again. Just that once.

I waited, but nothing more happened.

Finally, I went and dragged my coat and scarf from a hanger and bundled up.

"I'll let you know how things turn out," Beef said.

I looked at him from the front door.

"I can be the guinea pig, yeah? Anything goes wrong with the op—it's my skin, right?"

"How'd you get Cleo's bag?"

"Gave it to me."

"Cheap gift."

"I'm flat, I wasn't kidding."

"Tell Pidge I said good night."

"Sure." He breathed down on his big smile. "When's Carnegie Hall?"

"Day after tomorrow."

"Be good, youse guys."

I was still looking at him.

"And, hey, Grinner: Merry Christmas."

"Stuff it, Beef."

23
Obit

Jack Laudermilch got a squinty bead on a tumored gray bitch, cocked his right thumb and fired three make-believe rounds—"Chu-chu-chu!"—from his crooked index finger. The dog studied him glassily, then slinked off, dragging her belly and her long, horizontally flattened beaver tail. Laudermilch rubbed his nose on his jacket sleeve, turned and looked back toward us—toward Niles Sharkey and me. He dug a handkerchief from his pocket and blew. He gazed up at the overcast, down at the bay, across the water at the New York City skyline.

When Sharkey had called before breakfast I said all right, I'd meet him at Bayside Park after lunch.

He unwrapped a deli sandwich and drained pickle juice from the waxed paper. Laid the sandwich between us on the concrete bench.

He wasn't wearing his spacer ring.

"We've left you alone," he said. "We thought that was best. What have you got?"

I had a headful of salt and a burning stomach from too many cups of almos-coffee.

Reeni hadn't come home from Skully's last night. I'd rung her at three: she'd answered. At four: she hadn't. I'd dressed and hurried over, I'd found her vacuuming the carpet in her mother's disintegrating sealskin coat, her father's galoshes: "What the well-dressed adulteress is wearing this season." I'd called her a zombie and gone back to the house.

"I don't know where the fish are," I said. "I don't know where he is. How long you been a spacer?"

"What an asinine question! Spacer? You know what I am."

"I do," I said. "I do. Tell me something: are you willing to buy those fish?"

"Is he willing to sell them?"

"I don't know, I didn't ask. I was just wondering. You'd buy them?"

"There's that possibility."

"Funny narc."

"Not really," and picked sesame seeds from his roll.

"You ever hear of a girl named Cleo? Her father was named Follet. He was a spacer, too. You know the girl?"

Sharkey smiled, stretching out his arms along the back of the bench. "Called herself Cleo Nothing? A nihilist? I've heard of her, yes. And . . . ?"

"She told me about you. Your project. And I been trying to figure out what goldfish got to do with it. And death eggs. So what I've figured is this. They're not death eggs at all. Are they? I also figure you guys were responsible for Caliban's Night."

"Caliban's Night? What is this, kitchen-sink day?"

"Right," I said. "Kitchen-sink day. I could go to the cops, you know. I could go to the newspapers. Or I could tell somebody I know. And he'd go. In a minute. A second."

"Cleo Nothing," Sharkey said.

"She told me enough," I said.

"She did."

"Enough. And then there's Sam LaPilusa."

Sharkey moistened his lips and stood. He chucked his sandwich at a graffitoed bronze soldier bust. "I don't know what you're talking about, Mr. Fistick. But, here, let's walk. I'm getting cold."

Laudermilch scuffed behind us, breath ragging from the side of his mouth.

"What's this project you mentioned?" Sharkey jiggled his cigarette pack at me, I waved it away.

"Mind rockets. Ring a bell? Minds instead of ships? Scouts?"

"Sounds bizarre."

"Microwaves? Veiled Elements?"

He shrugged.

"Come on, already! You spacers were fooling around with all that shit on Blofeld Street in the eighties. Something went the matter and blew up. The fallout put gills on me and green eggs in the pet goldfish. And those eggs are what you guys wanted all the time, only you didn't know it. Am I correct? You didn't know it until the eggs went on sale. Nobody's going to heaven, just to space. And the god-lights—"

"Stars?"

"So you admit."

"I was just one step ahead of you. Logically."

"It's the truth."

"What do I know about that? I'm just a law-enforcement officer."

We'd come out of the park, were heading for the red Solaris parked at the curb. I ducked slightly, checking to see if anyone was seated in the back. No one was.

"I could go to the cops."

"They've come to you."

"Bullshit."

Sharkey leaned against the hood of the car and smoked. "Now that you've said this much, tell me the last line of your story."

"The last line is this: Go away, leave me alone. And tell Ralph Studebaker it's okay, you don't mind if I work."

"Mr. Fistick—"

"I'm letting you off cheap."

"Cheap?"

"With what I know, I could make you pay for my operation."

"We've already offered to pay."

"I could *make* you pay. With no strings."

"Finished?"

"I'm finished."

"Fine. Now I have something to say. I've never left the planet in my life."

"That's not what Cleo says."

"Now how the hell would she know anything about me?"

"Cut the shit. You've met. You just told me you knew her!"

"You asked me if I'd *heard* of her, and I answered yes. Honestly. In fact, I *just* heard of her this morning." He filliped his butt and held up one finger. Unlocked the car door, leaned in and grabbed a tubed *New York Times*. "Just this morning." He rattled through the paper, folded it back, pointed to a headline buried in the fifth news section:

RADICAL NIHILIST FOUND DEAD IN SOHO LOFT

I backed off from Sharkey, bumped into Laudermilch, and slid away fast.

"Says here, she blew herself up. Bagging gravy," Sharkey said after a skim. "You were right, though, about her father. Mentions he'd been a spacer. Died in California two years ago. Poor bastard was taken out by some union cabbie during the fleet's biennial rundown strike." He tossed away the paper, the sheets burst apart, were gusted up the block. "And *she* told you all that stuff about projects? If I were you and wanted to be so paranoid, I'd at least try to find a better source for my suspicions."

"You saw her with me that day, didn't you?"

"And killed her? God, you really are paranoid, aren't you?"

"I could still go—"

"Go anywhere you please, Mr. Fistick. But if you want to simplify things, why don't you go to your brother and take us along? Or just tell us where he is."

I was thinking, then: "You'd buy his fish? And then leave?"

"I said once, there's that possibility. We'd have to be assured, though, that he was selling them all."

"And if I arranged that? You'd still give us the money for Dr. Sleet?"

"We'd even splurge and let you have all the pictures we took of your wife. Plus negatives."

"Call me tonight."

Sharkey nodded. "But if your brother doesn't want to sell, that doesn't let you—or your wife—off the hook."

"Just call me tonight, huh?"

Dinah Murphy lived on Van Nostrand Avenue.

She answered my rings holding a sterling cake server partially wrapped in a flannel cloth pinked with silver polish.

She listened to me, then shut the door.

I spent what was left of the afternoon neatening Reeni's new bridemask.

24
Flour's Christmas Spirit

After buttered spaghetti, I coaxed Reeni into modeling the Ms. Sears bridemask, and it was perfect, lovely—although it mocked her squat physique and humongous hands. I made her walk up and down, up and down. She quietly obliged. I ran to embrace her, and she suffered even that, but stiffly.

She said: "Do you mind if I take this off to do the dishes?"

I said: "Let's truce."

She said: "Let's not."

Those green glass eyes looked so genuine, so mentholated, so Normal, that I couldn't be angry.

I hooded my new groomhead over a plastic brandy snifter and sat admiring it while I waited for the telephone to ring.

Reeni finished in the kitchen and came back, minus mask, and put on headphones and played a video cassette, an old Time-Life remainder, *Epilog for Elephants*.

Dinah called at eight: "He says you can't trust narcotics agents. He says you can't trust Normals. He says he thought he told you that."

"Won't he even quote a freaken price—just to see?"

"He says he could ask for the city of Minneapolis. He says but what's that gonna mean? They won't give it."

"What about, they give *me* the money first, then I—"

"He says you really shouldn't be hanging around with those sort of people. He says you might catch the Normal flu—if you haven't already."

"And that's all he said?"

"He said to find out what size shirt you wear. In case he felt like giving you a Christmas present. He says to tell you that he's got enough belts this year but that a pos-negative scarf would be appreciated."

"He didn't even consider the offer. Did he?"

"He says you can't trust narcotics agents. He says he thought—"

"You tell *him* that Grinner says: From now on, I'm gonna decide who to trust and who not."

"He says he thought there was a chance you might say that. And he says you've always been a lousy judge."

I hung up.

Elephants lumbered through a forest of tree stumps. At their plight, Reeni beat her knuckles together.

Sharkey phoned at the dot of nine.

"No," I told him.

"Well, that's it."

I said: "I guess it is."

He said: "Now, where's your brother?"

"I wish I knew."

"You're not going to Skully's house tonight," I said. "You stay here. He can keep. Tomorrow we got a show and I want you here."

Without a word, Reeni threw off her coat. She lugged her video player up to the bedroom. I started turning off the downstairs lights. I walked into the kitchen, wet a fingertip and stuck it in the salt cannister, licked. Killed the fluorescents over the sink, and spotted the bridemask lying face side down on the popping radiator below the window. When I peeled it away, gummy sections of cheek, nose, brow and chin, and one green eye ringed by socket, adhered to the hot coils.

The mask, the beautiful mask, looked just like a monster now, a beast with gleaming yellow hair. A Freak.

I went tight across the chest, clutched the ruined latex in a fist and stormed upstairs.

But there was no sense in shouting at Ugly Irene: like the elephants that littered the wasteland on the screen of her tabled video player, she was dead.

25
Studebaker Incensed

Next day, I borrowed Pigeon Mary's Ford, and Reeni and I, mute and edgy, drove into New York City.

After resurrecting, she'd apologized for destroying the bridemask. I'd refused to accept it. She'd called it an accident, thoughtlessness. I'd refused to believe it.

I'd had to leave Mr. Sears-Roebuck-face at home, still fitted over the brandy snifter. What good was it without its mate?

We'd taken our old papier-mâchés with us, inside their striped hatboxes.

We parked at Eighth Avenue and Fifty-fifth Street, in a six-tiered garage, and the young Puerto Rican attendant measured us up and down with a smirk. He called in a Spanish babble to a fat white man in the glass foreman's office who was straining a tea bag. Then, pointing after us as we hurried up the ramp with the claim ticket, the kid chanted: *"Rarezas, rarezas, rarezas . . ."*

Ralph Studebaker was pacing in front of Carnegie Hall. No large surprise, he recognized us through our disguises. He was wearing a long buff coat imprinted on both front and back with blown-up facsimiles of his ChemBank savings account, deposits and withdrawals.

"I was getting worried," he said. "One fifteen tops—didn't I tell you that in my letter? It's already one thirty!"

We followed him to the artists' entrance.

On the sidewalk there were two manned card tables overspread with clear bags of rock candy, rock salt, gravel and unshelled macadamia nuts for sale.

Reeni and I had separate dressing rooms: a class hall.

Ralph followed me into mine and while I stripped, washed my face and did some calisthenics, he chewed on his false candy-coated fingernails. I put on my tux. "What's the house like?"

"Not a sellout, but not bad," he said.

"I thought I mighta heard from you, Ralph—about my suggestion."

"It was a dumb idea, Grinner. I didn't think it deserved a reply. Call yourself Barracuda, call yourself Fillet of Flounder—you don't think those guys would know it was you?"

I put on my tie, my cummerbund.

"I keep checking the news every day," he said. "Checking to see if they got your brother."

"So you know what Sharkey wants."

"They paid me a second visit. Yeah, I know. And, like I say, I keep checking the papers to see if I can pick up the phone and give you a call."

"That's nice of you, Ralph."

"I'm a nice guy. I don't want to see a talented Freak go on the dole. It breaks my heart. I got contracts, all colors and sizes, that I'm dying for you to sign."

"Who's going to Canada? Instead of us?"

"Did I have to settle for less than great on that one," he said. "Some shrimpy guy with feet like snowshoes, some glommy broad with a puss fulla artichoke hearts, they look like. No comparison with you and Reeni. Just no crackle." He bit off a thumbnail tip and minced it between his teeth. "Grinner . . . can't you help Sharkey?"

"If I do, Ralph, you wouldn't like it."

"I wouldn't? Why?" And cropped his ringfingernail.

I'd never told Ralph about my plans: it wouldn't have been very smart. Once, he'd overheard a Freak at the Sycorax mention how she was saving for Syntha-skin and he fired her on the spot.

"*Why* wouldn't I?"

"Never mind, Ralph."

"No, no, come on. What'd you mean by that?"

I shrugged, couldn't think of a lie quickly enough, said a stupid thing: "If I find Flour. I mean, find him for *them*— they pay for my operation. And Reeni's."

"Operation?" He was gaping, there were purpled nail flecks on his underlip.

"That's what Sharkey offered."

"You *want* one of those things?" Gape turned to squint.

"Well . . . I've thought about it."

"You little *shit!*"

"Ralph, it's no big thing. I only thought about it once or twice, maybe. It'll never happen—"

"Here I've been supporting you and you turn around and want to use *my* money for an operation? So you can go live among people who don't know what you're like, how you behave, what you *do!*"

"You never *gave* me a dollar!"

He spat a nail curl and pulled open the dressing-room door.

"Ralph! Ralph, hey . . . it's never gonna happen, it was just an idea."

"You'd better hope," he said, "that it *does* happen. Because I got no more use for you as a Freak. Fishdick."

When he was gone I locked the door and chewed salt, I stared at my reflection in the table mirror. The stage manager rapped and I put on the mask.

26
Return of Freaks
on the Boards

. . . Mask flung aside, I move to the looking glass. A Freak now, my face is scored by scales, gills cantilever on my throat. I raise my arms . . . tear at my clothes . . . but as I turn toward the bed, my "bride," still in her mask, isn't cowering: she beckons with her hands while her shoulders twitch, as though shaken by laughter.

—What's she *do*ing?—

I'm circling the bed in a low crouch, Reeni signals me: come closer, closer. I do, and she hurls herself from the mattress, her white-gloved fingers bent and tearing at my neck. I'm thrown off balance and crash to the hard stage, twisting an ankle, the right ankle. Reeni lifts her white-stockinged foot and drives the heel powerfully into my chest. Her other foot lashes out and cracks me in the ribs.

Out of breath, completely dizzed, I blink up at her: she stands straddling me . . . haughty . . . still in her bride-mask, still as a Normal. I see her raise a foot again, this time I clamp the ankle and wrench it, and Reeni falls back, spilling onto the bed.

I attack, trying to chop at her mask's spring point in order to cleave it. But she deflects my aim, she bats my wrist.

And we kneel on the bed, breathing hard . . . spines belligerently oblique. Antagonists. Normal and Freak.

"What the hell are you *do*ing?" I hiss at her.

She laughs again, that rattles me, she builds a mace with

both of her hands, she lifts it above her mask. I push off with my knees, butting her shoulder hard with my head. Grab handfuls of gown to rip it, she rolls away—some material tears, but not much. Not enough. Then she rolls right back, her elbow flipping up and stunning my adam's apple. I'm choking, still choking, when she clips me a good one on the temple and I see all colors of splintered light . . .

27
Laudermilch Stew

I was alone on stage with a bloody nose, with a dented brainpan, I was staggering around in a red blur. My eyes began to clear, the sea-whumps faded, segueing into applause. Applause. Arms . . . out there . . . were moving, hands were beating hands. I looked behind me: Reeni still hadn't returned. Shakily, I wandered downstage, took a very cautious bow. No stones, no bad meat, no soft fruits. Just applause. I thumbed closed a nostril, the left nostril, and took another bow, from the waist that time.

I spotted a few overdressed zoms, and even they were clapping, but in slow motion.

The balconies were blears of flickas, were noisy, shouty. Piercing whistles came from the loges. The orchestra rippled.

And seated there in the orchestra, on the aisle, tenth or eleventh row: Sharkey and Laudermilch. Sharkey was clapping wimpily, Laudermilch not at all.

Then the applause turned abruptly to boos, to catcalls, and the rocks and the cinders, the crisp rose stems and the greenmolded cheeses, the little corked tubes of piss— they all were in the air at once, catching light.

But nothing struck me: only Reeni, who'd come back out and was standing across the stage like a statue. Still in her bridemask, still in her white dress spotted now with my blood, still as a Normal. They were jeering only her, slinging their ammo just her way.

I couldn't figure it.

I glanced back over the house again. Individual faces moved into focus: Normals with gray hair, red hair, white skin, black skin. Normals with contorted faces stoning the personification of themselves.

I couldn't figure it.

I felt like shouting: *Stop it!* Felt like shouting: *Me! Throw at me!* Felt like shouting: *What's the matter? What is the matter?*

Felt like shouting, but didn't: instead, I watched Reeni be splattered with homemade slime and with chicken blood, watched as butternuts and shriveled tubering potatoes, chunks of glass, cup handles, empty trank bottles and hacked-up dolls, even a child's small replica of an American orbiter, even a snowy paperweight, even a control box from pos-negative pants, even a cleric's cross, struck mercilessly at her mask and bashed off frags of painted papier-mâché. Finally, something small and round and silver grazed the spring release, and Reeni's mask fell in half and shattered on the stage.

And the audience lost its roar, its arms fell to its sides.

I bent and picked up the small and round and silver thing: it was a brooch minted with the face of a monkey. I closed my fist around it, let its pin zag across my palm, bloodying it.

I was angry, almost sick.

I couldn't figure it.

The audience was reaching for its coats.

And then I saw him: down there in the second row, left of center, a good-looking young Normal with brown hair and squinty eyes, strong-jawed, clean-shaven.

Mr. Sears-Roebuck. The face I'd constructed in my cellar, the mask I'd made.

Mr. Sears-Roebuck had soap-white hands and long, very long fingers. He lifted those fingers now and fluttered them. At me. At Reeni, who turned and half ran across the stage. She tore a strip of buttery-soft sleeve from her gown and dabbed my bloody nose with it, she laughed, she said: "Now it's all over. Last show. Now we can go home. Grinner, I love you, Grinner."

I shrugged away her touch, I looked back toward the slowly emptying house, I caught Sharkey's eye.

Then I turned my stare on Mr. Sears-Roebuck.

And tipped up my chin, and tipped it down: a nod.

Reeni screamed, her eyes mobbed with red specks: Laudermilch was lumbering down the aisle.

—Was seizing Mr. Sears-Roebuck, Flourface, was seizing my brother in a stranglehold. Immediately, a mask cheek was corduroyed, the chin was torn—and through that hole I saw a patch of bleached skin.

Reeni cracked me hard across the face with an open hand. I cracked her back.

"They're not gonna hurt him," I said. "They're not gonna hurt him. Not gonna hurt him!"

She'd begun to scream again . . . and down in the orchestra, openmouthed men and women Normals were pushing and shoving, tripping and sprawling into the aisles.

Flour was trying to pry his fingers between Laudermilch's forearm and his own trachea: pasty fingers scrabbling, wiggling, flexing.

I saw Sharkey shouldering his way through the crowd that was fleeing toward the exits. He was blocked, and, shouting, was currented rearward.

Reeni almost jumped from the stage. But I caught her in time, grabbed both of her wrists.

Flourface was grinding his thumb into Laudermilch's eye, he pressed his first finger against the bridge of Laudermilch's nose, until the fingertip broke off and stuck.

Three, four, five seconds later, Jack Laudermilch's skull exploded into a potluck of bone chips and brain samples. His body quivered, lifted slightly and toppled, smoking and geysering, over the back of an upholstered seat.

Flour wailed and tore at his melted mask, it came away in gooey strings that blistered his already bleeding hands. His real face was scorched raw. He bolted toward a side aisle.

And I pulled Reeni upstage without a struggle: she'd gone suddenly limp.

28
Backstage with the Fisticks, Plus One

Niles Sharkey turned his folded hands inside out and his knuckles popped. We were in my dressing room. I sat scrunched low in a rainbowy ragchair gazing mostly at my toes, their webbing. I couldn't look at Reeni, who was chain-smoking and grunting, chuckling like some lunatic with secrets.

Somehow, Flour had managed to duck from the hall and escape.

A single filament of clotting blood meandered across the instep of Sharkey's suede loafer.

I let my gaze climb from shoe to cuff, from cuff to knee, then I jumped it to his grim face, to his blinking gray eyes. His hair was peaked and rumpled. "How'd he get here?" And there was some browning blood on his shirt cuff.

"Don't ask me," I said. "Ask her! You knew he'd be here, didn't you, Reeni? You melted your mask on goddamn purpose. And you messed with the show just to give him a laugh. Didn't you?" Talking to Reeni, I talked at Sharkey.

"Did you know your brother-in-law would be here this afternoon, Mrs. Fistick?"

"What if I did? I was supposed to tell you? I'm not the person you have an arrangement with."

"Wait a second! I never made any arrangement with these—" I broke off as I swung my head around and met

Reeni's gaze, steady and fatal, the eyeballs cauliflower-pale, no flagellums in the whites. "Sharkey. Tell this girl. Was I ever less than creepy to youse? Reeni. What, you think—? Sharkey, *tell* her. Tell *me*. How'd you know that was my brother? Did you see him wave? Reeni—the asshole shouldn't have waved. Why'd he wave?"

She kept staring like a mechanical gypsy in a coin-op tarot booth. Then said she was going next door to change. And if anybody minded, well, shit.

When she was gone, I clenched an impotent fist, then burst it open as if there were dice to be tumbled. "I hope you know you just ruined my entire fucking life! Why didn't you wait? Youse coulda grabbed him outside—what was with that rhino shit down the aisle?"

"It wasn't my idea. Unfortunately, it was Jack's."

"Thanks a lot!"

"Jack Laudermilch doesn't have a head."

"You're telling me?"

Sharkey picked his coat up from the chaise longue. He put it on and stuffed his hands in the pockets, he played with some coins. "Why'd you tip us? Finally?"

"Shit. I don't know."

"You surprised me."

"*I* surprised me. I can't figure it. Maybe I didn't even. Maybe I was just *looking* at Flour and you seen his hands. Poss—"

He started to leave, there were cops swarming the hall, you could hear leather squeak, walkie-talkies. "I'll be in touch."

"Hold on! What about your part of the deal?"

"It stands."

"Stands, crap. It best start walking. You *owe* me!"

"I don't see any fish. Present company excluded."

Alone, I stood in my robe at the cheval mirror, nodding over and over again, as curtly as a commandant at a military execution, as leisurely as an emperor opening court, and trying to decide: had it been deliberate, my gesture to Sharkey? Yes. Hold on, hold on—*no!*

Yes.

I took out my salt bottle.

Reeni didn't come back. I finally went next door and found her chunked bridemask—a welter of stains, a riddle of pits—plus her spattered wedding gown, stuffed together in a wastebasket. She'd gone without me.

And so, wrecked on sodium chloride, I dressed by trial and error, made up slovenly, collected all of my things and found my swaying way outside and down to the car-park.

Pigeon's steering wheel was slippery with pomade, the driver's cushion was poulticed with used tea bags.

No tip for the grinning garage attendant.

Part Six:
The Cavewoman
(January, 2011)

29
Egg in an Ice Cube

Ma handed me the claw hammer. I had nails in my mouth, I spat out a few and whacked them into plywood. I'd already boarded up two porch windows, last one to go. Done. I tossed the hammer back in the toolbox and Ma flipped the lid closed with her foot. "They bothered you again last night?" she asked.

"Didn't know they had so much energy. Were outside until almost six o'clock. Shifts."

"They didn't try to break in, though?"

"Nah—but if I'd left the door unlocked, they sure woulda *walked* in. At the knob for hours, twisting."

"You shoulda come stay with us."

"If Reeni shows, I wanna be here."

"They bother you again tonight, I want you to move in with your father and me tomorrow. I mean this."

"I'll be all right, it's not zombies I'm worried about."

"What about sleep, are you getting any rest?"

"Ma . . ."

She whipped around, pressed her groin against the porch rail and glared across Neptune Avenue: half a dozen communard zoms, all Normal and all bundled up for a blizzard, milled on their front steps. Their hatted heads lifted slackly when Ma cupped her mouth and shouted: "You leave my son alone! He's done nothing to you!"

"Ma, quit it—please? Let's go inside."

"Well, but why are they hounding *you*?"

"I tried to harm their eggman."

"You did no such thing!"

"That's what the papers said." The papers said I'd "co-operated with drug enforcement authorities."

"A little twitch in the wrong direction and they have you passing signals to the police. It makes me sick."

The newspapers had also reported a few "facts" about Jack Laudermilch, deceased: 39, a bachelor, a decorated marine who'd seen action in Kuwait and California, where he'd suffered a chest wound in Sacramento during the seventeen-day Western Secession of '98; an agent of the Bureau of Restricted Drugs, a six-year veteran. But there'd been nothing, in either news stories or sidebars, that connected him with the spacers.

The hell with Laudermilch. Reeni was missing.

I hadn't seen her in ten full days, not since backstage at Carnegie Hall.

Christmas had come (Ma had fixed a plate of reheated turkey and brought it over to me in the evening), and Christmas had gone ("Make just one resolution, Grinner," Da had suggested when he phoned on New Year's Eve. "Only one: a hermit's life for me!").

Ten full days, and each day I'd gone and passed several boring hours in Skully's apartment, waiting. No Reeni. Just Mrs. Scocco, who dropped in occasionally with tins of anise cookies and made sure that old Lazarus had enough blankets, sponge-bathed him and cooked his pablums.

Nine long nights, and each night I'd come home and lock my doors and stay clear of the windows, and wait. No Reeni. Just zombies, who stationed themselves like stooped totems on the frosted lawn or tramped across the porch stammering threats and warnings.

No Reeni, no messages, no anything . . .

Squatted, Ma slid a pan of open-face cheese sandwiches under the broiler. She got up and sniffed at encrusted stove pots, raised her state trooper shades and scrutinized dishes for smudges and cemented bits of food. "What is this, animal land? Should I even bother to ask whether you've been sleeping in a bed? If I looked, be honest, would I find a salt ring in the bathtub?"

"What've you heard, Ma? Anything?"

"I heard he's doing all right, thank God," and screwed the catch basket into the sink drain, ran hot water. "He's got a bad burn on his face. But you already knew that." And squirted green detergent.

"What about Reeni?"

"I heard she's with him. Doing nursey stuff."

"Where?"

Ma shook suds from her fingers, threw me a vague, and vaguely scolding, glance: "I don't know."

"Who's been giving you these bulletins? Dinah Murphy?"

"For one." And brilloed crusties from the burger grill, rinsed it. She dried her hands and checked on the sandwiches. The provolone was blistered and puffy, the muffin halves were burnt. She grabbed a plate and a spatula. But I couldn't eat, not a bite: the cheese goo gave me a fresh hit of the guilts.

Flour wailed and tore at his melted mask . . .

"And what's she been saying about me? Dinah?"

"Nothing. What, you want a piece of cake instead?"

"I'm not in the mood."

Ma sat down. "You've seen that policeman again?"

"No."

"He called you, though."

"Twice."

"And? Come on, we can't talk?"

"The same old stuff. Where's Flour? I go, I don't know. He goes, I'll be in touch. Dinah really didn't say anything? I put them boards up more on account of the Dragon than zombies."

"I'm sure Alan's friends are gonna realize it wasn't your fault. Eventually."

"So she did say something. What?"

"Just don't be seen with that policeman. If he comes here, you don't be home."

"She said that?"

"What you call, implied."

"They're watching me?"

"They won't hurt you."

"Who says?"

"Your brother Alan says. That's what I heard."

"Alan says."

"Grinner . . . if you're not going to eat your food, at least don't play with it."

I dropped the sandwich, molten side to plate, that I'd piked with a knife.

It wasn't until after Ma left that I realized she'd called me Grinner. For the very first time, to the best of my recollection.

That same afternoon, I got a postcard from Beef, a matte picture of the New York Hospital for Special Surgery, under glossy blue skies. The food was great (he'd scrawled), his readjustment counselor was a redhead with "bombs where they count," and the op was scheduled for Wednesday.

Today.

He'd signed the note: "Your friend, Big Jim," and jotted a phone number—"In case you want it."

I tossed the card into a garbage can on my way over to Skully's. The pair of zombies who were trailing me fetched it out, tore it into strips and smidgens—in case it was a coded message for narcs.

With bombs where they count.

Two Newsboys had been arrested yesterday for the killing of Cleo Nothing.

They admitted blowing her body up, as a proper send-off, but claimed she'd already been dead and rigored when they found her on the studio floor blanketed with primed canvas unraveled from a bolt.

On television, I'd seen one of the accused, a thirteen-year-old kid with rope burns on his neck who called himself Aftermath Nothing: "She looked pretty with her head on backwards," he said. "Somebody bust her neck, but not us." Beef's op was today.

"Skully. Shit. Don't you ever take a breather?"

He was standing on a bedroom chair, pushing up a ceiling panel. He reached in and brought out a shoe box. I helped him step down.

The shoe box was filled with French's mustard jars. He opened one and began to feed himself death eggs, shells and all.

"So have you heard from your daughter?"

He thought for a moment then mouthed the word: *once.*

"What'd she say?"

He shrugged then mouthed the words: *hello . . . phoned.*

"Hello, that's all? Shows how much she really cares. Go off and desert you like that. They do that, don't they? Desert a guy."

He lay down on the bed and shut his eyes.

I shrouded him with a great-grandmother's quilt.

I discovered three more shoe boxes hidden away in the drop ceiling and spent three quarters of an hour bombing eggs into the toilet, flushing them away . . .

Sometime past midnight, I heard Skully moving around in his bedroom. He came quaking into the parlor and stood there, encysted head thrust forward, shoulders hunched, an empty mustard jar in each bony grip. Openmouthed, he stared at me. I brushed salt from my jeans, refolded the bag. "Whyn't you sit? Something I wanna tell you."

With a moist howl, he pegged his jars. One bounced off my kneecap, the other missed and burst against a table. He shuffled out to the kitchen and worked a long ice-cube tray from the freezer. He put it down on top of the stove, bridging two burners. Several green shapes showed below frozen bubbles: his emergency stash.

He guarded the stove with a bread knife.

Like a desperado with the posse's drop on him, I raised my hands. "I'm just trying to do you a favor, Dad. Nothing malicious. What do you think I am, anyhow—malicious?" And gave a snort. "I just don't wanna see you fooling yourself, wasting your time. You're still a young guy, you know?"

Without removing his gaze from my face, he tested an ice cube with a finger. It was still frozen solid.

With some effort I partly cleared my head of salt fog, and started: "Some things," I said, "you can get, if you try hard enough. Isn't that right?" I'd rehearsed.

Skully sucked in his lips, narrowed his eyes. I wasn't expecting sarcasm from such a gone zombie. I was just hoping for a little comprehension.

"I mean," I said, "you work and you bust your balls and you accomplish something—that's the way of the world outside, yeah? Normals don't have an exclusive on that. I always wanted Reeni, for instance. Always. Ever since I was a kid. I mean, there were others—I bet—who wanted her. Maybe just as much as me. But I worked harder, you know, at it. And I won—'cause I could give her what she wanted most. You see?"

He was frowning, he turned the burner flame on low.

"And what she wanted," I said, "was to be free. Not to worry. Come-and-go free."

There was some water shining now on the surface of the ice cubes.

"And if I try—if I *wanna* try, and I *do*—I can get Reeni to come home again. Now. And remember what she wanted. What she *wants*. If I see her I can work hard, I can get results."

Skully turned up the flame a little.

"On the other hand," I said, "there's some things you can't get no matter *what* you do. Skully, I'm talking about

Olga now. I'm talking about you can't have her back.
Dead is dead, Skully. Even if you egg down till you're
ninety-five, you'll never see her. Maybe—how do I know?
—you'll see her when you finally go for good. But not before. You been fooled, Skully. It's not fair but you been
fooled."

He pulled up gently on the tray handle—a squeak, a
crunch.

I said: "It's dark when you do eggs, isn't it? Just about
as dark as you can imagine. Just about as dark as space
must be—when you get out there where there's no stars. Or
maybe just a few stars—two or three. Or six."

He selected a cube and cupped it in his hands, trying to
melt it faster with body heat. Water trickled through his
fingers.

I told him about Niles Sharkey. "He *admitted* what he
was, Skully. A spacer."

I told him what Niles Sharkey wanted, and why. "The
eggs don't free the soul, Skully. Just the mind. You're not
gonna find Olga waiting in some elbow of the universe for
you, Dad. You been fooled. Everybody's been fooled. And
you know whose fault it is? Same person who fooled Reeni.
Who's been feeding you eggs and feeding her lines. Who's
been promising the both of you happiness where you can't
find it. You can't find it in space, Skully, and she can't find
it in Freaktown."

He was shaking his head back and forth. I started shaking
mine up and down. "I'm telling you, Skully, for your own
good. Why should anybody go on fooling himself? That
don't make any sense."

He shuffled from the kitchen with the melting cube still
closed in his fist. His eyes were shut, he was navigating by
memory.

"I figured you should know. I figured you could handle
it."

I stood in the kitchen, I heard his bedroom door shut.

I found the death egg, still skinned with ice, on a dampening patch of black dirt in a glazed white pot of withered English ivy.

"Oh my God!"

"I was sleeping, Ma. I didn't hear a thing."

"You'd think his weight woulda pulled the fixture right outta the ceiling."

"You haven't seen him, Ma. He weighed, like, seventy, eighty pounds."

"But still! Oh my God . . ."

"I'm taking care of everything. And Mrs. Scocco's here."

Mrs. Scocco was sitting on the couch, wringing her monstrous hands.

"Do you want me to come over?"

"No, Ma, it's all right. Just, if you could, call Dinah Murphy. We have to make sure Reeni gets word."

"I'll do that now. What about the wake?"

"Kessler and Kozakowski's: They'll have him ready tonight. So you tell Dinah—tell her that Reeni can come tonight."

"I can't believe the man did this."

"And I keep thinking: if I'd only been goddamn awake . . ."

"It's not your fault."

"I know," I said, "I know it, but . . ."

"I'll make that call."

We hung up.

Mrs. Scocco pressed her anemic lips together and stretched out her hand to me. I took it and squeezed it briefly, then I let it go: I didn't like touching such an ugly thing, and I didn't want to be touched.

"He's in heaven right this minute," she whispered. "I'm sure of it."

I stooped and snatched up my salt bag, closed it with a twist-tie.

If I see Reeni, I can work hard. I can get results.

I'd always worked hard. Trying for results. It was the way of the world outside. I belonged there. I tried for results. I wanted.

When I see her.

Tonight.

"Don't blame yourself, Grinner."

I looked at Mrs. Scocco. "I'll try not," I said.

30
Wake

The calling hours began at seven.

I came into the funeral chapel with Ma and we knelt down together at Skully's burnished-copper casket. Four golden crosses stood inside the open lid flanking, like bodyguards, an intentionally bleared holy-gram—a levitated unsmiling Christ bathed in a pearly aura, butterscotch grace flowing from his scarred palms.

In greasepaint, Skully's corpse-face looked almost Normal. The embalmers hadn't bothered resurfacing his hands —they'd just stuck gloves on them and plaited the fingers with rosary beads.

I blessed myself and sat down on a folding chair. I looked at the flowers:

There were flagging lilies from my parents.

There was a modest horseshoe wreath of yellow rosebuds from Mrs. Scocco.

There was a huge basket of American Beauties with a diagonal gold banner stamped *Dad*, and, in smaller script, *Irene & Charles*. I'd ordered that.

And finally there was a tall wickerwork choked with burnt-orange hydrocephalic bulbs, fog-lemon legumes as moistly ribbed as vagina barrels, electric-blue sunflowers eyeballed with bituminous-black membranes, fleshy bellflowers whose tightly clustered pistils quivered and made a morbid ticking. Tiny graymold lozenges trimmed with silvery lice served as baby's breath. The pennant was sheet percale, hand-lettered: *Beloved Father*.

Ma took the seat next to mine. She picked through her bag, pulled out a tissue and blew her nose. She sniffled and stared at Reeni's bouquet. "Where'd she find those? In the Blofeld Hole?"

"You think?"

"Well, they're not FTD, are they?" Gingerly, she removed her snowy hat from her black wig.

Da came in and paid his respects at the coffin, making the sign of the cross with his clickity steel hand.

I leaned over and asked Ma: "You two . . . all right these days?"

"Oh, yes, things are back to normal. At last."

"He hasn't gotten rough again?"

"Just that once," she whispered. "Just that one time." And smiled.

Da was wearing sunglasses and a false epidermis of pallid lotion and rosy powder. He was wearing an overcoat and overshoes, a quizzical frown. He sat and crossed his legs, then uncrossed them. He put his head back. He seemed to shrink a tiny bit with each breath he expelled, as if blood and organ atoms were hitching themselves to the carbon dioxide.

I'd tried speaking with him earlier while Ma dressed and deliberated over sundry wigs. I'd found him seated at his cleared desk listlessly notching the mahogany top with his mechanical fingertips. I said: "You can't be serious, you can't just lose all your curiosity on account of what happened with Ma. We should sit down together, we could work out some arrangement." He looked pained, he looked tempted, he went off to put on his makeup . . .

When I went out to grab a smoke, Niles Sharkey was deferring to Dinah Murphy at the register book. He goggled at her quartet of breasts and grinned. I ignored him and thanked Dinah for coming. Her eyes—chilly little citrine balls—darted to mine and darted away. She walked into the chapel.

"Let me," said Sharkey, "offer my condolences."

"Screw your condolences. You got no business here."

"Is she coming?"

He followed me around a corner and into the lounge.

"I asked you if she was coming."

"Wouldn't you come?" I sat down, lit up and pulled over an ashtray stand.

"Do you figure she's been with him all this time?"

"No, I figure she's been in Bermuda."

"Let me have one of those, Grinner."

I hesitated, then tossed him my cigarette pack. He had his own lighter, a black one engraved with the spacer insignia.

"If she comes, Grinner, we can wrap this up tonight. You and me."

"You're a careless mother, Sharkey. Or is it deliberate this time?"

He looked at his lighter, he looked at me. "I guess it's deliberate." He sat back and stretched out his long legs and crossed them at the ankles. "I'm going to tell you something, in the cause of mutual trust. It's this. You guessed right about the fish. About me."

"And about the death eggs?"

His torso rolled forward. "About the *mind* eggs—yes, about those, too."

"How?"

"Beats us. A fluke, serendipity—it happened. Same way you Freaks happened. Start with microwaves, stir in some exotic radiation, season with electricity, add chemicals and maybe even a pinch of native air pollution. You fool around long enough in the kitchen, sometimes you bake a cake, sometimes you make a mess. Other times you wind up with a messy cake."

"Nice fucking attitude."

"Look, I wasn't even with the spacers in 1988. Christ, they were still called astronauts and I was still in college. Blame Halley Tumpel, if you have to blame somebody. But what's the point? Calamity happens every day, all over the world. That's *our* point. We're working against a deadline, we're trying to find a new home—is that so villainous? Tell the truth. There has to be thousands of earth-type planets out there just waiting for Americans. We want a second chance."

"Who's Halley Tumpel?"

"Your Thomas Poole."

"So you find some planet," I said. "How's everybody gonna get there? You plan on running buses?"

"You mentioned Sam LaPilusa to me once. Well, Sam's research wasn't involved with mind rockets. He was working on something we call a Beeline—a molecular scrambler. You move objects—or people—from here to there same as they were voices on a radio."

"Did it work?"

"We understand he scrambled a cufflink from one oven into the other but it melted. However, it's a start. Some spacers in Georgia are doing similar experiments using corpses. We'll have success, eventually. Soon, maybe. But first we have to find a suitable planet."

"The eggs won't help you. The trip don't include planets. Just six faraway . . . lights."

"But when we *get* the fish, we can *work* with them, try to make them produce slightly different eggs, eggs that'll take us to more interesting places. We'll change their diet, the composition of the water they swim in, we'll irradiate them a little more . . . we'll grind them up and feed them to larger fish. And maybe the larger fish'll shit better eggs. We'll see what happens. We'll fool around."

"Fool around."

"More or less." He stubbed out his butt and blew smoke down his nose. "By the way, we think we finally figured out where, specifically, in space every zombie's mind is zooming. On a computer it prints out as seven Roman letters, three Greeks and fourteen hyphenated numerals. The *Everlasting Streak* passed the zone about a month ago."

"I seen."

"You and more than a few zombies. But I understand they interpreted it just as an awesome green-and-silver seraph. Those people are so banal you wonder if they're even worth saving."

"That's all you talk, save. From what?"

Sharkey looked amused, then vexed. "Where've you been? The world's got skin cancer, Grinner. It's got lung cancer. Brain cancer. It's dying. We want to survive, we take our leave."

"That's what Cleo said. It's dying, she said." I patted all of my pockets, searching for the little film canister that I'd loaded with salt tabs. I found it. Save, I thought. Brain cancer. Bullshit. Not fair! Not true, couldn't be true. Nobody calls the game till I've had my turn at bat. "And Cleo was crazy."

"But only," said Sharkey, "in her response to reality. About reality itself, she was quite perceptive. Unlike some people. But let's talk about your brother again. And see what we're going to do."

"Wait one more second. One more. You answer me something first. This guy Tumpel, why'd he do his fooling around in a house in the middle of a city?"

"Why'd Sam LaPilusa conduct his research in Toledo? So he could be near the art museum. He used to wander over there every afternoon to look at the glass collection. Swear to God. Funny guy. Mother ought to be shot. And Halley, Halley always said he got inspired by the smell of coffee in the air. Another funny bird. He said on Blofeld Street he could smell the beans from the Maxwell House factory. See? Everybody looks for wormy conspiracies when, mostly, things are simple. Things are more like comic books than Rosetta Stones."

"Caliban's Night happened 'cause some shithead liked to whiff coffee? This is what you're telling me?"

"You try to pamper genius. You try to take care of those

that really count. Because in the end your pampering bene-
fits everybody.”

“That house was in the middle of a city!”

“Who expected it to blow like that?”

“A city, we’re talking.”

“Of a few hundred thousand.” He shrugged. “A few, hundred, thousand. Fortunately, Halley Tumpel wasn’t home
the night the furnace exploded.”

“Furnace?”

“Right. It wasn’t even his fault—the cellar furnace went
and took everything else with it. It was in the Blast Report.”

“My father never mentioned a furnace. And he read that
report a million times.”

“I guess it must’ve been in Wilma’s classified report. Not
to contradict what I just said, but occasionally—*occasionally*—there are some conspiracies. Some. Benevolent.”

I lit a fresh smoke, it scorched my tonsils, I crushed it out
and stood up. “Why’d you tell me? You wouldn’t before.”

“Before I didn’t think I could trust you. You proved I
can. And as I told you earlier: I want you to trust me. We
need each other, we’re in the clinch. Bad guys and good
guys. Choose and be chosen. I can’t stay around here tonight. Your brother’s friends all know my face now. But
you’ll be here. And when your wife arrives—well, either
you find out where she’s just come *from*, or you follow her
where she’s going back *to*. And then you let me know about
it.”

“Don’t trust me, Sharkey. I don’t want you to.”

“Ah, Grinner, we’ve come this far. Let’s finish things up.
And tomorrow you’ll feel like a new man. Exactly like a
new man.”

“You suppose I’m gonna keep quiet about Caliban’s
Night? When I know?”

“Certainly I do. Why should you make any stink? Do you
really care about ancient history? I think you’re more concerned with the rest of your life. I’m a good judge of char-

acter, Grinner. Besides, we'd deny it and you'd be dead inside of a month." He buttoned on his carcoat. "Grinner . . . I was wondering. About the wake, I mean. Couldn't have come at a better time. Very neat. I was just wondering if you had anything to do with her father's—"

"You must be crazy! What do you think I am, anyhow?"

"I think," he said, "that you're much like me. And it's certainly something I would've considered." He picked up one of Skully's memorial cards from a plate and wrote a phone number across the picture of Christ praying in Gethsemane. "When you find out from Maureen, you let me know about it."

I sat alone in the lounge. Sharkey *must* be crazy, I thought. I had nothing to do with Skully's suicide, it wasn't my fault! I'd only been trying to help him . . .

I tore the holy card in two but pocketed the halves.

Tomorrow you'll feel like a new man.

But I already felt like a new man, somehow. Everything I did lately seemed right and natural at first—only later on, later on, all seemed unreal, the actions of a crazy stranger. I *felt* changed but didn't look it. And my hands were flapping now on my knees like two hooked sunfish cut loose on a lakeside dock. Too much salt, too much salt. Should lay off for a week, just lay the hell off . . .

I started back to the chapel. Cutting across the vestibule I heard someone knocking at the front door. Veered to answer. (Where was the funeral director? And caught a glimpse of him—he was a Normal whose pituitary glands had turned him so hulking he looked almost kin to Freaks—presiding languidly over his alcoved desk, a wrinkled circular from a men's clothier in his hands, caramel cubes and black tranks arranged on the blotter like two enemy platoons of toy soldiers.) Answered the door (be-Reeni, be-Reeni . . .), and called to Pigeon Mary. She was already down at the bottom of the steps.

The night was swirled with corn snow, the ground was

blanketed, telephone wires and tree branches sagged under white piping.

"Grinner, what's the idea? The door's locked."

I looked, and she was right: someone had turned the bar to the vertical on the inside knob.

Pidge came in unraveling her scarf. She blew on her hands even though her feathers had grown seasonally thicker. Thicker plumage on her cheeks, too. She was carrying Cleo Nothing's flicka-bag. "Did she come yet? Reeni?"

"Not yet."

"Grinner? Have you heard from Beef?"

"I got a postcard—when? Yesterday."

"No, I mean in person. Because I phoned him before at the hospital but he's gone. And the people I talked to there— they sounded very strange. They asked me if *I'd* seen him!"

"He was supposed to stay a coupla weeks."

"Don't I know it. But he's gone."

"What do you mean, strange they sounded?"

"Like they were angry about something. And they were short with me—wouldn't answer any of my questions."

I took her into the chapel, then stationed myself against the baize wall. Mrs. Scocco had arrived. She was speaking to Ma. Da was still gazing openmouthed at the chinky plaster ceiling. Dinah Murphy stood up, folded her coat on the seat of her chair and slipped out.

I waited a few seconds and walked after her. She wasn't in the vestibule but the front door had been locked again. And the door below the staircase leading to the basement mortuary was ajar. I took the steps down and passed through a large room where caskets were stockpiled, through a smaller room filled with bottled chemicals, and into a long and chilly slab-floored room: three steel sinks, a white porcelain cabinet and a sheeted corpse on a table with coaster-wheels.

"She coming now, Di?"

Dinah jumped, as though broomhandled in the southernmost spinal knob, and spun around from the receiving doors. She puffed air. "Pretty soon," and squinted. "I expect you unlocked the upstairs door on me."

"No. But you don't have to worry about Sharkey. He's gone. It's safe."

I shouldered past Dinah when there was an easy tap on the receiving doors. I rolled them open.

Reeni stood at the bottom of the driveway with flakes of coarse snow melting in her scalp fur. Her jacket shoulders and sleeves were soggy. She looked at me for a long moment with a null expression. She came in. I closed the doors. I blew a cough into my fist. She sent Dinah back upstairs.

I said: "Reen, I'm real sorry. I was asleep when he did it."

All of Reeni's fingertips were about twenty millimeters too long.

She said: "Did you find where Daddy kept all his papers? About the cemetery plot, and like that?"

"Haven't looked. We can look for them together later tonight. After the wake."

"I'm not going home with you after the wake. Don't kid yourself. I'm going back."

"You're not serious."

"He needs me. Thanks to you." A lonesome red strand birthed from her left iris and went floating lazily around the eyeball. Three, four, five strands were squiggling already through the right one.

"Reeni, I didn't betray him on purpose. It was an accident. I was all grogged—I mean, that was some surprise you pulled on stage."

She said nothing. She wasn't looking at me. She was looking at the tabled cadaver.

"But how is he? Flour. Is he all right?"

"He'll be all right."

"I'm glad to hear that, Reen. Honest to God, I'm glad to hear that."

Slowly, she raised her teeming eyes to my face, forced a laugh.

"When he's better but—you are gonna come back, aren't you, Reen? We'll start fresh, right Reen? I been sick, I haven't—"

"Shut up and lemme see my father."

We started up the stairs. She led. Green thorns and mashed fruit pulp were mingled with snow and mud clods that dribbled and slid from her rubber boots. Some bits of the pulp burned coldly, like fireflies.

Reeni braced herself inside the chapel. She filled her lungs and walked stiffly up to the bier. Pigeon Mary and Mrs. Scocco were gone. Dinah Murphy sat alone twisting her rings. My father, head still thrown back, seemed fast asleep. My mother cocked her chin, lifted her eyebrows interrogatively. I shrugged at her, I crossed my fingers.

Reeni dropped onto the padded kneeler and covered her face with her hands.

I sat down next to Da. I could see that his eyes were open behind his sunglasses. He'd wrung a memorial card into a torsade. Suddenly, I wanted to tell him all about Sharkey and about Caliban's, free of charge. Then I didn't want. Then I did. Didn't. All within a span of ten seconds, no longer. I thought I might fall off the chair so I held on with two hands.

I thought I might laugh out loud.

I got an idea to hold my breath till my brain starved.

I curled my toes until the arches cramped.

Ma leaned across Da to peck at my knee. "You're breathing strange. Are you all right?"

"Fine," and watched Reeni stand up, her knees buckle. She steadied herself and lifted her right hand like an oath taker, let it fall onto her father's face. It lay there a few moments. Then she curled her fingers slightly and raked them gently down Skully's cheek, thick pancake grouting anthropoid nails. When she withdrew the hand finally there were four parallel plow lines on her father's face. Yellow knobs were visible in them.

She turned around dry-eyed and gazed at Ma, at Da, at me. She nodded, she tucked her chin and walked rapidly from the chapel.

Da snagged my shirt cuff with his stainless fingers when I jumped to my feet—flannel ripped. "Leave her be, let her breathe!" Da blazed. "You goddamn traitor—goddamn monster!"

He burst into tears. I'd never seen him cry before. He shook and sobbed and his right-hand fingers tinkled emptily, like wind chimes.

I ran from the room.

Dinah tried blocking me at the basement door. I shoved her aside. Caught up to Reeni in the embalming room . . .

There was the time I'd caught up to Reeni in Columbia Park. We'd been racing, tagging, and I'd tackled her on the brown October grass and her fur had felt thick and soft, so good. And she'd said: *I love you*. We were thirteen.

There was the time I'd caught up to Reeni at the end of an alley in back of a transients' hotel near Journal Square. We'd been chased by half a dozen Normal kids in satiny coach jackets, we'd outrun them. Reeni was panting, her teeth were chattering like telegraph keys. Her eyes were wet. She'd pressed herself against me. And said: *I'm scared*. We were sixteen.

And there was the time I'd caught up to Reeni after she bolted during one of the first Normal parties that Studebaker booked for us. One minute she'd been standing naked in the cloakroom, the next minute she was gone. I'd found her wandering the dewy grounds of the big house in East Hampton. I'd walked with her, my arm encircling her waist, telling her, *Don't listen to any remarks, it's okay, it's all right, forget it. Soon we'll be just as good as these people.* And she'd said: *Take me home, I wanna go home* . . . We were twenty.

I caught up to Reeni in the embalming room, I snatched her wrist, babbled apologies, pleaded: "Don't!"

And this time, at this catching-up, she said nothing at all.

She squeezed through the half-open doors and slogged up the drive toward the street. Toward the gray Mercury Dallas parked at the curb and chauffeured and shotgunned by fat Bobby Lumps and Gulchface from the shoe store. Before jumping in, Reeni turned and saw me charging up the snowy slope behind her. She swung her head from side to side to side to side . . .

31
Starring the Beefstone

The silent film had a title: *Death of an Exhausted Species: A Paradigm.* The title was painted on a cue card, and the cue card was signed: Cleo Nothing.

They were showing the film on the late television news.

I stood watching it in Pigeon Mary's parlor while she sat slumped in an armchair. I'd come straight here from the funeral parlor, intending to borrow her car. I had a yellow bag of her iodized salt tucked in my elbow like a football.

The Christmas tree was still in place. Most of its needles had fallen, the branches were dry, the strung lights weren't burning. Even the topping angel was dark . . .

The film began with a tight shot of Cleo Nothing's head, the back of it—awry sprigs of jet hair. Then: columnar throat, naked shoulders dusted with tiny freckles. A moment out of focus, a brown blur, as Cleo moved away from the camera lens—

The newscaster had said she'd concealed her camera inside of a wall.

—to reveal Beef parked in a sand chair. He was frowning, studying his hands. Cleo reentered the frame. She was nude, her vertebrae were protuberant, her buttocks long and flat and speckled with blackheads. She knelt in front of Beef. Her heels and soles were dirty, her calves blistered with oil paint—cerulean blue, raw sienna, titanium white. Beef's expression grew slowly pained, then swiftly angry. His eyes cut from the crown of Cleo's head to a boneyard of seared stretcher strips, to a stack of newspapers, to a bundled drop cloth. He shook his head in vehement refusal, pushed Cleo away and stood up. She followed him to the windows. They were taped over with broad sheets of parcel paper.

Beef gummed his lips and rolled his eyes. Cleo shouted and jerked on his forearm. She thumbed her fingers like a moneylender. Grudgingly, Beef nodded consent, and Cleo lowered herself meltingly to the floor, she lopped her head. Beef stood above her, he made fists—

Pigeon Mary lurched forward, dry-heaving.

—but then he shook his head again, no! And turned, and started crossing the room. Cleo, her face frenzied now, snatched up a charred strip of wood and flung it. It grazed Beef in the small of his back, tearing a gash in dark-red stewmeaty skin.

Cleo's mouth moved, her lips split wide open.

Beef picked up the strip and slapped it against his palm, he strode back to Cleo. Then, with his eyes closed and his face blank, he raised the club and brought it down crushingly hard on the base of her skull. He flung it away, exited from the frame.

Furry white glare, film sprockets, inky blackness . . .

Pigeon Mary, doubled over with cramps, hugged herself and rocked.

The newsman was saying the police had found several dozen "so-called" manifestos in the wall, as well as the camera and the exposed film. "Insane" manifestos that "rambled" about new races and old races, about what new ones should do to old ones: "usurp and destroy." Cleo Nothing had also left behind a signed statement excusing Martin Stein from all blame. "The monster [she'd written] was correct. The monster was coaxed."

Nevertheless, the police were searching for the "monster," who'd apparently learned about the discovery of the "damaging" film and "fled" from the New York Hospital for Special Surgery "sometime after lunch today."

On a screen behind the newsman: a film clip of a tall

cowboy ambling down a dusty Western street, spinning around, drawing his six-gun and squeezing off three shots. The image froze. "Anyone seeing this man should contact police at . . ."

Slowly, Pigeon Mary got up from the chair. I glanced at her—she bent toward me—and then I glanced back at the set.

On the screen now was a sample of Cleo's work: I was the subject. With erection, I stood on a wet black rock, staring straight ahead, grinning. Below, a hand was breaking the muddy flood waters, its bleached and puffy fingers were curled, its wrist was surrounded by eddies. Splintered boards, bread wrappers, and condoms resembling jellyfish swirled past.

I stared until the weatherman appeared with his pointer: the snowstorm, he said, was moving out to the Atlantic, the front was Canadian, the flakes were carcinogenic . . .

Pigeon Mary switched off the TV. I stood where I was. She said: "What's he going to do?"

I said: "Pidge, I need your car. It's important."

She started to cry again, she flung her arms around me, she pressed her face against my chest.

I walked into the room and found Reeni with her arms around Flour, her face against his chest.

Pigeon Mary wanted to know what Beef was going to do. I wanted her car keys.

I stood on a wet black rock, staring straight ahead, grinning.

Reeni's mother was dead. She wasn't waiting in some elbow of the universe for Skully.

Skully was everlastingly dead.

I caught up to Reeni in the embalming room. She said nothing. Cleo Nothing was dead, too.

Pigeon held me, seeking comfort. I wanted her car but I closed my arms around her back. I squeezed, her feathers yielded, blood pounded in my fingertips. I wanted to leave but I stayed all night. She fell asleep. I sat on a wet black rock, staring. At Reeni, who flung a short-sleeved shirt over a shoulder. At Flour, as Mr. Sears-Roebuck, who sat waving at me from the second row, left of center. At an iced-over death egg melting slowly on black soil in a glazed white pot.

I had such a headful of blues. Greenmold. And clay . . .

32
Down the Hole

I fitted the two halves of the memorial card together and called Sharkey's number. It was a local exchange. I wondered where he'd set up base. A man with a hoarse voice answered. "He's not here but I can take a message. Is this Mr. Fistick?"

"Yeah. You can tell him to meet me at the shoe store, he knows which one. In about forty minutes. Tell him to wait in his car. Tell him I got what he wants."

"He'll be there."

"Who am I talking to? Is this Mr. Poole?"

He hung up.

Pigeon Mary watched me over the top of her juice glass. Her eyes were rimmed red, her facial feathers rumpled. I pocketed her car keys. "This Sharkey," she said. "Is he the same one I read about in the papers? The one whose partner—"

"It's the same guy."

"Then you just hand back those keys, Grinner. And get the hell out of here! I didn't believe what I'd heard about you, about what you'd done on stage. But I should've, huh? You and Beef, you and Beef—"

"You don't understand. I got it all figured out, it'll be okay."

"Give them back! Right now!"

"Would you just listen? I'm not gonna do anything, I just wanna see Reeni."

"And bring Sharkey along for—what? Marriage counseling?"

"I'm not going to the shoe store, Pidge. I just wanna be sure *he's* there. I'm going up Blofeld."

"Why?"

"I told you already. To see Reeni." Along with some salt tabs and some coins, I pulled out a few green thorns and a chunk of dried fruit pulp from my pocket. I held up the fruit. "This came off Reeni's boot last night. It's gotta be from the Hole. Another time, she was out with the Dragon selling eggs, and she came in with a bunch of freak mushrooms sticking to her coat. I should've thought, but I didn't: she went down Blofeld to pick up the eggs 'cause that's where the fish are. That's where Flour is. Why Lumps and the Dragon took me to the Hole: Flour lives in it. And that's why a guy named Four-quarters is buried in it—he was killed down there after he seen the fish."

Da's gumshoe chromosomes.

"Flour's in the Hole," I said.

But Reeni hadn't told me. That night at Skully's when I'd scraped the fungus from my jeans, she hadn't told me. She could've, but she didn't.

She didn't trust me.

Flour didn't trust me.

Flour says you can't trust Normals. He says he thought he told you that.

"I want her back, Pidge. I never intended all this shit to happen." I jiggled the car keys. "You still want these?"

"Poor Grinner," she said.

"I coulda stole them when you were asleep. But I didn't. I stayed with you, Pidge."

You get points for being human to people when they're blown down.

I walked into the room and found Skully twisting at the end of a urine-soaked sheet.

"I never intended everything to get so crazy."

"Neither did Beef," said Pigeon Mary. "I guess."

I went and dug out her car, I warmed the engine, I walked into rooms, onto stages. I pulled away from the curb just as a New York City police car turned into the street.

The snow hadn't been plowed, so it took me close to an hour to make it up to Blofeld. I parked on the Boulevard, looked to see if anyone was watching, then squeezed through the fence. As I walked down the slope, the snow (it was squelched with footprints, both coming and going) gradually thinned out until finally the fractured pavement was clean and dry. Ahead, I could see the tops of the botanical weirdworks. And got shivved with groin cramps, felt salt pangs start behind my sternum. But I was glad I hadn't taken any pills with me. I wanted a clear head. Because Reeni hadn't said anything when I caught up to her in the embalming room. And because everything I'd done lately seemed unreal now, the actions of a crazy stranger. His name was Charlie Fistick. He lived beneath scales, in back of a grin. And he'd begun to frighten me. He was twenty-two years old, but he'd never been born. He was a desperate spook, but I'd welcomed him in.

I ducked inside one of the shaky ticket booths when I spotted Bobby Lumps and the Dragon, Gulchface and the fox-headed dwarf come tramping through a clump of milky ivy. They each had flight bags on their shoulders, two bags apiece. They each lugged a cardboard box full of Mason jars. They lumbered past me and ducked through gaps in the cyclone fence.

I waded into the ivy (its oddly clustered berries bore a close resemblance to teaching models of complex atomic structures), located the steep path behind it and followed it cautiously down into the Hole. At the bottom, the air turned sultry, the ground spongy, the foliage denser. Pink sandpapery leaves like goliath cat tongues languished from gnarled, driftwood-gray branches. Underfoot, limp blades

of black-and-yellow striped grass parodied unconscious gar-
ter snakes. Thorn bushes barbwired every avenue. I'd borrowed Pigeon Mary's long bread knife. I used it now.

I found the place in less than five minutes. Dumb luck,
maybe, or maybe I'd been led there instinctively, by some
frail memory transistor. The shack. The shack that we'd
built—Flour and me and Reeni and Beefy and Lumps and
all the other Freak kids we'd played with—in two months
of summer Sunday afternoons way back in the middle of
the nineties.

It was as big as a pioneer cabin, banged together from
junk doors and scrap lumber—nothing mitered, chinks
galore. Windowless, and the roof had been tacked with tar
paper, was flocculent now with grapy moss. It stood canted
in a mushy clearing hieroglyphic with tracks.

Inside that cabin, Reeni had first taken off all of her
clothes for me. She'd stripped, I'd looked and said, *Nice*,
and she'd dressed again, slowly. We were nine years old.
You next, she'd urged, but I'd refused. So she'd teased:
What're you ascared of?

Nothing!

Well, do it then.

I don't feel like it—you mind?

What're you ascared of?

About her nakedness, I'd said, *Nice*. About my own, I
was terrified she'd laugh. Or, worse, flinch—as local Normals often did when they passed me on the street, as my
mother always did whenever she bathed me or smeared my
chest with mentholated decongestant.

What're you ascared of?

*Nothing! Just shut up, Reeni! And why'd you color your
dumb fur anyhow—it looks stupid!*

First I'd said: *Nice*. And meant it. Then I'd said: *Stupid!*
And meant that, too.

I slogged across the clearing and stood outside the cabin,
listening. A humming of pumps. Fish tanks.

I walked in and found Reeni with her arms around my brother, her brow buried in his chest.

I stood outside the cabin on a wet black rock, listening to the water filters hum.

I twisted the knob and pushed, the door eased open.

And there was Flourface sitting bare-chested on a stripped twin mattress. Whitewash flesh, his nipples like two licorice drops. Short black lips. His nine bulbs of rinsed-red hair. He wore beige jeans, fluffy white socks and a thick dressing on half his face. His right hand was swaddled in gauze. Surrounding him on the mattress were fish eggs on paper plates, loose cigarettes, a jar of ointment. Reeni was sprawled, facedown, on a second mattress.

There were fish tanks on bookshelves, on magazine tables, on the wide-plank floor. And swimming inside them were bloated goldfish the size of baseballs. Green eggs littered the gravel. Nets on helical wire handles hung from brads in the shack walls.

Flour closed his eyes and smiled. He opened his eyes and frowned. "Who's with you?"

"She dead?"

"Sleeping just. Sleeping Beauty. You come alone?"

"Yeah."

"Honest to God?"

"I wanna talk to you, Flour."

"Maybe you *think* you came alone." He was getting up. "Or maybe you're pulling another fasty."

"I'm telling you, don't worry. Sharkey's down Freaktown. It's okay. Trust me."

"Lemme see for myself." He grabbed a handful of fingertips from a soup bowl on the cold hotplate. He took a peek through the shack door.

"Satisfied?"

"Blame me for being nervous, do you, Grinner?"

"She really sleeping?"

"Shake her, for Christ's sake, if you don't believe me."

"I'll wait. We should talk first."

"Should we?" And folded himself down again on the mattress, kept the fingertips closed in a fist. "About what?"

"I wanna say I'm sorry."

"Oh, shit, keep it. You and your sorries, man. Is that all you came to say?"

"No, there's more."

Reeni shifted in her sleep, drew her knees to her chest, mumbled.

"See," said Flour. "Alive. Hasn't dropped one egg since she's been here. I'd like to think it was symbolic. But, truth is, she's just a conscientious nurse."

I watched a goldfish leak bubbles, extrude an egg. "Why'd you come to the show? Why'd you do that?"

" 'Cause I felt like it. 'Cause Reeni asked me. And 'cause it was my idea to change the rape around. A bunch of us were talking one night here and I said, That's the kind of Freak show *I'd* like to see. And Reeni said her too—why not? It was the last show youse were doing. Why not?"

"Your idea. So you gotta take blame for what happened."

"No kidding. I do? Well, if you say so, Grinny—you being the expert on blames and guilts."

"I didn't start this trouble."

"No, course you didn't." He threw a glance at Reeni, who'd just flung an arm across her face, sniffled, cleared her throat. He smiled. "*She did.* All her fault, really! Never could make up her mind. You, you always knew you were a monster. Reeni, she'd have doubts. Yes, I am. No, I'm not. I'd tell her, No, you're not. You'd go, Yes, you are."

"She chose me."

"That's right, she did. Not that you were ever convinced. A coward can't trust anybody."

"I'm gonna wake her up and she'll come home with me."

"She will, probably. I'm healing, Grinny, and you're bleeding. She always had a weakness for the pathetic. Like you say, she chose you."

"Okay, you're right. I admit it. I'm a coward. But I only wanna be safe, that's all. Me and Reeni. Safe."

Flour pinched up an egg and smirked at it. "You got a lot in common with my clients. I mean, what's safer than dead as a rock? And just to be more safe—not dead for good."

I sat down on Reeni's mattress and started rubbing her calf.

"Yeah, Reeni'll leave with you—don't worry," Flour said. "When she showed up here the day everything happened in New York, I figured *finally, finally*. It didn't take long but, to realize she wasn't gonna stay. I was hoping but I knew she wouldn't. 'Cause the thing about Reeni is— do you know what I'm gonna tell you?—the thing is, she wants safety as much as you do. Except you got different blueprints lately. You still say it's in the lay and texture of the skin, the color of the eyes. She thinks now maybe it's just a roof, a running toilet, a long night in a warm room, with videotapes."

"Reeni," I called, "wake up." She gave some quizzical grunts.

"Grin," Flour said. "When youse went on tour. Grinny, you listening? When youse went, Reeni didn't wanna help me distribute eggs. She was scared. But I told her, hey, just one favor. And you make some extra cash—help you guys save faster for your skins. She was scared but. So I said, please, *please*—and you know how she responds to that. I coulda done without her help. But I was hoping she'd discover she liked taking risks. My roof leaks here and the plumbing is primitive. Called no-plumbing."

"Reen," I said, "it's me."

She didn't want to wake up.

"Then once youse got back," Flour said, "I offered her more work. She didn't want it. She told me youse both were set on playing it . . . safe from here on. No more shows. No more running around with death eggs. *Freaks' Amour*, domestic style: take it soft and easy. But you had other ideas, so she wound up back here. And she ended up doing as many eggs as Skully done. A shitty kind of safe and not very happy."

Reeni rolled onto her back. She opened her eyes and saw me. Jerked up, shoulders banging the shack wall, busting scabs of antique paint.

"It's okay," I said. "I'm alone, it's all right."

She slumped once Flour had shown her a flickering smile and said: "Yeah, it's safe." I took her hand. She didn't snatch it back. "Reen," I whispered, "I can't find your father's papers, Reeni. You gotta help me." She began to cry, quietly.

While she collected her few personal items—a couple of blouses, some balled socks, three clippings of her father's obit—I stood watching goldfish.

Flour walked over and kissed her on the brow, he squeezed her shoulder and, "You took real good care of me," he said. "Sorry I couldn't do the same for you." He threw me a sidelong glance and shrugged.

Reeni came and joined me at the door, looking bowed as some crone.

"Grin?" I heard my brother call as we were turning to go. "You should tell me the story before you take off. Should I be outta here by this afternoon? In other words, will Sharkey be coming?"

Reeni's eyelids flipped up. The brown coloring vanished from her eyeballs. Her emotional syringe was poised ready to squirt blood.

I said: "Nobody's gonna come. Not Sharkey. Not me. Not Reeni."

"Fair enough."

"But what about you? How long you plan on staying down here?"

"Don't know. But I wouldn't concern myself, if I were you, Grinny. I like it. The climate's right. And I feel at home. Always have, here. Probably something you've never felt anywhere. At home."

He followed us outside, walked us to the edge of the clearing where there was a thick curtain of switchy branches and leathery brown leafage. Reeni was breathing heavily, traipsing slowly. It struck me then that she hadn't uttered a single word since waking: she'd wept as I spoke of Skully, she'd listened placidly to my apologies, blinked and sniffled when I kissed her woolly fingers and warty knuckles. Then she'd stood up, stepped off the mattress and begun to search around for her belongings.

She'd said nothing, still nothing, but at least she realized she belonged with me.

There'd be plenty of time later to debate running toilets versus the texture of skin.

Flour put a hand, the bandaged hand, on my arm. "Grinner. What we were talking about? Nobody's safe. Not ever. As long as you're not dead, you're not safe. A house could blow up, a bomb could fall, there's maybe toxins in your tomato. You wanna be safe, you're gonna be scared. And scared, you're liable to do anything. To anybody. Look at the Norms—they launch orbiters and they strangle Brainstorm. Look at you."

A nest of albino mice burst squealing from the underbrush.

Reeni drew a sharp breath.

Flour's eyes widened, his jaw dropped, he twisted his head to the right.

I saw Niles Sharkey a fraction of a second before my brother did. Then there was an explosion, a puff of gray smoke and several of the leaves confettied in front of us. Reeni covered her face with her hands, spun away, cracked her wrist against a tree trunk. And Flour was running, zagging through the muck. A Normal with a boyish face and short-cropped yellow hair charged through brambles and into the clearing. He dropped to one knee, extended an arm. His gunshot blasted a jagged hole through one of the shack's hollow-core wall doors. The gunman wore a loose khaki uniform with a spacer patch sewn above the breast pocket. Flour dove into the shack and kicked the front door shut. Reeni was balled down in the mud, hands clasped behind her neck.

I looked around frantically for Sharkey. He'd popped down, wasn't in sight. I glanced back at the gunman who stood rigidly in the center of the clearing as though at a target range. He fired again at the shack. I reached down to grab Reeni's hand, to drag her into a thicket, to drag her to safety.

The gunman fired again.

Reeni screamed, she whipped her head around and glared up at me: her eyes were two bulging sacs of dark-red blood. She hissed.

The gunman squeezed off a fourth shot.

On hands and knees, Reeni shied off, crab style. She jumped to her feet, made to plunge back into the clearing. I tackled her, I leapfrogged her, I straggled out into the clearing myself. There was a vacuum in my belly, a sump pump in my skull. I wanted to run away, *had* to run away. Instead, I shouted to the gunman: "You want them fish, you better stop! You listen! Wanna bust every tank?"

I kept walking. He aimed the gun at my head. "What're you, crazy? Don't you know who I am? I'm with Sharkey. It's okay. Now, my brother, he's got no gun, so whyn't you just stop?"

When he lowered the barrel and flicked his eyes to the shack, I drove Mary's bread knife deep into his forearm. His fingers sprang apart, the gun fell, I snatched it up. I waved it above my head—*Look, Reeni, look!* Only she wasn't looking at me: her face was turned toward Niles Sharkey, who'd reappeared holding an ugly blue-metal gun of his own. "You told me not to trust you, Grinner," he said. "So I didn't. I sat outside your friend's house all last night."

I raised my gun and felt giddy doing it. The small of my back tickled with electric flakes. The spacer I'd stabbed was walking in a tight circle. He was cursing and using a hand clamp as a tourniquet.

"Are we going to stand here the rest of the morning, Grinner?"

"Would you go away, Sharkey? Will you promise to go away?"

He smiled. "If I get what I want, I'll go. Sure."

"And the three of us?"

"The *three* of you?"

"Three. Reeni and me, you give us what you promised. And Flour, you let him walk. You take the fish and he walks."

"It's not that simple any more—"

"It's simple, it's simple! The three of us leave now and you cart the fish. Or else we stand here and wait for the other Freaks to come back. That's simple, isn't it?"

"I suppose."

"Well?"

"Agreed. Now get your brother to come out and let me see my fish."

I backstepped to the shack, rapped knuckles on the door. "Flour? You heard? You gotta leave now. You got no choice."

Reeni was walking toward me. Sharkey was walking toward me.

"Flour?" I said. Then, to Sharkey: "Just wait!" And to Reeni: "Go up to the street. I got Mary's car. We'll meet you."

She shook her head no. "Don't trust this man, Grinner. Please, I'm begging you!" The first words she'd spoken.

"Dammit, I know what I'm doing!"

"You can't trust him!"

"Well, how about you start trusting me? Do what I ask you, Reen. Just do it."

She looked at me, she looked at the mud.

Her shoes made digestive sounds as she walked across the flat and disappeared through the curtain of leathery leaves.

The young spacer sat on a tably root, pressing his cut with the heel of a hand.

I told Sharkey: "You go stand with him. Lemme see my brother for one minute. So he understands the bargain."

I knocked again. "I'm coming in, okay? You got this locked? Unlock."

I heard Flour thumbing several hooks from several metal eyes. The door opened a crevice, opened wider, and I slipped inside: "Who's a coward, huh? Did you see me out there?"

Flour slammed the door but let the hooks dangle. There's just two, Grinny? How many? Two just?"

"I asked you if you seen me out—" I broke off when I caught sight of my brother's left leg: from the knee down it was wet with high-gloss blood.

One of the fish tanks had been struck with a bullet, too. All its water had splashed out, goldfish were squirming on the soggy gravel.

Flour rubbed his cheek, glanced around and grabbed a newspaper from Reeni's mattress, a bunch of fingertip bombs from his soup bowl. "Grinny. Listen up good. They won't let me leave, not after what happened in New York. No way! They're just fooling you—so we haveta fool them right back."

"No, I believe him."

"You would."

"Really! He only wants the fish."

"Right." He grimaced when he stooped and laid out several straight rows of fingertips on the shack floor, in front of the door. Then he overspread the bombs with newspaper. "Whoever walks in first gets blown—all right? The guy behind gets shook long enough for you to put a bullet in his neck."

"What're you talking? Let's just get outta here."

"Then gimme the gun."

"I'll hold it, you don't mind."

"Tell him to come in, he can look at the fish."

"You're being a fucken cowboy. They're giving you a break—"

"Step over the newspaper . . . open the door . . . and tell 'em to come in. Then stand back and shut up."

"Flour . . ."

"Fuckit, Grinner—either you side with me or you side with Sharkey. You trust your own brother or you trust some cop. I'm a Freak and he's a Normal. Now, you just choose who you wanna save, and let me know. But don't take too long deciding."

I opened the door a crack and called to Sharkey and the ashen young spacer: "Youse can come in and see what's here. And when you seen, me and my brother go. Yes?"

I told Flour: "They're coming."

He'd flattened himself against the back wall, between a pair of tanks on black-enameled stands. "Grinner, move over here by me. You don't wanna get burnt."

I didn't move, I dropped my eyes to the newspaper mat.

"Grinner!"

"Screw you! Just let me handle things—okay? I'll get you outta here. I know what I'm doing." And crouched, and whipped away the newspaper, collected up the fingertips. "They don't care about your ass. It'll be cool, we can go. And I can get my op—"

Flour drove his elbow through a fish tank, another. He toppled a third.

When the shack door opened, several fish flowed and flopped over the sill, were beached in the muck outside.

Gravel thick with death eggs made spits and keys across the floor.

I remember that Flour was laughing.

I remember that Niles Sharkey was smiling.

And I know that I was grinning.

But it wasn't my fault.

I was grinning like a skull but it wasn't my fault!

33
The End of Everything

Water sloshed in the trunk of the Solaris.

Niles Sharkey and the young spacer (his name was Raymond Wilks, he spoke with a Southern drawl) had collected all of the goldfish, both the living and the dead goldfish, from the puddly shack floor and from the muddy front yard. They'd dumped them into a pair of tanks, the only two Flour hadn't had the time to destroy.

Sharkey had come outside and walked over to the bush-line, where I'd done most of my vomiting. He'd taken the gun from my waistband, the fingertips from my fist. After the shooting I'd nearly squeezed those fingertips, I'd nearly blown my arm into cat food. Deliberately.

Nearly done it.

Sharkey had said: "Why'd he smash them?"

And I'd said: "Why'd you shoot him?"

Neither of us had answered the other one's question.

Nobody's gonna wind up dead with a bullet in his face . . . Don't talk bad luck.

Sharkey had given me a box of salty sunflower seeds.

Water sloshed in the trunk of the Solaris.

"We're going to the Holland Tunnel," Sharkey said.

I drove. Wilks rode up in front with me. In the back seat, Reeni was sandwiched between Sharkey and an older man, the same older man I'd seen with Sharkey and Laudermilch in New York City, outside Dr. Sleet's office. A man with wavy gray-flecked brown hair. Wearing a shiny bluish-green

winter raincoat and a charcoal woolen scarf twirled around
his neck. But no neck brace. The brace was lying on the
back window sill.

In the rearview I watched Reeni chew on her fingernails.
Her eyes were as clear and pale yellow as serum. She looked
sedated.

When Reeni had seen me come through the Blofeld fence
with Sharkey instead of Flour, her eyes pimentoed.

Raymond Wilks had set down his tank of fish and blocked
her as she tried to race back to the Hole.

And I'd tried to look like Sharkey's prisoner. I'd hoped
she'd believe it. I wished it were true myself. I wished it,
I wanted it. I stood with my back bent and my head down.
My grinning lips were syrupy with vomit. I stood there
holding a fish tank.

Sharkey trusted me not to drop and shatter it.

The Solaris had rolled from down the street and stopped
in front of us.

The older man had climbed out of the car and while the
tanks were being loaded into the trunk he'd walked over
to the Blofeld fence with his hands in his coat pockets.
Smiling a ripply smile he'd gazed through the diamondy
chinks and down the slope. His eyes misted. He looked very
hopeful.

Water sloshed in the trunk of the Solaris.

Reeni was still nibbling on her fingernails.

"Are there any more fish?" Sharkey asked her. "That you
know of? Anyplace else?"

She nibbled: her eyes met mine in the rearview. Her eyes
closed and opened. Her eyes were paler now and still dilut-
ing. I could see far back into her eyes, far, far back: they
were caves. Her eyes met mine in the rearview, and nothing
was communicated. Nothing. And everything.

Water sloshed in the trunk of the Solaris.

At the fence, she'd pulled away from Raymond Wilks.
She began to tremble like a zombie but didn't try to run.

We'd looked at each other. Nothing was communicated.
That's when the blood started to leave her eyes, her eyes
to pale . . .

Water sloshed in the trunk of the Solaris.

Raymond Wilks tightened the knot on the bandage he'd
made from a sleeve of one of Flour's shirts.

Raymond Wilks had skin like Sharkey's. The facial pores
were invisible, there was a pale-pink congenital blush.

Raymond Wilks took out his wallet and gave me money
for the tunnel toll. On one of the bills, Washington's eyes
were whited out. Money circulates. Blood circulates. Clay
does not circulate.

It was snowing again in Jersey City.

It was probably snowing across the river.

I glanced in the rearview and watched the older man
loosen his scarf: for just an instant, I saw a fat red wolf's
eye glowing on his throat. The brace was on the window sill.
He pulled a thermos from a gym bag on the floor. He twisted
off the top and sniffed. Coffee. Real coffee. He offered some
to Sharkey. Sharkey frowned and lit a cigarette.

Reeni was still nibbling on her nails.

I drove into the tunnel, then braked the car with a jolt.

Water splashed in the trunk of the Solaris.

I turned around, I looked at Reeni, I reached.

She pushed backward, she put her fingertips into her
mouth.

"I'm sorry, Reen. I swear to God, I'm sorry."

She had her fingertips in her mouth.

Her eyeballs were colorless.

She had fingertips in her mouth.

"Let's go," Sharkey said. "Come on."

Reeni had fingertips in her mouth.

I tipped up my chin and tipped it down: a nod.

She closed her eyes and squeezed those fingertips between
her tombstone teeth.

As long as you're not dead, you're not safe.

We want to survive, we take our leave.

On the wet lawn in back of a big house we'd walked naked, and she'd said: *I wanna go home* . . .

Suddenly: a chaos of fiery red lights . . .

Epilogue: At Home with the Zombie
(May 1, 2013)

I'm sitting in a chair in my bedroom, behind dark glasses, and Pigeon Mary and Archangelina think I'm asleep. I hear Pidge shush her kid, I hear the kid beat her wings, hear the wings strike some vase or jar and topple it. But it doesn't break. The kid is clumsy, the clumsiest. She weighs a hundred pounds, is two years old. Her wings are useless, they'll never lift her off the floor. Sometimes I'll touch her face, and the skin feels thick, meaty. I wonder if it's red, like Beef's used to be.

Archangelina begins to sing a song, singing very softly because her mother has warned her not to wake me.

I hear Pigeon Mary tiptoe up to my chair. She rewinds the tape on Da's old machine, presses the PLAY button: "Reeni had fingertips in her mouth." She presses another button, and it's quiet in here again, except for the kid singing.

Archangelina is singing nonsense words, a song she makes up as she goes along: ". . . you . . . me . . . bird in the tree . . ."

"I'm finished," I say to Pidge.

"Did I wake you?"

"Nah."

"Can I get you anything?"

"No. Thanks. What time is it?"

"A little after seven. At night."

Lina is still singing. I hear the points of her wings scrape across the floor. Sometimes I'll feel them, those wings:

they're heavy as surfboards, the feathers are coarse. She expects to fly with them, when she gets a little older. She tells me that all the time. She's been speaking for almost a year.

She also tells me that her father sends her gifts, every single month. From London—do I know where that is? Where he makes movies. In fact, the gifts—paste jewelry, sweaters, vitamin pills—are sent from Manchester, where, in fact, her father does make movies. But not the sort she imagines. The Beefstone—Martin Stein—appears in a genre of state-sponsored snuff films called "chaffs." As in, separate the wheat from the chaff. Beef does the separating, with a variety of metal and wood implements and very little dialogue.

Naturally, I've never seen one. Just heard about . . .

Archangelina tells me often that her father is coming home very soon. When she does, I say: "That'll be nice."

Occasionally, she wants to know what sorts of gifts I get from my father, so I tell her: "My father is dead," but she doesn't understand. She'll say, "Yes, but what kind of things does he like to give you *most*?"

If Da were alive, I'd want to give *him* a gift: these two dozen recording cassettes stacked on the table next to my chair. But he's dead. A year and a half. An accident, Ma called it, but I don't know. A walk through the Blofeld Hole, alone. A treacherous root, a long fall, a sharp rock. An accident, yes . . . but his stainless steel hand was found thunked into the wall of a rickety old Freak Pride ticket booth, and he hadn't been wearing makeup when he died, or a wig, so—

Disruption of your entire life without a good reason—well, that could drive anybody crazy.

Ma told me she'd selected a wavy black wig for him, and beige cosmetics. The funeral director prepared his body to her exact specifications. I was still in the hospital then. I think.

"Lina," says Pigeon Mary, "that's enough of that singing. Now, just quiet down."

"It sounds windy out," I say.

Pidge gives a short laugh. "It's been like this since last night. Seems to me it's getting stronger, but I don't know. They say not. On the news."

On the news, according to Pigeon Mary, they also say which species of bomb dropped where, dropped when, and dropped by whom is responsible for these storms. But I don't care about which, where, when, whom.

I don't want to know.

I don't want.

I listen to Pidge move across the room and push back a window curtain. "The sky is amazing," she tells me. "Green as a swimming pool." Clumsy Archangelina lugs her wings over to look, and she agrees with her mother. "*Just* like a swimming pool! You should see, Grinner." She takes a breath. "Oh, I'm sorry . . ."

I ask Lina to run, get me my salt pills, like a good girl. She runs and she falls: she's so clumsy, she weighs . . .

We're alone now, Pigeon Mary and me. I listen to her unwrap a candy bar, smell chocolate. I wonder how she can afford it, wonder if Beef sent her a box of them.

"I listened to most of the tapes," she says. "I hope you don't mind."

I smell chocolate and nougat.

"I told you to go right ahead. What do you think?"

She walks around the bedroom, touching things. She picks things up, puts things down. She doesn't answer my question.

Niles Sharkey is dead.

Thomas nmi Poole is dead.

And Reeni.

"What do you think?" I ask again.

She comes over and pries open my fingers and puts a

plastic bag into my palm. "Two was all I could get today."

"You still haven't answered my question."

Through plastic I feel tiny eggs.

Are there any more fish that you know of?

I hear Archangelina singing out in the hall: ". . . green as a pool . . . green, green, green as a pool . . ." Pigeon Mary calls her, then says to me: "We have to go."

"The wind," I say. "Have supper. Please."

But wind or no wind, they have to go. Lina comes and puts a bottle of salt pills on my table. She lifts my hand and places my fingers on the bottle. Her skin feels thick, stew-meaty. I imagine it must be red.

"What did you think of the tapes, really?" I ask Pidge again.

I picture the two of them, mother and daughter, standing by the door: Pigeon Mary slim and gray, Lina squat and blood-red. "Really," I say. "What did you think, really."

Pigeon Mary says: "Poor Grinner."

And Archangelina begins a new song: ". . . poor, poor, poor . . . no-more, more, more . . ."

You can hear the wind howl when they open the front door downstairs. You can't when they shut it but the house is rocking.

I feel around for the plastic bag and take out the death eggs. With a thumbnail I puncture both shells . . .

The six lights glimmer, and the darkness that flows around me doesn't flow empty. It's full. Of life. It must be, has to be. I can almost. Hear. Feel. Almost.

Reenie, I'm sorry . . .

Flour, forgive me . . .

Skully, Flour, Reenie . . .

Da.

The spacers are right: seven Roman letters, three Greek, fourteen hyphenated numerals. Space.

But the zombies are right, too. Death.

Reeni's here, must be, where I can reach her, tell her.
There's a chance I'll find her. A chance.

She closed her eyes and squeezed those fingertips between
her tombstone teeth. And left me.

They do that.

I'm shivering. I'm bundled in wool blankets and I'm shivering. Ma is shaking soot from her wig—what color today?
I wonder. She curses the winds and sits beside me, takes
off my glasses. I imagine she's moving her hand back and
forth in front of my face.

"What . . . time is it, Ma?"

"Almost eleven."

"Night?"

"Morning."

I feel a cool wetness on one cheek: she is painting me:
beige? pink? Painting over the scales, very very carefully.
I ask her about the winds.

I'm not interested in them, but I ask.

"Grinner, when are you gonna stop all this nonsense and
come live with me?"

I ask her about the winds. Have they stopped? Are they
stronger?

"You can't stay here alone."

Does that need a reply? No, so I don't give one. I open
the blankets and brush eggshells from my lap. "Would you
. . . make . . . me something . . . to eat?"

"When're you gonna stop this nonsense?"

"I'm . . . hungry," I tell Ma and she goes down to the
kitchen.

Baudelaire leaps to the arm of my chair, leaps again and
stretches out across the back, above my head. His purrs
sound like a Geiger counter.

"You know," Ma calls from the bottom of the stairs,
"you know you're going off your head. I hope you know it.
Just in case you don't, I'm pointing this out."

Directly opposite where I sit all the time is a mirror, a big oval mirror. It hangs on the wall, and I know it's there because I remember it. My face is reflected in it twenty hours a day, maybe more. But I can't see it. Just as well: I don't want to.

I'm waiting for Pigeon Mary to come back, for some eggs, for some food.

I'm waiting for Reeni.

I'm waiting to be Normal.

"Grinner?" Ma calls up. "Is soup all right? Tomato? Charlie, I'm asking you a question. Is tomato soup okay? Grinner . . . ?"

I pick up one of my tape cassettes and fumble it down into Da's machine:

"When we were twelve, thirteen, fourteen . . ."

"Soup," I call down, "is . . . fine."

". . . into our bedroom late at night . . ."

I'd forgotten Archangelina was in the room when I taped that. You can hear one of her silly little songs, vaguely, in back of my voice. Back there. Her silly little song, her nonsense: ". . . thirteen, fourteen . . . twenty thirteen . . ." And you can hear wings beating.

". . . we'd been conceived (pretty amazing odds . . .)"

Archangelina expects to fly with those wings of hers, when she gets a little older.

But she won't.

"Did you say tomato was all right? Yes or no! Answer me! Grinner? Charlie? Charles . . . ?"

ABOUT THE AUTHOR

Tom De Haven grew up Catholic in Bayonne, New Jersey, and graduated from Rutgers University. He received an M.F.A. in creative writing from Bowling Green State University and participated in a fiction workshop sponsored by the Academy of American Poets. He says he can't remember where the initial idea for *Freaks' Amour* came from, but he knows he was writing a story about a contemporary porno star and then one morning he didn't feel like doing any work on it and started noodling around with a paragraph about some guy who discovers his wife dead on the toilet with eggshells strewn around her feet. Second draft of paragraph: The wife had troglodytic tootsies and happened to resurrect. The Blofeld Blast had its origins, though, in real life, from an oil refinery explosion the author witnessed in Linden, New Jersey.

Tom De Haven currently earns his living as a free-lance writer and is working on a second novel, *Jersey Luck*. He and his wife, Santa Sergio, a painter, have recently bought a row house in Jersey City. His hobbies are drawing cartoons and collecting book reprints of classic American comic strips. *Freaks' Amour* was published just before his thirtieth birthday.